Read and

Buried

Also available by Eva Gates

Read and Buried

A LIGHTHOUSE LIBRARY MYSTERY

Eva Gates

CROOKED
LANE

NEW YORK

This is a work of fiction. All of the names, characters, organizations, places and events portrayed in this novel are either products of the author's imagination or are used fictitiously. Any resemblance to real or actual events, locales, or persons, living or dead, is entirely coincidental.

Copyright © 2019 by Vicki Delany

All rights reserved.

Published in the United States by Crooked Lane Books, an imprint of The Quick Brown Fox & Company LLC.

Crooked Lane Books and its logo are trademarks of The Quick Brown Fox & Company LLC.

Library of Congress Catalog-in-Publication data available upon request.

ISBN (mass market): 978-1-64385-572-1
ISBN (hardcover): 978-1-64385-233-1
ISBN (ePub): 978-1-64385-234-8

Cover illustration by Joe Burleson
Book design by Jennifer Canzone

Printed in the United States.

www.crookedlanebooks.com

Crooked Lane Books
34 West 27th St., 10th Floor
New York, NY 10001

Mass Market Edition: August 2020
Hardcover Edition: October 2019

10 9 8 7 6 5 4 3 2 1

To Joan Hall, beloved aunt
and keen reader

Chapter One

"Come in," Bertie James, the director of the Light-house Library, called in answer to a knock on her office door.

The door swung open and a man stood there, shifting awkwardly from foot to foot. The yellow construction helmet on his head hung low over his forehead; his overalls all but swallowed his thin frame, and when he walked, his steel-toed boots made slapping noises on the floor.

Normally exceptionally polite, he didn't bother apologizing for interrupting our meeting. "You're needed outside, Bertie."

"Can it wait a few minutes, Zack?" she asked. "Lucy and I are almost finished here."

He shook his head, and his hard hat fell over his eyes. He lifted one dirt-encrusted hand to push it back so he could see. "Dad says it's important."

Bertie stood up, as did I. I was in my boss's office having my quarterly performance review, and although it had started well, with a listing of all the things I'd achieved this quarter, I wasn't entirely disappointed to be called away. These things always start well, and then we get to the "needs improvement" part. I was confident I was doing a good job as the assistant director, but I've found that bosses can always find something that "needs improvement." I followed Zack, and Bertie followed me, down the hallway and through the main room of the library, where a handful of patrons browsed. Charlene Clayton staffed the circulation desk, and she threw me a questioning look. I returned it with a shrug. She stood up and joined us. Curious patrons fell into step behind the procession. Charles, another library staffer, woke from his nap in the comfortable wingback chair next to the magazine rack, yawned and stretched, and then realized something was happening. He leapt off the chair, ready to follow us outside.

"Not so fast, little fellow." Mabel Eastland scooped him up. "You and I will wait inside. Let the young people fuss." She settled into the chair and put the cat on her lap. Charles decided being stroked and cuddled was better than whatever might be happening outside, and settled down to enjoy the attention.

The moment we stepped out of the library, we were enveloped in a wave of hot, sticky air. It was mid-July and the temperatures had been in the high nineties all week, with barely a breath of the usual sea breezes to keep us cool. The library itself was comfortable, being enclosed in thick stone walls, but the outside felt like a sauna, and the normally green lawn was turning a crisp brown.

The section of lawn remaining, that is, because at the moment the grounds immediately surrounding the Bodie Island Lighthouse Library were a construction site.

Two construction sites, actually.

Ronald Burkowski, our children's librarian, and one of his volunteers were supervising the smaller site this afternoon. He'd brought in buckets of sand and some unused lumber and created a construction zone where kids could pretend to be working alongside the real project currently underway. Ronald and library patrons had provided child-sized hard hats and safety vests, along with shovels, pails, dump trucks, and other "heavy machinery." Heavy machinery in miniature and made of brightly colored plastic.

The kids loved it, and they didn't seem to mind the heat, although Ronald had put up umbrellas to keep everyone shaded, and jugs of water were kept on hand.

The real construction site was surrounded by a six-foot-high chain-link fence to protect passersby from falling into the enormous hole dug into the base of the lighthouse tower. I couldn't imagine being one of the workers, wrapped in their heavy construction gear and safety vests in this heat.

Over the winter, a large crack had appeared in the stone walls of the lighthouse that gives our library its name. To our horror, the crack began slowly, ominously to spread. When Grimshaw Construction checked it out, they told us a massive amount of work would be required to keep the historic old building from collapsing around our ears. The job was highly specialized and hugely expensive, and we'd feared that without a lot of money—money we didn't have—the library would be forced to close.

But the library community and the citizens of Nags Head, North Carolina, had come through, and we'd raised enough to get the job done.

Work began last week and, so we'd been told, was proceeding well and on plan. Scaffolding covered the eastern wall of the lighthouse tower, and an enormous hole chewed into the earth at its foot.

At this moment, all work had stopped, even in the children's zone.

The workers—the adult ones—stood in a circle staring into the hole. Their machinery had fallen silent. The kids watched them, shovels in hand, hard hats on heads. One little guy was enjoying a snack from the lunch pail his mom had provided.

"What's happening?" Louise Jane McKaughnan, today's playground volunteer, asked. "No one will tell me anything."

Bertie didn't answer. She picked her way across the lawn and through the gate in the fence. Ronald, Charlene, Louise Jane, and I, along with all the patrons, adults and children, followed.

George Grimshaw, the construction boss, turned to us with a scowl and put his hands on his hips. "This isn't a community picnic, people. I sent for Bertie, not everyone in town."

He might not have spoken for all the attention anyone paid him. George was in his sixties, a giant of a man with a heavy black beard, big round belly, and scratched and scarred hands. He was a tyrant on the jobsite. The men who worked for him admired and respected him and jumped when he told them to, but to everyone else in the community, he was just George, whose bark was a great deal louder than his bite.

Taking care to avoid hitting our heads on the scaffolding or falling into the hole, we gathered around. Ronald tried to keep the children back, but in that he got no help from Louise Jane, who pushed her way to the front and peered into the dark depths.

"What do you want to show me?" Bertie asked.

George handed her a yellow hat.

She threw up her hands in horror and stepped back. "I'm not going down there."

"You need to see," he said.

"You can tell me," she said. "Please don't say it's worse than you estimated?"

"No problem with the job," George said. "All's going according to plan on that front. You need to see what we found for yourself. You're the boss lady."

"I manage the library, but I'm not the owner. Perhaps we should contact the library board or get a representative of the town out here."

George grumbled something about political interference.

"Before calling anyone," Charlene said, "we need to know what we're dealing with. It might be nothing."

"If it's nothing," Bertie said, "then I don't see why—"

"Time is money," George said. "My men are getting paid while they're standing around watching us yammer."

The men didn't look entirely unhappy at the forced break. They pulled out bottles of water or granola bars and wiped sweat off their brows.

"Can't you just tell me?" Bertie said.

George didn't reply. Zack shifted from one foot to another. Zack, short and scrawny, was George's son. Except for the identical eyes and chin, the two men couldn't have been more different physically.

Library patrons murmured among themselves. None of the construction crew said anything. The children looked from one adult to another. Ronald grabbed a collar as one little boy prepared to leap into the hole.

"It's too hot to stand around all day," Louise Jane said. "Get on with it, Bertie."

"I'm sorry, but I can't," Bertie said in a voice I'd never heard from her before. One of pure terror. She shuddered and the last of the blood drained from her face. "I . . . I can't go down there. I just can't. I can't abide closed dark spaces." She grabbed the hard hat, but rather than putting it on, she shoved it at the person standing nearest to her. Which just happened to be me. I took it without thinking, and she said, "Lucy will go in my place."

"I will?"

"If you don't mind," Bertie said.

"I'll go," shouted six-year-old Charlotte Washington.

"No, I'll go." Her sister Emily jumped up and down so enthusiastically her pigtails bounced. Emily's hair was wrapped in red ribbons, Charlotte's in blue. That was the only way anyone could tell the twins apart.

"Neither of you are going anywhere," Ronald said. The girls pouted.

"I'll do it." Louise Jane reached for the hard hat. I pulled it out of her way. I don't know why I did that. I wasn't all that keen to climb into that hole either, to face whatever George wasn't telling us. Conscious of having been interrupted in the middle of my performance review, and the pending "needs improvement" part, I put the hat on. It was far too big, and I felt it crushing my curly hair and slipping over my eyebrows. "What am I going to find down there?" I said.

"You'll see," George replied.

"Not a body. Please, not a body. Not even a mouse. Especially not a mouse."

He grunted. "Nothin' like that."

"Can't you bring it up?" I asked.

"Hurry up, Lucy," eighty-six year old Mr. Snyder, who came into the library every day to read magazines and enjoy some company, said. "A man could grow old listening to you lot bicker."

"We're not bickering," Charlene said. "We're deciding on the most optimal allocation of resources."

"We called that bickering in my day."

"You need to see it in place," George said, "before we bring it up."

"I bet it's an old skeleton," Charlotte said. "Wouldn't that be neat?"

"You might be right, young lady," Mr. Snyder said. "Building this lighthouse was a dangerous job."

I let out a long breath and tried to summon some vestige of courage. "Okay. Let's do this."

Dodging people, scaffolding, and random pieces of equipment, I hesitantly approached the chasm at the base of the lighthouse tower. Zack jumped nimbly in and pointed to a section of wood protruding from the dark earth. "Put your feet on that. Steps all the way down. I'll go first; you follow."

My right foot found the first step, and I tested it to be sure it could support my weight. It didn't shift, so I stepped gingerly onto it. Step by cautious step, I descended into the dark depths of the earth. I'm only five foot three, so I quickly passed below the level of the earth and the feet of the onlookers. The heat dropped almost immediately, and I was conscious of the enormous weight of the black-and-white-striped lighthouse above me. I looked up, to see a ring of curious faces peering down.

"What do you see, Lucy?" someone called. I didn't answer, because I didn't see anything at all.

I didn't care for the feeling of the earth closing in around me. I shivered, whether from the sudden damp coolness of the air or a sense of being in a place in which I didn't belong, I didn't know. The light on Zack's construction hat shone on nothing but dirt on one side, the solid foundations of the lighthouse on the other, and the empty blackness below.

"Almost there," Zack said. His voice was calm and steady. "You're doing great, Lucy."

I continued climbing down. I forced myself to take deep breaths, to keep myself from panicking. Zack's bright light lit up the space, and above me the sun shone in a blue sky, but I couldn't help but think that at any moment the lights would go out and I'd be trapped down here. I felt as though I'd descended into the center of the earth, but probably hadn't taken more than twenty steps when Zack said, "Stop."

I stopped. We'd reached the bottom of the excavation.

"There," he said. He focused his beam onto the ground, and the light caught a flash of metal. I blinked and peered closer. I saw a tin box. Old, battered, scratched, dirt-encrusted, about one square foot. The dirt surrounding it had been scraped away, and it rested at the base of the hole. A single modern shovel was propped against a wall of earth next to it.

I let out an enormous sigh of relief. Despite George's assurances, I'd been afraid they'd found the remains of a long-ago lighthouse builder. "It's a box."

"Yes," Zack said.

"How'd it get here?" I asked, perhaps stupidly.

"Don't know," he said.

"Why didn't you just bring it up?"

"Dad said it has to be seen where it was found before we move it. It might be historically important. Take a picture."

"What?"

"Take a picture. Then we'll take it up."

"Is it heavy?"

"Don't know."

I glanced around me. "Did you find anything else?"

"No. We looked, but the box seems to be down here all on its own."

No one had suggested I bring a camera, but today I was dressed in loose linen pants, and I'd slipped my phone into a pocket. I took it out and snapped a few shots.

Zack picked up the nearby shovel and gently and carefully levered the box out of the earth. He then bent over and picked it up. It came easily, meaning the contents couldn't be too heavy.

I stared at it.

Nothing appeared to be written on it. I wondered how it came to be here. Had someone hidden it deliberately, or maybe they dropped it and didn't care enough to go in after it?

It must have been here for a long time. It was unlikely anyone had been down here since work on the building had begun in 1871.

"How are we going to get it up?" I asked, thinking of pulleys and levers and rows of heaving men.

"I'll carry it," Zack said. "Up you go, Lucy."

I climbed back up, grateful to be heading toward light rather than away. Zack followed nimbly, cradling the box in his arms.

I'd been down in the hole less than five minutes, but when my head emerged into the clear fresh air of the Outer Banks and I felt the warm sunshine on my face, I was very glad I hadn't taken up the life of a miner.

George reached down a hand and pulled me out of the excavation.

"Was it a skeleton?" Charlotte asked very eagerly.

"What did you see?" Louise Jane asked, equally eagerly.

Zack handed the box to Bertie, and she took it. "Oh, my goodness," she said.

Everyone gathered around, shouting questions.

Charlotte and Emily groaned in disappointment. "It's nothing but a dirty box."

"A very old box," Ronald said. "I wonder what's inside."

"Go on, Bertie," Louise Jane said, "open it."

"It's like Christmas," another one of the children said.

"Do you think I should?" Bertie said. "Open it, I mean? Maybe we should wait for Mrs. Fitzgerald and the library board. Or even the mayor."

"Let's open it now and not tell them," Louise Jane said.

"For once, I agree with Louise Jane," Charlene said. "Come on, Bertie, I'm dying to see what's inside."

"Okay," Bertie said. "Let's go into the library and open it there."

And we trooped back inside.

Mrs. Eastland and Charles looked up when we all, including George, Zack, the entire construction crew, and the children came in. "Goodness," Mrs. Eastland said. Charles leapt off her lap.

Ronald cleared a place on the table in the alcove, and Bertie put the box down. Charles jumped onto the table. I picked him up. Better keep him away until we knew what we were dealing with.

We stood in a circle staring at the box. Bertie reached out a hand.

"Before you open it," Charlene said, "let me do my Sherlock Holmes bit." Charlene was our academic librarian. The nautical history of the East Coast of North America was her specialty. "That sort of box was used in the eighteenth and nineteenth centuries to—"

"All well and good," Mr. Snyder said, "but I want to know what's inside."

"It doesn't appear to be locked," Ronald said.

The lid had a metal clasp that a padlock could fit through, but if it had ever been secured by a lock, it wasn't any longer.

Once again, Bertie put out her hand.

"Hold on," Charlene said. "We need to take a picture." Out came her phone. "Okay, go ahead."

Bertie picked up the box and shook it. Something inside rattled. She opened it slowly while Charlene took pictures.

I'd guessed by the ease with which first Zack and then Bertie had carried it, that nothing of any weight was inside, and I'd been right: the box was empty except for a small leather-bound notebook. The leather was cracking and red with age.

The children groaned in disappointment. "Boooooring," Emily proclaimed.

Charlene's eyes glimmered with excitement, and Louise Jane sucked in a breath.

"I was hoping for treasure," one of the construction workers said. "Like pirates' gold or somethin'."

Charles yawned and I put him on the floor. He returned to the chair near the magazine rack to resume his nap.

"Back to work, men," George said. "Excitement's over."

"Don't think that qualifies as excitement," one of them said as, grumbling, they left.

"Okay, kids," Ronald said. "Outside. Louise Jane?"

"What?"

"Time go to outside. The children have to be supervised."

"You go," she said. "I want to see what it says."

He knew better than to waste his time arguing, and herded the children ahead of him.

"Maybe there's something else down there," Charlotte said. "Something that got missed. I can check if you want."

"No, I'll check!" Emily said.

Ronald told them to hurry up and the twins ran for the door.

The patrons returned to what they were doing, and eventually only Mrs. Eastland, Bertie, Charlene, Louise Jane, and I were left standing in a circle around the box. Bertie hadn't taken the notebook out. We simply stared at it for a long time.

"Don't touch anything," Charlene said, "until I get back."

She ran upstairs and returned almost immediately with a pair of tweezers and two pairs of white cotton gloves. She handed the gloves to Bertie. "Put these on."

Bertie did so.

"Regardless of what this is," Charlene said, "it wasn't put there last week, meaning it's a historical document. It might be of some significance. It might not. I, for one, am more excited than if the box had been stuffed full of pirates' gold."

Slowly, carefully, Bertie lifted the notebook out of the box.

"Time for me to be off," one of the patrons called. "Lucy, I'm not going to my granddaughter's this week after all, so I can come to book club. I hope I can still get a copy of the book. What is it again?"

"*Journey to the Center of the Earth*, by Jules Verne," I said.

Charlene's eyebrows rose. "Tell me you're kidding."

"Nope. That's what we decided on at the last meeting."

Chapter Two

Charlene grabbed two hardcover books off the nearest shelf and put them on the table, four inches apart. "Here. Prop the notebook against these, one on each side. Don't bend the spine back, or it might crack. Use these tweezers to open the pages, and do it very, very slowly. If they seem to be stuck together, don't try to separate them, or they'll tear."

Bertie rested the notebook into the supports. As it moved, a piece of paper shifted so a fraction of an inch stuck out of the book.

Mrs. Eastland groaned. "Oh no, a page is ripping. Be careful the whole spine doesn't crack."

Bertie gritted her teeth against the onslaught of advice but said nothing. She might not be a rare books expert, like Charlene, but she knew how to handle fragile documents. "That hasn't torn. It's a separate sheet tucked in here. See? The color's slightly darker than the rest of the book."

"Careful," Charlene warned. "Paper is fragile."

Bertie opened the book ever so slightly and fastened her tweezers onto the edge peeking out. She pulled at it slowly, carefully, and it came easily without the dreaded sound of ripping.

I leaned closer for a better look, and I realized I was holding my breath. Bertie laid the page on the table. It was a single sheet of paper, fractionally smaller than the pages of the notebook, but the edges weren't torn, meaning this page had been slipped in after the book had been bound.

"It looks like a hand-drawn map," Bertie said. "I think it might be of the Outer Banks. Something seems to be off about it, though."

"That's as it was back in the nineteenth century," Charlene said.

"The sands are constantly shifting, and the currants move things around all the time," Louise Jane said. "Roanoke Inlet closed in 1811, and Bodie Island became part of the peninsula. This map was drawn later than that— you can see the island's gone. I'd guess it's about mid-to-late nineteenth century."

"Around the time the lighthouse was built," I said. "After the Civil War."

"Right."

"Strange map, though," I said. "It doesn't have the names of any towns or bodies of water or other landmarks marked on it. Just those numbers."

The map, if that's what it was, was rough and hand drawn, the ink dark with age but still clear. Lines outlined the shape of the land, and a handful of squiggles were probably meant to indicate the ocean and the straits. In no pattern that I could see, numbers from one to eight were scatted across the landscape. Number two was in the approximate location of the lighthouse where we now stood.

"Do the numbers indicate where towns used to be?" I asked.

"No," Louise Jane said. "Nags Head's always been where Nags Head is now, and it's not marked. The five seems to be at Jockey's Ridge. Nothing but sand dunes even then, as far as I know. I could check with my grandmother."

"What does the book have to say?" Charlene asked. "Open it."

Bertie carefully pulled back the cover. The center of the first page was marked by a small, neat signature: Mrs. Jeremiah Crawbingham. And a date: 1858.

"Never heard of her. Or of him," Louise Jane said. "Or anyone by that surname. It's an unusual one." If anyone would know, Louise Jane would. Her family went almost as far back as the first European settlers on these shores. She was a keen amateur historian and a well-regarded storyteller of Outer Banks history and legends. Unfortunately, Louise Jane didn't always worry about the legends part leaking into the history part. And, I sometimes suspected, if she didn't know something, she simply made it up.

Bertie turned to the next page. We sighed in collective disappointment. The date, July 2, was written at the top of the page, and underneath:

Fair and sunny. No wind.

Then the next day, July 3: *A soft breeze bringing the threat of rain. High tide at 11:55.*

And on it went. Every entry was the same. Dates and weather and tide reports.

"Her husband might have been a fisherman," Louise Jane pointed out. "Nothing was more important in their lives than the weather."

"True," Charlene said.

Bertie flipped to the last page. It was empty.

"I wonder how it ended up underneath the lighthouse," Charlene said. "Paper was expensive in those days, and you didn't just throw away all those blank pages. Our Mrs. Crawbingham seems to have been somewhat wasteful, the way she barely fills the page before starting another. The book itself wouldn't have been cheap, not with that good-quality leather binding. She must have had more money than I'd expect for an Outer Banks fisherman's family."

"As for how it got underneath our lighthouse," I said, "maybe someone dropped the box and couldn't find it in the dark, and then they built the lighthouse on top of it."

"I don't suppose we'll ever know." Bertie turned another page.

While all this had been going on, I'd been aware of what was happening in the library. Some patrons had left, and new ones had arrived. The shouts of playing children came from outside, as did the sound of men's voices and the rat-tat-tat of a jackhammer or the roar of the engine of a heavy truck.

Our library was never a peaceful place—modern public libraries aren't. But the constant noise of the construction was threatening to drive us all mad.

Still, a bit of noise was better than the lighthouse tower collapsing on top of us.

And considering that I lived on the fourth floor, in a small apartment I call my Lighthouse Aerie, the noise was much, much better than the building collapsing. Fortunately, work outside stopped at a reasonable time, and the nights remained peaceful.

"What's this I hear about pirate bones buried under the lighthouse?" Janelle Washington, the twins' mother, joined us.

"That story's growing quickly," I said.

"It's all the kids outside are talking about," she said with a smile. "I know to take it with a grain of salt." Janelle was an attractive black woman in her early thirties. She brought her girls to the children's programs at the library regularly and always ensured they left with book bags stuffed full. She was such a lover of literature, she'd named her children after the best known of the Bronte sisters.

"More like a bucket of salt," Charlene said. "Rather than a pirate, we found this old book."

"More interesting, I'm sure, than a pile of moldy bones," Janelle said.

"I've checked the girls' books out already," I said. "Their book bags are behind the desk. Let me get them for you."

"Thanks."

I half-turned to go back to work, leaving the others to read Mrs. Crawbingham's weather reports, when Bertie said, "Oh. How strange."

She'd turned a page to find a second loose piece of paper. This one was not covered in Mrs. Crawbingham's neat script giving daily reports on the weather.

The page was full of lines of rough printing forming rows and rows of closely packed letters in a mad jumble that made no sense to me.

"What on earth?" Bertie said.

"Is it in another language, do you think?" Louise Jane asked.

"That can't be it," Charlene said. "There aren't enough vowels."

"Many of the words, if they are words," Bertie said, "are very long."

The letters were organized into groups. The shorter ones had only two or three letters, some without vowels, but many contained ten or more characters. They were mostly letters—from A to Z—but a few numerals were sprinkled among them.

"Is there more?" Louise Jane asked.

"Nothing I can see," Bertie said.

"Is it some sort of code?" Janelle asked.

"Might be," Charlene said.

"The weather diary entries were written just before and during the war," Louise Jane said. "Somehow this book got into someone else's hands after that."

"A man, judging by the handwriting," Charlene said. "But that's only a guess."

"Someone either stole this notebook or was given it," Louise Jane said. "And then the war started, and they used it as a code book. This must be a record of troop movements or names of spies or the like. Wow! It's quite a find after all."

"Your imagination is running ahead of you, Louise Jane," Bertie said. "We can conclude nothing of the sort."

"This is the same hand as put the numbers on the map," I said. "Look at the two." I pointed to the drawing and then to the notebook. "It has an identical little curl at the end as the one here."

"So it does," Bertie said.

"Numbers are mixed in among the letters. Numbers one through eight, nothing higher than an eight. Look at the map. No nine and no double digits."

"The code page—if it is in code—might be referencing the map," Charlene said.

"I think it must be," I said.

"If it is a map," Bertie said.

"This is no spy's report," Louise Jane said. "It's a treasure map."

"Don't be ridiculous, Louise Jane," Bertie said. "Treasure map, indeed. It's been a long time since I read *Journey to the Center of the Earth*, but as I recall it begins with the discovery of coded directions to a passage in an Icelandic volcano that leads to the center of the earth."

"Thus the book's title," Charlene said. "I agree with Bertie. You're letting that book lead your imagination, L.J."

I bit my tongue. I'd also been reading the Jules Verne classic in preparation for book club, and I'd been about to say the same thing Louise Jane had.

"Rather than lead my imagination, as you put it," Louise Jane said, "my recent reading has helped me to arrive at the logical conclusion quicker than I might otherwise."

"A treasure map," Janelle said. "That's cool."

"Sorry," I said. "I've left you waiting."

"Not a problem. This is much more interesting, and the girls are perfectly happy outside for a while longer."

"Treasure!" Mrs. Eastland said. "There have been rumors, you know. The pirates who sailed in the Caribbean often came up this coast."

"The days of the Caribbean pirates were long over by the nineteenth century," Charlene said. "And even if they weren't, seamen didn't stuff chests full of gold coins and jewels and bury them in the sand and forget to come back."

"Who says?" Mrs. Eastland asked.

"Reputable historians," Charlene replied.

"Doesn't mean it didn't happen," Louise Jane said. "There have also been rumors through the ages about valuables families hid during the War Between the States. Valuables they were never able, for one reason or another, to come back and reclaim."

"Those stories have as much validity as Captain Jack Sparrow and his merry crew," Charlene said. "The Outer Banks was a poor place in the nineteenth century, occupied by hardworking people struggling to make a living out of the sea and poor soil."

"Still is," Janelle said. "Families like mine."

"And mine," Charlene said. "Fishing families didn't have diamonds and jewels to hide from potential invaders."

"Don't be so sure," Louise Jane said. "Valuable doesn't always mean—"

"Goodness me, but it sounds tense in here." Theodore Kowalski joined our little group. I hadn't even heard the door open. So engrossed were we in studying the map and the code page (I couldn't now think of it as anything else), I'd lost track of my surroundings. "What do you have there? Oh my, is that written in some sort of code?"

"We think it must be," Louise Jane said.

"We think nothing of the sort," Bertie said.

"I agree with Louise Jane," Janelle said.

"I do too," Mrs. Eastland said.

Charles jumped onto the table and sniffed at the book. I snatched him up before he could give it a lick.

"Ronald told me a historic book had been found underground," Theodore said. "I was hoping he meant a book as in a novel. But this looks better." Theodore was a rare book collector and dealer. He adjusted the spectacles on his nose and bent over to peer at the lines of print. He didn't need help seeing, and the lenses were made of clear glass. He was not an Englishman and not in his fifties, and he didn't smoke a pipe. But he thought all those things gave him more gravitas in the world of book collecting than the nonsmoking thirty-something Nags Head native with a soft North Carolina accent and perfect eyesight that he was.

"Hmm," he said. "This makes no sense."

"Yeah, Teddy," Louise Jane said, "we kinda noticed that."

"Have you tried reading it backward, like in *Journey to the Center of the Earth*?"

I didn't admit that I'd tried that already. But backward made nothing any clearer.

"No," he said after a moment. "That doesn't help. Perhaps it's not in English."

Bertie closed the book, tucked the map and code page inside, and put it back in the box. "That's enough of that for now. We have work to do everyone. Mabel, so sorry to keep you. Come into my office. Lucy, can you join us? We'll be discussing plans for Settlers' Day."

"Sure," I said.

"Leave it with me." Louise Jane reached out a hand for the box. "I'll protect it."

Bertie placed her right hand firmly on top of it. "This doesn't leave the library until I know what we're dealing with. It might not lead to buried treasure; it might be the ravings of a lunatic or a couple of schoolboys playing pirates. But it is a historical document, and we'll treat it as such."

"What are we going to do with it?" Charlene asked.

"My fellow members of the Bodie Island Historical Society would love to see it," Mrs. Eastland said. "One of them might have heard of this Mrs. Crawbingham and be able to tell us about her."

"No one by that name ever lived on the Outer Banks," Louise Jane said.

Mrs. Eastland sniffed. "I doubt even you, Louise Jane, know the identity of every person who ever passed this way."

"I know the old families . . ."

"At the least," Mrs. Eastland went on, "the society can check the weather records and see if this book is at all accurate. Mrs. Crawbingham might not have been living in these parts. Perhaps she gave the book to someone who brought it here and put the map in later."

"That's possible," Louise Jane said.

"I can try and find the weather records for the dates mentioned," Charlene said, "but I've got a lot on my plate these days, so some help would be good, as would researching the Crawbingham family."

"Not that there's anything to find on that accord," Louise Jane said.

"Can I tell the society about it, Bertie?" Mrs. Eastland asked.

"I see no reason not to," Bertie said. "Besides, everyone in town will know about it soon enough."

"No better way to spread a secret than to give it to a six-year-old," Janelle said. "And that goes double for my twins."

"Nothing the society loves more than a historical mystery," Mrs. Eastland said. "Please invite the group in to have a look. Jeremy Hughes in particular will be thrilled."

"Jeremy Hughes?" Charlene said. "What's he got to do with anything?" Her tone turned sharp, and I gave her a curious look. A touch of red had come into her cheeks, and she avoided my eyes.

"Jeremy's the new head of the historical society," Mrs. Eastland said.

"And the primary force behind the forthcoming Settlers' Day Fair," Bertie said.

"I didn't know that," Charlene muttered.

"We've been working out the details while you've been on vacation," Bertie said. "I haven't thought it necessary to involve you, Charlene, because the library's not doing much more than providing the space."

"The historical society has everything well in hand," Mrs. Eastland said. "I myself am on the committee. It's all coming together perfectly."

"Can we get back to this book?" Theodore said. "I'll ask my mother about the Crawbingham family. Her knowledge of Outer Banks history surpasses even yours, Louise Jane."

"As if," she said.

"And if my mother doesn't know, she won't pretend she does."

"Hey! I never—"

"I'll talk to the society today," Mrs. Eastland said. "We don't need to check official weather records; we have plenty of diaries from the times, and many of them recorded the weather regularly."

"Thank you," Bertie said. "We close early on Mondays. Invite them to come in tomorrow morning, if they'd like, for a quick peek. In the meantime, I haven't forgotten that the town owns this library. Thus, I will assume, until I'm told otherwise, the town owns the contents of the box. Lucy, when you get a chance, can you call the mayor and inform him of the find?"

"Happy to," I said, feeling a warm flush on my cheeks. The mayor of Nags Head just happens to be my boyfriend, Connor McNeil. I knew Connor would also be interested in our find on a personal level. Like Louise Jane and Theodore, he was descended from a proud longtime Outer Banks fishing family.

"I don't want any talk about codes and treasure maps," Bertie said, "or we'll have every crank in town wanting to have a go at deciphering it." She studied our faces. "Am I understood?"

"Sure."

"Fine."

"My lips are sealed."

"Got it."

"I hear you."

"Meow," added Charles.

"Good. In the meantime," Bertie said, "I'll lock this away in my desk drawer."

She reached for the box, but I snapped it up. "Let me help you," I said with a smile.

"It's not heavy."

"Happy to be of assistance."

The front door flew open, and Ronald, surrounded by a pack of kids, came in. "I could have used some help out there, Louise Jane," he said.

"I've been busy," she replied. "My historical expertise was needed."

"Whatever," he said.

*　*　*

"I assume you want to talk to me about something before Mabel joins us for the meeting?" Bertie said when I'd put the box on her desk.

"I'd like to take some pictures of the map and the code page. If it is a code page. I'm rather good at anagrams and word puzzles, if I do say so myself. I can take a crack at figuring it out."

"I don't see a problem with that. As long as you do it on your own time."

*　*　*

In telling us to keep the contents of our find a secret, Bertie might as well have saved her breath. Not an hour passed before people began pouring through the doors. And not just "every crank in town." A good number of highly respected citizens showed up as well.

Including His Honor, the Mayor.

My heart lifted at the unexpected sight of him. Although he was the mayor of our town, Connor was only a year older than me, and heart-stoppingly handsome, with dark hair that curled in the mist off the sea, prominent cheekbones, eyes the color of the ocean on a sunny day. He'd come from the office, so was dressed in a dark blue business suit, crisp white shirt, and red tie. It was mid-afternoon, but traces of dark stubble were already breaking through his jawline.

"I thought you said you were in meetings all afternoon." That's what he'd told me when I called to tell him about the find.

He formed his lips into a pucker and threw me a silent kiss. As I was facing into the room, and people were standing behind him, I didn't return the gesture, but I gave him a private smile.

"On the phone, you said George had dug up a historic relic. I assumed you meant a farm implement or uniform buckle, but word's spreading that it's a map to pirate treasure."

"Oh dear," I said.

"Meaning it's not? My ten-year-old self is mighty disappointed." He put on an exaggerated pout that was so cute I laughed.

"I'll let Bertie show it to you. You can go on in."

"Still on for dinner tonight?"

"Not even a chest full of Spanish doubloons will keep me away. What's a Spanish doubloon anyway?"

"A gold coin. You close at five tonight, right? I'll pick you up at six."

"I'll be ready."

Connor went down the hallway to Bertie's office. A room full of people watched him go. A few tried to follow. I called out, "Sorry, staff only past that point."

One or two didn't intend to let my protests stop them, but the presence of Charlene, looming up to block the hallway, did.

*   *   *

For the rest of the afternoon, I felt the photo of the code (if it was a code) burning a hole in my pocket. I kept touching the phone, as though I could read the words through my fingers.

I didn't dare take a moment to check it. If I did, I'd become so quickly engrossed in trying to solve the puzzle, I'd forget to go back to work.

I wondered if Connor would mind if we spent our dinner huddling over a printout of the picture.

Probably not. It would appeal to the ten-year-old boy in him.

It appealed to the ten-year-old girl in me.

Chapter Three

At quarter to five the library was clearing out for the day. Connor had left, giving me a wink, and when Bertie didn't come out of her office to address the waiting crowds or show them the map, they drifted away. The construction crew finished work at the regular time of four thirty. Their machinery fell silent, and their trucks and cars revved up as they drove away.

"Never a dull day at the Bodie Island Lighthouse Library," Ronald said as he headed for the door.

I looked up from the computer. "You can say that again. How's the construction playground working out?"

"Stroke of absolute genius. The kids love it; the parents are happy to have their children playing in the fresh air; and upstairs I'm pulling out picture books about construction work and reminding the girls that all trades are open to them. See you tomorrow."

"Good night."

Ronald left as Charlene clattered down the stairs. "I'm late, I'm late," she said. "See you tomorrow, Lucy."

At that moment the door opened, and four people came in. Mrs. Eastland was among them. and I recognized two of the others as members of the Bodie Island Historical Society, a group of amateurs with a keen interest in the history of our area and the preservation of historic buildings and artifacts. They often consulted with

Charlene about the library's collection of old documents and had been in and out of Bertie's office over the past few weeks, keeping her up to date on plans for the forthcoming Settlers' Day event.

When she saw them, Charlene sucked in a breath. Her shoulders and neck stiffened, and color flooded into her face. She dropped her head and kept her eyes on the floor. "Night, Lucy," she mumbled. "Excuse me. Sorry—gotta run. I'm late."

The man I didn't know broke into a huge smile the moment he spotted her. He said, "Charlene! I've been hoping we'd run into each other," in a booming voice. She avoided his eyes and mumbled something as she pushed her way past the new arrivals and almost sprinted out of the library.

He watched her go, his smile getting even bigger. He was in his early to mid-fifties, not bad looking, but there was something I didn't like or trust about that smile or the way he turned to me and almost leered. "Hi there," he said. "We're here to see the notebook you found."

I threw a questioning look at Mrs. Eastland.

"Have you two not met?" she said. "Lucy, this is Jeremy Hughes, the newest member of our little group of history lovers."

"We're so lucky to have him. It was Jeremy's idea for Settlers' Day," the other woman giggled. Giggling, I thought, didn't suit her. Her name was Lynne Feingold, and she was a short round woman in her fifties, full of nervous mannerisms and bursting with an excess of enthusiasm. She was involved in anything and everything to do with arts and culture in Nags Head, and had once been on the library board, although she was no longer.

"I told them Bertie gave us permission to examine your find," Mrs. Eastland said.

The others nodded.

"I believe I said you could see it in the morning." Bertie came into the room. "The library's closing now."

"We couldn't wait a minute longer," Jeremy said.

"We knew you wouldn't mind," Lynne said.

"I told them it's absolutely marvelous," Mrs. Eastland added.

"Tomorrow," Bertie said.

"Tonight," Jeremy said, "Right now. Come on, Bertie. It's not even five o'clock yet. We should be able to make a quick judgment as to authenticity. If it's not of the era you claim, then we don't need to waste anyone's time tomorrow."

"I haven't claimed it's anything at all, but it wasn't buried at the base of the lighthouse tower last week," Bertie said.

"Allow me to be the judge of that," Jeremy said.

I saw Bertie's back stiffen. This man was already rubbing her the wrong way. If he wasn't careful, he'd find himself barred from seeing the notebook at any time. From his spot on the top of a bookshelf, Charles hissed at Jeremy.

Phil Cahill, the fourth member of the group, coughed lightly, and said in his quiet, polite voice. "If it wouldn't be too inconvenient Bertie, we would appreciate it. Just a quick peek." Phil was around sixty, reserved and taciturn, a passionate lover of the Outer Banks, and the author of popular nonfiction books about the earliest settlers to the eastern seaboard. He did much of his research in our rare books room and was a vocal supporter of the library. He'd donated generously to the building restoration fund over the winter.

Bertie gave in. "I suppose a quick peek wouldn't hurt. Lucy, can you lock up, please."

I headed for the door, but I arrived too late. It flew open to admit two more people, almost hitting me in the face. I suppressed a groan. Professors Elizabeth McArthur and Norman Hoskins from Blacklock College.

"What's this?" Elizabeth shouted, "You've found wartime letters from President Lincoln? We came the moment we heard."

"Lincoln!" Lynne's hands fluttered. "Oh, my goodness, I never dreamed. I wonder how they came to be here?"

"We've found nothing of the sort," Bertie said. "It's an old journal. A fishing wife's record of the weather and the tides."

The newcomers' faces fell.

"What it is remains to be seen," Jeremy said. "Which is why we're here. I don't recall inviting you to join us, Professor McArthur."

"I don't recall you being invited to invite anyone," Bertie muttered under her breath.

"I don't know that I need an invitation from you or anyone else," Elizabeth McArthur replied. "If this is a document of potential historical importance, it needs to be examined by professionals, not a pack of enthusiastic amateurs."

"I don't consider myself—" Phil began.

Elizabeth cut him off. "You, Mr. Cahill, merely write up in popular format what others have spent years of scholarly devotion studying."

Phil bristled. "My books bring history to life so folks can appreciate—"

Bertie didn't allow him to finish his explanation. "What are you doing here, Professors?"

We'd encountered Norman Hoskins and Elizabeth McArthur before. They were professors of North

Carolina history at Blacklock College in Elizabeth City, and last year they'd been in competition with us for possession of a valuable collection of seventeenth- and eighteenth-century maps and sea charts. In the end, no one got the collection when the owner died and his granddaughter assumed management of it. The methods McArthur and Hoskins employed in their attempts to secure the papers were not entirely aboveboard.

"Word reached us," Elizabeth said, "of this discovery. Naturally we decided to come and take a look for ourselves." Norman said nothing, but he nodded enthusiastically as she spoke.

"Might as well make a party of it," Bertie said.

"Oh good, I'm not late." Louise Jane burst into the room, panting heavily, as though she'd run the entire way. "Accident at Whalebone Junction, and I got delayed. A couple of cars turned into the driveway behind me. I think one of them is Diane and Curtis."

"This is ridiculous!" Jeremy said. "We're here on an important, perhaps vitally important, historical mission, and everyone and their cat"—he threw a hostile look at Charles—"thinks they can barge in."

"It is my library," Bertie said.

"Barge in!" Louise Jane shouted. "I'll have you know I was present when the notebook was found. I've already seen it. You're lucky I agreed with Bertie that it should stay in the library. She wanted me to take it home so my grandmother could examine it."

"I didn't—" Bertie said.

"Your grandmother!" Lynne yelled. "That old fraud."

"Notebook?" Norman said. "You mean they're not letters from President Lincoln?"

"My grandmother and her family before her were part of the history of the Outer Banks when your ancestors were living in New York City, Lynne." Louise Jane managed to make it sound as though living in New York was some sort of crime.

Maybe to her it was.

Lynne sputtered, but Phil spoke over her. "Lynne is as proud a Banker as you and your grandmother, Louise Jane. At least she's not chasing ghosts up and down the coast."

"Paranormal research is an important part—"

"You people aren't still insisting this library is haunted, are you?" Elizabeth said.

"We've never . . ." I said.

"Look who we found." Diane Uppiton and Curtis Gardner were next through our doors. An apologetic-looking Connor McNeil tagged along behind them.

"Sorry I'm early, Lucy," Connor said. "I stopped into Josie's to grab a coffee after a meeting, and I ran into Diane and Curtis, and . . ." His voice trailed off.

Diane was dressed in one of her pastel Chanel suits. She must have come directly from the hairdresser: the scent of the hair spray holding her solid black helmet in place surrounded her like a noxious cloud. "I asked Connor what was going on at the library, but he wouldn't tell us. We decided we had to come and have a look for ourselves. Good thing we did. We seem to be the only representatives of the library board on hand."

"Figured you'd want us here," Curtis said.

Charles jumped off the bookshelf where he'd been sitting to best hear the conversation, and hurried over to greet the new arrivals. By *greet*, I mean he stretched out his claws and took a swipe at Diane's leg. She screeched and leapt out of the way before he could ruin her stockings. Goal achieved, he smirked and leapt back to his place.

Charles didn't like Diane and Curtis, and he rarely failed to display his disapproval. I didn't like them either, but I was never so obvious about it. Curtis and Diane might be members of our board, but they were no friends of the library. Diane inherited her position when her husband, who'd been chair of the board, died. At the time of his death, they were going through a highly acrimonious and very public divorce. She'd hated everything he cared about, and she still did. Including the Bodie Island Lighthouse Library. She and Curtis took up housekeeping together shortly after Diane's husband's death, and she managed to get Curtis on the board to serve as her ally. He didn't care about the library one way or another, but he knew who was paying his bills—Diane—and he took her side on every matter, whether he understood it or not.

"Lucy, lock that door!" Bertie shouted.

I did so before the remainder of the population of Nags Head and environs could get wind of what was happening and decide to join us.

Bertie clapped her hands in an attempt to be heard over the babble of voices. No one paid the slightest bit of attention, so I decided it was time for me to intervene. I have three older brothers, and growing up I'd learned a trick or two.

One of which is to whistle.

I put my fingers in my mouth and blew. To my intense satisfaction, the sound rang throughout the room and bounced off the curving, whitewashed stone walls. Everyone stopped arguing in mid-sentence.

"I didn't know you could do that," Connor said with what sounded like genuine admiration.

"Thank you, Lucy," Bertie said. "Now that I have your attention, we will proceed in an orderly fashion into my office. I'll lay out the notebook, and you can all have a look. But no touching."

"What do you mean, *no touching*?" Jeremy said. "If you want us to examine it, we have to have a close look."

"Examine what, exactly?" Diane asked. "Bertie what's going on here?"

"See what I mean about amateurs?" Elizabeth McArthur said. "Proper analysis needs to be done to authenticate the age of the document. We have the facilities at Blacklock College. I can take it tonight and start work tomorrow."

"It's a fisherman's wife's journal," Mrs. Eastland said, "not a lost copy of the Magna Carta."

"What's a *carta*?" Curtis asked.

"You mean all this fuss is over some diary?" Diane said. "My mother's kept a diary her whole life. Most boring thing I can imagine."

"A great many documents of considerable importance have been mistaken at first for common or garden items," Elizabeth pointed out.

"I for one would prefer a settler's diary," Louise Jane said. "The Magna Carta's been read already."

Bertie led the way, and I brought up the rear. "Don't say anything about the map," I whispered to Connor. "Bertie doesn't want to start rumors of buried treasure."

"Too late," he said. "I have a mental image of everyone in town out with picks and shovels digging up the shoreline." Connor dipped his chin to indicate Curtis. "Led by you-know-who."

I shuddered. "Perish the thought."

Chapter Four

A painting hung on the wall behind Bertie's desk. It showed a woman on the beach, doing a downward dog, framed by the light of the rising sun. It was beautiful and calming, and I always gave it an admiring look when I came in here.

I did so now, but I was the only one. Everyone else gathered expectantly around the desk. Curtis and Norman elbowed each other in some sort of display of dominance as they jostled for the best place to stand. Diane didn't bother to be discreet. She simply stepped directly in front of Mrs. Eastland. Lynne trod on Elizabeth McArthur's toes, and the professor yelped. I was conscious of Jeremy behind me, standing, I thought, far too close. Everyone scrambled to see better. Everyone except for Connor, who stood off to one side with a wry smile on his handsome face.

Bertie unlocked her desk drawer. She slipped on the white gloves and then carefully lifted up the tin box. I cleared a space on her desk and placed two books on either side to help support the diary. Bertie put the book down, carefully opened the first page, and everyone leaned in.

"No touching," Bertie said.

"No breathing," Connor muttered. I suppressed a giggle.

Jeremy's hand brushed my lower back as he leaned forward, and I squirmed out of the way. "At first glance," he said, "it looks to be well preserved. The leather binding is in good shape, and there's little deterioration of the paper."

"You say it was found inside that box," Elizabeth said. "That would preserve the paper quite well."

"The handwriting is good," Norman said. "Perfectly legible. That indicates the author received an excellent education."

"Or she was taught at home by a mother with good penmanship," Lynne said.

"That's what I thought," Mrs. Eastland said.

"The first thing we'd like to determine," Bertie said, "is if this was written in the Outer Banks. The weather entries should give you a place to start."

"I told the others we could help with that," Mrs. Eastland said.

"How much is it worth?" Curtis asked.

"Nothing," Lynne said. "Not in monetary value."

"Oh." Curtis lost interest. He broke out of the circle and went to lean against the door. He checked his phone.

"Not everything in this world can be judged by its monetary value," Mrs. Eastland said.

"Lynne, Phil, and Mabel can come back tomorrow and read it here," Bertie said.

"I'll assume you didn't deliberately slight me," Jeremy said. "I'll be part of that group."

"We wouldn't dream of working without you," Lynne said.

"Thank you." He gave her a slight bow.

Lynne preened. Mrs. Eastland snickered.

"If that's okay with you, Mr. Mayor?" Bertie asked.

"Sure," Connor said.

"The history department at Blacklock College is eminently qualified to examine it." Elizabeth said.

"I'm sure you are," Connor said. "But as this is, as far as we know, an Outer Banks relic, and of no monetary significance, we'll keep it for now. Thanks for coming."

"You're welcome to use our facilities at the college," Norman said to Jeremy.

"I might do that if it proves necessary," Jeremy replied.

"You might not," Phil said. "I'm with Connor. If we let it leave town, we'll never get it back."

"I'm not going to steal it," Norman said.

"Not in so many words, perhaps," Lynne said.

"I'll remind you, Jeremy," Mrs. Eastland said, "we are a society. We do not work as individuals."

"Is that so?" he said, "I don't recall you turning down my financial contribution on the grounds that you only want money raised collectively."

"That's completely different," Mrs. Eastland said.

"Jeremy's right," Lynne said, "he—"

"If Jeremy said the sky was green, you'd agree with him," Mrs. Eastland said.

Jeremy smirked. He was, I realized, enjoying this.

"Who cares?" Curtis put away his phone. "Anyone feel like going for a drink?"

"You should tell Eunice about this, Bertie," Diane said. Eunice Fitzgerald was the chair of the library board.

"Thank you for your advice, Diane," my boss replied. "That was certainly worth you coming all the way out here."

Diane tossed her head. Her hair didn't move. She took Curtis's arm and they headed for the door.

"But what about the coded page and the treasure map?" Mrs. Eastland said. "Are you going to show them those?"

Curtis and Diane swung around. Norman sucked in a breath. Elizabeth's eyes opened wide. Lynne gasped. Jeremy said, his voice low and calm, "There's a treasure map?"

"That's what people are saying in town," Phil said, "I assumed it was nothing but a wild rumor. Is it true then?"

"Mabel!" Bertie said, "We agreed to keep that quiet for now."

Mrs. Eastland's hands flew to her face. "Oh, dear. My husband always says my big mouth is my worst enemy. I didn't mean it. There isn't any treasure map. No, really. I made that up."

"Bertie?" Jeremy asked.

"If you found a map, it might have some historical significance," Elizabeth said. "Not that it's any treasure map, of course. That's nothing but overly dramatic pirate stories invented by writers of popular fiction."

"If that's a dig at me," Phil said, "you missed the mark. I don't write fiction."

"Or," Bertie said, "it might be someone's sketch of where their friends live or a child's attempt to be clever."

Curtis snapped his fingers. "Let's see this map, Bertie."

She glanced at Connor. He gave her a slight nod. Bertie took the separate sheet of paper out of the box and spread it on her desk.

Curtis stepped forward and gave it a quick glance. "That's supposed to be a map? It could be anywhere." He went back to the wall and resumed the study of his phone.

"What do those numbers mean?" Diane asked.

"It's a map of the Outer Banks," Norman said. "As it once was. At Blacklock we have an extensive collection of old maps. I'll take it back and compare, try to date it."

"And what's this about a code page?" Elizabeth said. "Let's see it. It might be the key to the map."

"Enough," Connor said. "Everything stays here. If the help of Blacklock College is needed, we'll be in touch. As for the here and now, I don't believe you were invited to join us today. Lucy, can you show our guests to the door, please."

"Now see here," Norman said.

"Don't bother arguing," Elizabeth said. "We'll go, because we've been asked. But we'll be back. With a court order. You people, amateurs and librarians, don't know what you have here."

"May I remind you," Bertie said, "that we have Charlene Clayton, a librarian so qualified you tried to steal her from us to handle the Ruddle legacy."

Norman sputtered. "We never!"

"Charlene will be in charge of the care of the note-book and its contents," Bertie said, "if you agree, Mr. Mayor?"

"An excellent suggestion," Connor said.

After giving Bertie one last poisonous glare and a sniff of disapproval, Elizabeth followed me out. Norman followed her.

When I got back to the office, having ensured the door was securely locked behind me, I was not at all surprised to find that an argument had broken out.

"It's not even six o'clock," Jeremy said. "We can get hours of work done yet. You haven't showed us this code page yet."

"Not until Charlene can supervise," Bertie said. "And that is that."

"Your suggestion is insulting," Lynne said, with a peek at Jeremy out of the corner of her eyes. "We at the historical society have handled plenty of old papers before, isn't that right, Jeremy? Some of them more valuable than this fishwife's diary."

"For once I agree with Jeremy and Lynne." Phil said. "And that doesn't happen often. But I'll concede your point, Bertie. Phone Charlene and tell her to get down here."

"It's Monday," I said.

"So?" Jeremy asked.

"Sundays and Mondays are Mrs. Clayton's caregiver's days off. . On Monday, Charlene gets a friend to stay with her mom until five. She won't come out now and leave her mom alone."

Even Jeremy couldn't argue with that.

Charlene was an expert in the care of historic documents. She'd worked in the Bodleian Library at Oxford University, among papers far older than anything found in North Carolina. She'd given up the job she loved to come home to Nags Head when her mother fell ill and needed care.

"Tomorrow it is then," Phil said. "What time does Charlene get in?"

"Nine," Bertie said.

"We'll be back at nine then."

Curtis looked up from his phone. "Anyone for that drink?"

"I can't," Diane said. "I have to go to my mother's for dinner. I told you that."

"Oh, right. Jeremy, Phil, Connor, you free?"

"No thanks," Connor said. "Lucy and I have dinner plans."

Phil shook his head, but Jeremy said, "Sure."

"I'm sorry, but I have another appointment," said Lynne, who had not been invited.

Bertie put the diary into the tin box, placed the two separate pages on top, closed the lid with a thud, put it in her desk drawer, gave the key a satisfying twist, and dropped the key into her purse.

Chapter Five

"I have something to confess," I said to Connor after the waiter had taken our drink orders.

"I figured you did," he said.

"You did not. I'm not that readable. Am I?"

"The words 'open book' come to mind." He smiled at me. "I can even guess what your secret is. You have a picture of the map and code page on your phone."

"Oh."

He laughed. "Don't worry, I didn't detect anything in the manner of Sherlock Holmes. Bertie told me you took a picture of them. Can I see it?"

"Even better," I said. "I printed copies when you and Bertie were chatting." Before I did my usual after-closing quick sweep and last-minute check of the library, looking for left-behind items, and then ran upstairs to my apartment to change for dinner.

We were at Jake's Seafood Bar, our favorite restaurant. The intense heat of the day lingered, but a soft breeze was blowing off Roanoke Sound, making it comfortable enough to sit outside. Lights were coming on in the houses lining the shore of Roanoke Island and on boats bobbing gently in the calm waters of the harbor. The fourth-order Fresnel lens of the reproduction Roanoke Marshes Lighthouse flashed its rhythm. A large white candle burned in the hurricane lamp on our table and threw shadows under Connor's sharp cheekbones.

The waiter arrived with our drinks while I dug in my bag for the sheets of paper and spread them out in front of me.

Connor moved his seat so he was beside me, not across the table. "I see letters," he said. "Lots of handwritten letters. But no recognizable words."

"I know something about cryptography. When I was young, one or another of my brothers was always sneaking into my room to rifle through my school notebooks for letters from my friends or in an attempt find my diary. I came up with codes so they couldn't read them. I got my girlfriends into it, and we wrote back and forth in code for a while."

"You mean you can tell what this says?"

"Haven't a clue. It looks like a substitution code to me."

"And that means?"

"Simply, one letter is substituted for another. Use a *b* in place of a *w*, for example." I studied the printout, looking for a pattern. Nothing was immediately apparent.

"How do you know what's substituted for what?" Connor asked.

"That's the problem. You don't. Not if the originator of the code doesn't tell you. But words have patterns, so all we have to do is find the patterns. The most common letter in English is *e*."

"There aren't many *e*'s used here."

"But there are a lot of *w*'s. So we speculate that perhaps *w* has been used in place of *e* and see what we get."

We studied the paper in silence for a while.

"Nothing stands out," Connor said at last.

"It doesn't, does it? But that would be too simple. The most common method of substitution is to simply reverse the order of the letters. Replace *a* with *z*, and *b* with *y*, and so on. That's what my friends and I did at first, thinking we were so clever." I dug in my purse for a pen and the scrap of paper on which I'd scribbled a shopping list. On the back of the list, I began writing out the letters as they were in the diary page, using the formula I'd told Connor about.

I ended up with a line of gibberish.

"That doesn't make any more sense," he said.

"How far have you gotten into *Journey to the Center of the Earth*?"

"As I suspect that question is related to our puzzle here, I can't bluff, so I'll confess I haven't started."

"The book club meeting is Wednesday."

He hung his head. "Sorry, no excuse—just too busy."

"The story begins when our hero and his scientist uncle discover a coded page in an old book. The solution turns out to be much simpler than they initially thought. Meaning they were making it more complicated than it needed to be."

"Fine, but in a book like that one, the code is created so the characters can break it, right?"

"Unfortunately, yes. Otherwise, you'd have no story. The problem with a substitution code, if it's not merely replacing one letter with another, is that you need a key."

"What sort of key?"

"Sometimes it can be in a book agreed upon ahead of time that both parties have access to. Like the first letter in the first word in the fifth paragraph on the two hundred and fifty-fourth page represents an *a*."

Connor's eyebrows rose. "Meaning without the book you don't have a chance."

"You do have a chance, even without the key. If you can find the pattern—if there *is* a pattern."

"Okay," he said. "Do you see any pattern here?" He touched the paper with his index finger.

"No, but that doesn't mean there isn't one. Sometimes even figuring out the pattern isn't enough. The substitution might change at a predetermined place; the fifth letter in the fourth line, for example. You can see how long some of these words are. That means they aren't likely to be individual words, but several words strung together in order to confuse the search for a pattern."

"You're also assuming it's in English."

"I guess I am, but all languages have patterns, and if we can detect the pattern, a linguist should be able to tell us what it is."

"A linguist such as found at Blacklock College?"

"Yes, but not Norm and Lizzie. I don't trust them one little bit. If we give them the code page or the map, we'll never see them again. Bertie's friend Professor McClanahan might be able to help with linguistics. If we get that far." I mentally began moving letters about.

The waiter appeared at our table, carrying a plate. "A treat from the kitchen."

I jerked. "What? Oh, sorry. Thanks." I hastily picked up the papers so the waiter could place the dish in front of us.

"I told Jake you're here. He says hi."

"Say hi back," Connor said. "And thank him."

I picked up a plump, glistening hush puppy and dipped it into the spicy sauce provided. Jake Greenblatt, owner and head chef, was married to my cousin Josie, and he knew how much I love these tasty little lumps of fried dough.

"Ready to order?" The waiter asked.

I hadn't even checked the menu. I didn't need to: I know it by heart. I asked for the shrimp and grits, as I usually did. Jake's were the best in Nags Head, if not the entire Outer Banks. Maybe all of North Carolina. Connor ordered a steak, rare, with a baked potato and Caesar salad, and we handed our unopened menus to the waiter.

"I never understand why you come to a seafood place as special as Jake's and have steak and potatoes," I said.

Connor just grinned at me and took a sip of his beer. "If the code used here is complicated, does that mean it's more than a fishing wife hiding something from her husband or a couple of kids playing at pirate treasure?"

"Might be. Might not be. Might be a determined fishing wife or a very clever child. I came up with some pretty imaginative ways of keeping my brothers out of my diary. Although the code page—if it is a code page—was written by a different person than the diarist. The handwriting is totally different."

"I'd like to have a peek at that diary of yours," he said.

"It would bore you silly. I was anything but a rebellious child." That was true. My biggest act of rebellion was to move to the Outer Banks to work in the Lighthouse Library. That, and to turn down the proposal from the man my mother had selected for me.

"Wugmunch," Connor said.

"What's that?"

"The only word I can make out is *wugmunch*."

"*Wugmunch* isn't a word."

"My point exactly. If you propose that the letter *f*, which seems to be quite common on the page, is a *u*, in order to have some vowels, then that"—he pointed at a line of print—"says *wugmunch*. Or maybe it's an *e*, so the word becomes *wegmench*."

"Do you know of a place called Wegmench? The town of Wegmench?"

"Lake Wugmunch?"

"Wugmunch Bay?"

"You want that?" Connor pointed to the last hush puppy.

"Help yourself," I said, and he did.

The waiter brought our meals, and once again I shoved the papers to one side.

"It might not make any sense at all, Lucy," Connor said as we dug into the delicious food. "There might well be no rhyme or reason to it. The person who wrote that page might not have even been literate. They could have been just copying out letters at random."

"But the handwriting is so good, and so neat, although a bit rough."

"Imitation maybe? Or someone who'd lost their mental faculties trying to recreate something they remembered?"

"That's discouraging."

"I'm only being practical. As for it giving clues to the meaning of the map, that's a mighty big stretch too. The map might just be a map and the numbers have no meaning other than to the map drawer."

I sighed. "You're probably right. I'm letting myself be influenced by Jules Verne."

"If it does give directions to the center of the earth, I don't know that I'd want to go there," Connor said. "Isn't it hot?"

"Can't be much hotter down there than it is up here this week. Mr. Verne's knowledge of chemistry and physics wasn't extensive. The science in the book is absolute rubbish. Other than that, it's a good story."

"Hey!" Connor leapt up, almost upsetting his beer. As often happens along the coast, out of seemingly nowhere, a storm struck. A sudden gust of wind lifted the printout off the table and hurled it toward the deck railing. Connor snatched it out of the air in the nick of time.

"Nice catch," I said.

"Close one," he said, securing it on the table with a salt shaker.

Around us people scurried for cover, and waiters adjusted umbrellas. Our table was under an awning, and we remained snug and dry as rain pounded on the roof and splashed at our feet. The temperature dropped about ten degrees in a matter of minutes, and I was glad of it.

I folded the printout, put it and my shopping list in my bag, and settled down to enjoy my dinner and the company.

When we finished eating—with me having declined dessert and Connor vacuuming up an enormous slice of key lime pie made at my cousin's bakery—and were relaxing over our coffee, Connor said, "You can look at it again, if you want."

"Look at what?"

"The so-called code."

"More mind reading?" I had been thinking about it.

"More like I'd like another peek."

We studied the page in silence. The back of the grocery list was now covered with seemingly random letters, many of them scratched out or overwritten. The rain stopped as quickly as it had begun, leaving the wooden boards of the deck glistening and clear drops dripping off the umbrellas.

"I could stare at this all night," I said, "and make no more sense of it than when I first saw it. We need that key."

"If there is a key."

"Do you want me to make you a copy?"

Connor threw up his hands. "Oh no. I'd never get any work done—and probably get no sleep either. I'd keep thinking, *One more try.*"

"Which is likely to be what I'll be doing the rest of the night."

"Ready to go?"

"Yes. Sorry if I seemed distracted."

"You were distracted. And so was I. There's something about word puzzles. We simply can't let go. It's early still. I hear good things about that band playing at The Tidal Wave Lounge. Want to go and hear a set?"

"I'd like that," I said.

We left the restaurant and splashed through newly formed puddles to Connor's car.

*   *   *

The band had been good and we'd stayed to listen to several sets. It was after ten before we headed back to my place.

"How are the plans for Settlers' Day going?" Connor asked as he drove through the dark, wet streets.

"Well, as far as I know. It's nice not to have much to do. The historical society's taking care of all the details. They're in charge of the day. We're just providing the space on our lawn."

"I've heard good things about that Jeremy Hughes," Connor said. "He put the money up to get the plans underway, and he's been generous about donating to some of the environmental initiatives."

I considered telling Connor I had a bad feeling about Jeremy. I hadn't liked the way Charlene ducked her head and fled at the sight of him, or the way he looked at me and "accidently" brushed up against me. Charles had clearly not taken to him. Charles, I had found, is an excellent judge of character.

I decided to say nothing. If Charlene had a problem with him, it was up to her to tell us, if she wanted to. I would try to ensure I wasn't ever alone with the man.

"Speaking of environmental issues, what's happening with that controversial development you've been worried about?" I asked.

"My allies on the town council and I are working hard at our end to keep it under some sort of control, so it matches the needs of the environment and the desires of people in the adjacent streets, but powerful forces want to see that resort built into the biggest and the flashiest around."

"Why has this come up now?"

"Most of that land has been in the Monaghan family for generations. Nathanial Monaghan was a local legend, fiercely dedicated to the preservation of the Outer Banks. He refused to sell off any of the land, no matter how much he was offered, determined that it wouldn't be developed. And so that parcel has been untouched for more than seventy years while the Outer Banks built up around it. The old man died two years ago, leaving the property without condition to Rick, his only child. Rick's arguing that he can do what he wants with it. On the positive side, his company's having some trouble raising the last of the needed cash before they can get the final permits and start work. Without that, they'll have to scale back their plans."

"Let's hope," I said.

"Rick Monaghan has badly overstretched himself, but once people started opposing his plans, he dug his heels in, and now he can't allow himself to be seen to back down. He refuses to admit that the smaller hotel is a better option for everyone. Including his family."

We drove in silence for a few minutes. When the flash of the lighthouse beam appeared in the distance, I said, "It would be fun, wouldn't it, if we had found an important historic document buried literally under our feet?"

"I don't know about 'fun.' Without even knowing what it is, you had the university people and the historical society squabbling about it. Not to mention Louise Jane wanting her grandmother's take, and everyone's ears pricking up the moment someone mentioned treasure."

"Are you coming to book club on Wednesday?"

"I plan to. I guess I know what I'll be doing for the next couple of nights."

"The book's not overly long. Not like some classic works."

"I'm glad to hear that."

He pulled into the long, winding lane that led between rows of tall red pines to the lighthouse and the marshes surrounding it. The road was wet and the BMW's tires spat rainwater on either side of the car. Overhead the clouds had moved on, and a three-quarters moon had come out.

Two cars were in the parking lot: my teal Yaris and one other I didn't recognize. It hadn't been there when we left, but I gave it no mind. People often came to see the lighthouse at night or to enjoy a moonlight stroll along the boardwalk to the marsh.

Connor parked at the top of the path.

"Far be it from me to interrupt your reading," I said, "but do you want to come in for a bit?"

He didn't turn to look at me.

"Connor?"

"Lucy, did you lock the door?"

"Of course I . . . oh."

The front entrance to the library was open. Images flashed through my mind. I'd been the last to leave. Connor and Bertie had been outside, chatting while Connor waited for me. All the others, those here to argue over the notebook and the map, had gotten into their cars and driven away before us.

It was possible Ronald or Charlene had come back for something, but their cars weren't here. And they wouldn't have left the door open.

I might have forgotten to lock up, although I didn't think so, but I never would have left the front door standing open.

"Charles!" I jumped out of the car.

"Lucy, no! Wait!" Connor ran up the path after me. He grabbed my arm. "Don't go in."

"But *Charles*."

"Charles can look after himself." He took his phone out of his pocket. "You were last to leave. Are you sure you shut the door?"

"Positive."

"Might Bertie have come back?"

"She might, but she would have locked up when she left."

"I'll go in and check it out. You wait here."

"I'm coming with you."

"Lucy."

I slipped my hand into his free one. "Let's go."

As soon as we got closer, we could see that no one had simply forgotten to set the lock. Shards of what had once been the door flapped in the wind. The wood around the lock and the handle had been smashed as though someone had gone after it with a sledgehammer.

Connor cautiously pushed the broken door aside, and we stepped into the library together. "Hello!" Connor yelled. "Anyone here? The police have been called."

We held our breath. All was quiet. Nothing seemed to be disturbed. The computer sat on the circulation desk, dark and quiet, as were the three computers used by our patrons. The books were neatly lined on the shelves, the magazine rack tidy.

I normally love being in a library at night. The peace, the quiet. Being surrounded by thousands of pages waiting to be turned, millions of words waiting to be read. But tonight, the silence was ominous, the dark foreboding.

Connor pointed to the spiral iron stairs, twisting upward into the dark. I shook my head. There would be no reason for anyone to go up there. My apartment had a good solid door and its own lock, and the only window was a hundred feet above the ground. The rare books room, where we kept items of value, was accessible by the back staircase, and it also had its own lock.

I was desperately worried about Charles. He hadn't come out to greet us, as he always did—not, I was sure, because he was happy to see me, but to remind me it was time to fill the food bowl.

It was always time to fill the food bowl.

"Office," I whispered.

Barely breathing, we crept down the hallway. Connor gripped my hand firmly, and I clung to his in return. The door to Bertie's office was closed, but a thin line of light leaked out. Bertie was a tyrant in terms of electricity use. She never would have left a light on.

Behind the door a shadow moved across the light.

I yelped.

Connor pushed buttons on his phone and spoke quickly but calmly. "This is Mayor McNeil. There's an intruder at the lighthouse library."

"I'm sending someone now, Your Honor. Please keep this line open and wait for us outside."

"Will do," he said. He stepped backward, pulling me along with him.

A screech that might have come from the center of the earth broke the silence. Charles! I didn't even think of what else might be lying in wait behind that door. I dropped Connor's hand as he cried, "Lucy, no!" and I wrenched open the office door.

I'd last been in this room about four hours ago. It had changed totally since. The visitor's chair was over-turned, and books had fallen off the shelves and lay tum-bled on the floor. The computer monitor was face down on the desk, and the keyboard and mouse were nowhere to be seen. Papers littered the floor like giant snowflakes.

Only the painting of the woman doing yoga on the beach was still in place, silent and serene and now look-ing so very out of place.

Charles sat on the desk, next to the overturned com-puter monitor, staring at me as if to say, *"About time you showed up."* He jumped down, landing on the far side of Bertie's desk.

I walked slowly across the room, feeling Connor close behind me as we rounded the desk. The keyboard and mouse dangled in the air, swinging at the end of their cords. The drawer where Bertie had locked up the tin box and its contents was open, the lock smashed.

A man lay on the floor. Charles sat beside him, but he made no attempt to push the cat away. It was Jeremy Hughes. Leather gloves were on his hands, and his eyes were open. He stared at the ceiling, unseeing, not moving.

Chapter Six

"Tea?"

"What? Oh yes. Tea. Thank you."

"I put extra sugar in."

"Thank you." I accepted the steaming mug.

"Where did you get a cup of hot tea out here at this time of night?" Connor asked.

"It's mine," the young police officer said. "I carry a thermos when I'm working nights. My mother's from England. Nothing better than a cup of hot tea, she always says. Although she calls it tea, not hot tea."

I breathed in the warm, herby, sweet fragrance. "Because *hot* tea goes without saying in England."

"Right." She held out her hand, and I accepted it. She was short and stocky and very young, with a sprinkling of freckles across her pale face and frizzy red hair pulled into a tight ponytail. "I'm Holly Rankin. I started working here yesterday." She turned to Connor. "You must be Mayor McNeil."

They shook hands. "Sorry to meet you this way, Officer Rankin," he said.

Connor and I were sitting outside on the steps of the library. Officers, including our friend Butch Greenblatt, had arrived shortly after we found the body of Jeremy Hughes, and we'd been hustled out of the building mighty quick. Officer Rankin had been assigned to watch over us. Why they thought we needed watching over, I didn't know. Maybe it was to give Holly Rankin something to do.

The storm had done nothing to break the heat; instead, it seemed to have only laid another level of humidity on top of it, but the hot tea was welcome nonetheless.

The moon had slipped behind a fresh bank of clouds, and this far from town it was very dark. The single lamp above the smashed and broken door threw a small circle of light onto the steps. At regular intervals the great 1000-watt bulb high above us flashed its steady rhythm of 2.5 seconds on, 2.5 seconds off, 2.5 seconds on, and 22.5 seconds off.

In these days of illuminated towns and cities and vast ribbons of highway, as well as radio satellites and GPS systems, lighthouses no longer perform the lifesaving function they were built for—to guide ships at sea— but I find the Bodie Island Light comforting in its regularity and reliability. Steady and unchanging in an unsure, constantly shifting world.

Back on the ground, more red and blue lights flashed as cars sped down the lane. An ambulance had been one of the first to arrive, and the medics had run inside. When they came out, they walked more slowly and did not have Jeremy with them.

Connor and I had known he was dead the moment we saw him, but Connor had dropped beside him to check for life signs, and we'd stayed with him until Butch arrived. A quick glance at the open tin box showed me that the diary was still nested within as it had been for more than a hundred years.

Charles had rubbed against my legs, and I bent down to stroke him, seeking comfort in his thick, warm fur.

For his pains, the big cat was now confined to the broom closet while the police did their work. He didn't sound very happy about that, and his plaintive cries echoed around the building.

"Evenin', Connor, Lucy."

I looked up at the sound of my name. Connor got to his feet and said, "Sam."

Detective Sam Watson—crew cut, strong square jaw, penetrating gray eyes—had arrived. "Want to tell me what you know before I go in there?"

I let Connor speak. Quickly and efficiently he told Watson about noticing the broken door and us venturing cautiously into the library to find . . . what we found.

"The nine-one-one operator told you to leave the building until a patrol could get here," Sam said. "Why didn't you? He could have been standing behind that door with a gun."

"I—" Connor said.

"It was me," I confessed. "I didn't think. I heard Charles cry out. I thought he needed me."

"Charles. You mean that dratted cat."

Detective Sam Watson was not a cat person.

"Charles alerted us to the presence of a body in the office," I said. "That's a good thing."

"Do you have any idea what he was doing in there?"

"He must have followed Jeremy and whoever was with him, and got trapped inside when the door shut as that person left," I said.

"I mean what the deceased was doing, not the cat."

"Oh. No, sorry."

"I can hazard a guess," Connor said, "but it's complicated."

"It's always complicated when the lighthouse library's involved," Watson said. "Lucy said his name was Jeremy. You know him?"

"Yes, we do. Jeremy Hughes from the Bodie Island Historical Society. He was here, at the library, earlier. As were a good number of people wanting to look at an artifact the diggers found."

"What sort of artifact?"

Connor and I exchanged a look.

"As I said," Connor said, "it's complicated. You might want to wait until Bertie gets here, and she can explain. I assume she's been called?"

"She has. Are you talking about the map leading to pirate treasure that was dug up earlier? Everyone at the station's talking about it, and I assumed it was nothing but a wild rumor. You're saying there's something to it?"

"We don't believe it's a treasure map," I said. "But right now we don't know what it is."

"Is it something worth killing over?" Watson asked.

Connor and I exchanged another glance. "I wouldn't have thought so," I said.

"But now you do?"

"I don't know, but someone broke the drawer where Bertie had locked the papers for the night. We found not only a map—guide to pirate treasure or not—but a leather-bound diary dating from the Civil War era, along with a couple of loose sheets of paper. They were in a tin box, buried underground next to the lighthouse tower. The box is still in Bertie's desk drawer. We have to assume Jeremy came back tonight either to steal it or to have a private look it."

"We have to assume that, do we?" Watson said.

"A reasonable assumption," Connor said. "It's also reasonable to assume someone else wanted to do the same.

You'll see what I mean when you see the office, Sam. You've been in there often enough to know Bertie is neat and well organized. Lucy and I touched nothing except for the man himself when I checked for signs of life."

At that moment the lighthouse light flashed high above us. Connor had stood up to talk to Detective Watson, and he caught the reflection of the light on something lying in the grass in the shadows at the base of the tower. "Hey. What's that?"

It was a sledgehammer. Almost certainly the one that had done the damage to our front door.

Officer Rankin, who'd been silently listening to us, took a step forward.

"Don't touch it," Watson said. "I'll send someone for it."

"It might have been left by the construction crew," I said. "After they finished for the day." I didn't believe that, but I wanted to point out the possibility.

"I know George Grimshaw," Watson said. "He's not careless with his tools, and he doesn't let his crew be. You two wait here." He turned to Officer Rankin. "Get a forensics officer to have a look at that, and then go up to the highway and prevent anyone from coming in who's not with us. Except for Albertina James. Tell Ms. James and everyone else to park over there"—he pointed—"next to the marsh. No closer."

"Why?" I asked.

"It rained earlier tonight. If we're lucky, we can get some prints of the car our person of interest came in."

Watson went inside and Officer Rankin trotted away.

Connor sat back down and cradled my hand in both of his. A small overhang protects the top of the steps from the rain, so at least we weren't sitting in a puddle.

An officer walked up, grunted a hello to us, took some pictures of the sledgehammer, and then bagged it and carried it away.

We didn't have long to wait before Bertie arrived. She parked in the far corner of the lot, as directed, and we watched her jog across the lawn. "What on earth has happened now?"

"Jeremy Hughes," Connor said. "In your office. He's dead. Probably killed by a blow to the head."

Bertie groaned and dropped beside me.

"He has to have been after the notebook," I said. "Your desk drawer was broken open. The box is still there, so it's likely he was interrupted in the act."

"That notebook is someone's diary. A record of their day," Bertie said. "Hardly something to kill a man over."

"Perhaps," Connor said. "Perhaps not. I'm not saying there's anything to that map or the coded writing, but some might think it significant that more than a hundred years ago someone went to the trouble of burying the box at the base of the lighthouse."

"It wasn't buried," Bertie said firmly. "It fell in and got covered up. Much ado about nothing."

I didn't reply. It was a considerable amount of ado to whoever killed Jeremy Hughes.

"Jeremy wasn't the only one here tonight," I said. "Someone killed him, and your office is a wreck."

"What you do mean 'a wreck'?"

"Jeremy and his killer must have fought," Connor said. "Whether they came together or just happened to arrive around the same time is something Sam will have to figure out."

The three of us sat in silence for a long time. We watched forensics officers moving around the parking lot, shining bright lights onto the ground. They seemed to have found something on the other side of the path from Connor's car, which caused a lot of interest. They did the same on the walkway, searching for footprints, but they didn't have much luck there. Connor and I had run up the path, followed by numerous police officers and the ambulance crew. The prints of anyone who'd gone before us would have been stomped on.

Eventually, Sam Watson came out. Butch was with him, and he gave us tight smiles. "Let's talk," Watson said. "Tell me about this notebook and why this man Hughes would have been in your office after dark."

Bertie outlined the finding of the tin box and opening it. She told him about the crowd in her office who'd come to see it.

"I told them to come back tomorrow when Charlene could supervise the handling of it, and then I shooed them all away. I locked the box in my drawer and—"

An image flashed through my mind, and I sucked in a breath.

"What?" Watson said.

"I remember now. Bertie, you put the notebook in the box first and then placed the papers on top. You didn't tuck the papers back into the diary where we'd first found them."

"I don't remember," she said, "but if you say so."

I turned to Connor. "While you checked on Jeremy, I looked into the box. I didn't touch anything else. I saw the notebook. But I did not see the map or the mysterious code page."

* * *

Watson escorted Bertie into her office so she could see if anything had been taken. I leapt to my feet to accompany them, and the detective told me to sit down.

Connor and I held hands, watched the police activity, and waited.

We didn't have to wait for long. When they rejoined us, Watson's face was, as usual, impassive, but Bertie gave me a shake of her head before she dropped onto the step beside me. "Gone," she said.

"Can you describe this map and the page with the strange writing?" Watson asked.

"I can do better than that." I pulled my photocopies out of my bag and handed them to him.

He studied them, flipping back and forth between one page and the other, as Butch looked over his shoulder. "It's nonsense," Watson said.

"Might be a code of some sort," Butch said, "Like in *Journey to the Center of the Earth*." Butch and his girlfriend Stephanie were members of my book club.

"CeeCee's reading that book now." Watson's wife also came to the club. "Let's not try to make things more complicated than they already are." He waved the paper in the air. "This is a page out of an old book that makes no sense. Who else knows about this?"

"Pretty much half of Nags Head," Connor said, "and those who didn't hear about it today will by tomorrow morning. Word's spreading that a treasure map has been found. You said yourself they're talking about it at the police station."

Watson rolled his eyes toward the night sky. "I'll keep this," he said, "if that's all right." I knew he wasn't asking my permission, but I answered anyway. "Sure. I have the photos on my phone."

"Send me the pictures so I have as close to an original as I can get."

I did so while Bertie told them about the after-hours meeting in her office and who'd been there. "It was arranged that the historical society, including Jeremy Hughes, could make a closer study of the notebook tomorrow. They were due at nine o'clock, as soon as we open. There was no reason for him to come sneaking back." She glanced at the shattered door. "And break in."

"He might have hoped you or I'd still be here and give him a sneak peek," I said. "But he was going to see it tomorrow at any rate. It seems excessively dramatic to break down the door."

"You never know what people will do with enough motivation, Lucy," Watson said.

We all turned and looked at the shattered door. Jeremy, or whoever else might have been here tonight, had not bothered trying to finesse the lock. He, or she, had simply smashed the door open using a sledgehammer. They would only have done that if their intent had been to steal the contents of the tin box.

Watson would ask George Grimshaw if the sledgehammer was one of his, but I thought it unlikely. Everything the construction crew used was either taken away at the end of the day or locked securely behind the wire fence. That fence showed no signs of having been tampered with.

"At least two people were here tonight," Watson said. "Which one opened the door—Hughes or his killer?— is one of many questions."

He asked Bertie for the names of everyone who'd seen the notebook. Including George and Zack and their workers, library staff and patrons, two board members, the people from the historical society, and the Blacklock College professors, it made an impressive list.

"Louise Jane McKaughnan and Theodore Kowalski were here too," I added. "Louise Jane when the box was found, and later when we gathered in Bertie's office, but Theodore was only here for the initial opening of the box."

"All the usual suspects," Watson muttered.

"When the meeting ended," Connor said, "Jeremy Hughes asked me if I wanted to go for a drink. I declined, as Lucy and I had plans."

"That's not exactly right," I said. "I'd forgotten about that until now. Jeremy didn't make the suggestion. Curtis Gardner did. And Jeremy said okay."

"Do you know if they went for this drink?" Watson asked.

I shook my head. "I didn't see anyone leave."

"If they did, they must have met up after," Connor said. "They came in separate cars, and both cars were gone when we left."

"Diane asked Curtis to drop her at home first. Something about dinner with her parents," I said.

"I'll have a talk with Curtis Gardner, then. But first, Bertie, I need you to come back with me into your office and see if anything else is missing. Lucy, you can go upstairs if you promise to say there for the rest of the night."

"We can't leave the door like this," Connor said. "I'll call a locksmith and see if someone can get over here tonight to fix this door and install a new lock."

"Thanks," I said, and then, turning to Watson, "Can I get Charles out of the broom closet?"

"Yes, please. Half of my officers say they can't hear themselves think over that racket, and the other half think I'm being mean to the poor kitty."

Bertie stood up and brushed at the seat of her pants. "Will we be able to open the library tomorrow, Sam?"

"So far, I see no reason not to, although I'll have to ask you to stay out of your office. I'll call you when we're finished tonight, to let you know."

Bertie and Watson went inside. Butch trotted down the path to talk to the forensic officers who were preparing to take casts of whatever they'd found in the parking lot.

Connor and I stood together, conscious of the buzz of people all around us.

He rubbed at the top of his head, leaving his hair sticking up in all directions. "I wish this hadn't happened here," he said. "Not again."

I resisted the urge to pat his hair back down. "But it did. Don't worry. I promise to stay completely out of it this time. I'll let Sam Watson handle it. I won't so much as speculate about what might have happened. Not even to myself."

He gave me a smile. "I can't see that promise lasting for long. It's late—time for me to be off. If you're okay? I'll call that locksmith now, but I can take you to Ellen's if you don't want to spend the night here. She never minds late-night guests." Ellen was my aunt Ellen, my mother's sister. Although I grew up in Boston, when we were children, my brothers and I spent a good part of every summer in the Outer Banks with Ellen; her husband, Amos; and their three kids. She and I were very close. Sometimes I thought I was closer to her than to my own mother.

"I'll be fine." I held my arms up and out to indicate the solid bulk of the building behind me. "Safe as lighthouses."

He smiled at me. My heart rolled over. I slipped my hand into his, and we walked to his car. A few feet away, Butch crouched down, studying a tire track in the fresh mud left by the storm.

"See anything?" Connor asked.

"We're lucky that storm blew in and then blew out again so fast," one of the forensics officers said. "The only prints we should find here were laid down this evening."

"Are tire tracks individual?" I asked. "Surely they're mass produced?"

"Every type of tire for every model of car has its own markings," Butch said. "Obviously, a heck of a lot of them are the same, but tires wear in distinctive patterns. So yeah, if we find something to match this with, we might get lucky. It all helps to build a case." He pushed himself to his feet. "The meeting in Bertie's office ended before the rain began?"

"Yes." I said. "It was at least an hour after that before it started to rain. We were at Jake's."

"You were the last ones to leave here tonight?"

"Yes, we were. Jeremy returned after everyone was gone. Jeremy and whoever was with him."

"Or whoever followed him," Connor said.

"That's his car over there," Butch said, indicating the one on the other side of mine. "The plate's registered to one Jeremy Hughes of Nags Head." He rubbed at the dark stubble on his chin.

"What is it?" I asked. "Something's bothering you, I can tell."

He gave his head a sharp jerk, telling us to follow, and took a step away from the forensic officer who was preparing to make a cast of the imprint. Butch kept his voice low. "I recognize that tire print."

"How can you?" I asked.

"It's an old tire, badly worn on the inside, meaning an alignment hasn't been done in a long time. It had a puncture recently when a nail went into it and a temporary patch was put on."

"That should make it easier to find than if it had been a new tire," I said.

"Thing is, Lucy, I'm pretty sure I fixed that puncture myself about a week ago. I told the owner to get her tires changed immediately. Obviously that didn't happen."

"Her?"

"Louise Jane."

Chapter Seven

I stood by Connor's car for a long time, wrapped in the warm strength of his arms.

Louise Jane and I had never gotten on. She wanted a job at the library and refused to believe I hadn't snatched the one she deserved out from under her nose. She tried to frighten me away by making up stories of the haunting of the lighthouse in general and my apartment in particular, and in turn I didn't take her at all seriously.

But I've never believed she has any real malice in her, not even toward me, and I couldn't believe she'd have fought with a man over an old book, killed him, and driven off into the night.

"You're sure you're going to be okay tonight?" Connor said into my hair. "I can . . . stay, if you like."

I shook my head. Connor had only ever been into my apartment once, to doze in an armchair and watch over me after I'd been attacked one night.

Our relationship was new, and we were still finding our way. But I had the feeling, and I think he did too, that this could turn into something deep and truly meaningful. I was determined not to rush into anything.

I was certainly not going to invite him up tonight, not with Butch Greenblatt, Sam Watson, and the rest of the police department watching us.

Reluctantly, I pulled myself out of his arms. "Safe as lighthouses," I said again, trying to sound cheerful.

He bent down and kissed me. I settled into the kiss. He put his arms around me. I was about to settle even further into the kiss when someone called, "Hey, you there! Rankin, or whatever your name is, bring that light over here."

Connor and I separated, feeling like teenagers caught necking behind the school bleachers after class. We grinned sheepishly at each other, and I stepped away. "Besides, you have reading to do if you're going to be ready for book club on Wednesday."

"I'll call you first thing tomorrow," he said. He got into his car. The BMW roared to life, the headlights came on, and Connor drove away.

I went back to the lighthouse, intending to grab Charles and head upstairs. Instead, Butch and Watson came out as I put my foot on the first step.

"Lucy," Watson said, "you told me Louise Jane was here earlier, when everyone was in Bertie's office examining the notebook."

"That's right."

"She left before you did?"

"I didn't see her go, but when I came out, her car was gone."

"That was before it rained," Butch said. "So that track wasn't laid down prior to this meeting."

"You're with us, Lucy," Watson said.

"I'm what?"

"You can come with us. I want to pay a call on Louise Jane."

"Now? Me?"

"It's late and we'll probably get her out of bed. I could take a female officer with me, but they're all tied up at the moment. You've seen this map and the so-called code page, and I haven't, except for your reproduction. If Louise Jane has them, you'll recognize them. You know Louise Jane as well as anyone. I want your reaction when we talk to her."

I felt my chest swelling with importance.

Detective Sam Watson wanted *me* along on his investigation. He valued *my* opinion.

"Besides," he said, "I see no point in telling you not to interfere. You will anyway."

My chest deflated. I decided not to tell Watson I'd promised Connor I wouldn't get involved. I never intended to find myself investigating murders. That just seemed to happen to me.

Somehow, I never ended up dead because of it, although I'd had a couple of close calls.

"Bring a car around," Watson told Butch. "We'll meet you at the edge of the marsh."

While we walked to the meeting point, Watson said to me, "Do you think this map means something, Lucy?"

"I honestly don't know, Detective, but I find it hard to believe it's anything important. Someone drew a rough sketch of the Outer Banks, which was a common enough thing to do before mass-produced maps were available at every gas station and long before Google Maps and GPS. Maybe they marked things on it that were important to them—places they'd seen or where they'd done significant things. The sort of things that aren't important or meaningful to anyone else. Where they met a future wife or husband for the first time, a first kiss . . ."

"It doesn't matter—not to me," he said, "if this map shows the route to an underground passageway leading to secret vaults of the Bank of England."

"I didn't know you were a Sherlock Holmes fan, Detective."

"What?"

"That's the plot of *The Red-Headed League*."

"I might have read a few of the stories. Anyway, it doesn't matter what it is. All that matters is someone may have considered it to be important enough to kill over."

Butch pulled up in a marked patrol car. Watson opened the rear door for me, and I climbed in.

I soon decided I didn't like it much back here. A wire partition separated me from the front seat, and no handles were on the doors or windows. It was like being in a cage.

"Hello?" I said.

"We can hear you, Lucy," Butch said with a chuckle. "If we pass anyone you know, duck."

"Most amusing." *Wouldn't that get the rumor mill working overtime!*

We drove toward town, passing no other traffic on Highway 12 until we arrived at Whalebone Junction. Butch carried on through and we drove into the town of Nags Head on the Croatan Highway. Eventually he made a left turn into a winding street of small homes and came to a halt. I'd never been to Louise Jane's house before. It was a small blue building with a single-car garage and a tiny yard consisting mostly of brown grass, sand, and a few scruffy bushes.

Louise Jane's car was parked in the driveway, next to two green trash bins. Butch switched off the engine, and he and Watson got out of the cruiser. Sam Watson held the back door open for me while Butch pulled his flashlight off his belt and knelt down next to the right back tire on Louise Jane's rusty old van. He shone the light on the tire, nodded once, and stood up.

"Yup," he said to Watson. "Same tire I fixed last week."

"Get some pictures," Watson said.

The lamp over the front door came on, the door opened, and Louise Jane stood there. The harsh light shining down on her emphasized her craggy face, flat chest, and bony frame, and threw deep circles under her eyes. She had changed her clothes since I'd seen her last and was dressed in a pair of baggy blue sweat pants and a well-worn T-shirt. Her lip was cut, and a dark bruise was forming on her left cheek. The tinny sound of a TV spilled out from the room behind her. "What on earth are you three doing poking around in the middle of the night?" she called.

"Evening, Louise Jane," Watson said. "May we come in?"

Louise Jane didn't look at either of the police officers. Instead, she studied my face. I automatically smiled at her before remembering this wasn't a social call. I dropped the smile.

"What's happened?" she asked.

"We can talk better inside," Watson said. "We don't want the neighbors gossiping."

"Don't see that that matters. They do nothing else anyway." But she stepped back and made a sweeping gesture with her arm.

The front door opened directly into a small living room. The furniture was cheap and plain, scarred with age, but everything was clean and tidy. The walls were hung with drawings and paintings of historic Outer Banks scenes, some old and yellowing, some fairly new, their colors bright and modern. A two-inch-high model of the Bodie Island Lighthouse sat on a table next to the TV. I didn't recognize the movie playing on the big flat-screen television that was the centerpiece of the room, or any of the actors dressed as medieval soldiers and peasants.

"I'd offer you a drink," Louise Jane said, "but I'm guessing this isn't a social call."

"No," Watson said.

"Can you turn the TV off, please?" Butch asked. I felt sorry for him, in his dark uniform and bulletproof vest. The house wasn't air-conditioned, and the two big fans did little but stir hot air around.

A remote control sat on a side table next to a brown La-Z-Boy, beside a half-finished mug of coffee and a library copy of *Journey to the Center of the Earth*. Louise snatched it up and pressed a button. The light of the screen faded, and silence filled the room.

"Thank you," Watson said.

"That's a bad cut on your face," Butch said. "How'd you get it?"

She lifted one hand and gingerly touched her lip. "I tripped over my own big feet. I was carrying groceries and did a face-plant into the countertop in the kitchen."

"Is that so?" Watson said. "Louise Jane, I need to ask where you were this evening, say between seven and ten o'clock."

Her eyes flicked toward me. "Here. Home."

"All that time?"

"Why are you asking?"

"Why doesn't matter. But I am asking."

"Okay, if you must know, I went to the library and then to the grocery store. I wanted to talk to Lucy, but she wasn't there."

"You're right," I said. "I wasn't there."

"What time was this?" Watson asked.

"I don't know for sure," she said. "It started to rain as I was leaving the house. It was still light out, but the sun was low. Seven thirty, eight o'clock maybe."

"When you discovered Lucy wasn't at the library, what did you do then?"

"I went to the market and came straight home. I carried the groceries in, and that was when I fell. I stepped in a puddle outside; my sneakers were wet, and I slipped on the kitchen floor."

"I've been told you were at the library around five. Why did you go back later?" Watson asked.

"I thought of something I wanted to ask Lucy." Her eyes moved around the room, not settling on any of the people facing her.

"Why did you need to ask her tonight? Rather than wait until tomorrow morning?"

Louise Jane shifted from one foot to the other and avoided looking at me again. "It wasn't late. I figured she'd still be up." Louise Jane was a good actor—she specialized in storytelling—but her nervousness was giving her away. She'd been up to something tonight, all right. And not just an after-hours social call.

"You drove all the way out there without calling first?" Watson said.

"It was a nice night for a drive. I didn't mind."

"By seven thirty, it was raining heavily," Watson said. "The wind was high, which you well know means a chance of waves washing over the road."

Her eyes flicked toward me, and then she faced Watson directly and spoke quickly. "I thought maybe Lucy'd let me have a peek at the notebook they'd found. Did you hear about that?"

"Yes."

"Bertie hustled everyone out awful fast, but I don't know why *I* couldn't examine it first instead of that ridiculous so-called historical society. Bunch of rank amateurs, if you ask me. I took a chance Lucy'd be in, that's all. I still don't know why you're asking me this. Did something happen?"

"Did you see anyone on the library grounds?" Watson asked.

"No."

"Any cars in the lot?"

"Just Lucy's."

"Did anyone arrive at any time while you were there?"

"No."

"Did you see anyone hanging about?"

"No. No one."

"It was raining when you say you left, raining hard. Did you see anyone walking along the road? Maybe someone hitching a ride?"

"Hitchhikers? Why are you asking me about hitchhikers? I know better than to pick up a hitchhiker on a lonely stretch of road."

"I didn't ask if you picked anyone up, Louise Jane. I asked if you saw anyone."

She shook her head firmly. "No. There wasn't much traffic at all. And no one ever walks along that stretch of highway. It's way too far out of town."

"You're sure about how you hurt your face?" Watson asked.

"Of course I'm sure. I didn't black out or anything. It was no big deal." She touched her lip again. "Maybe I was a little bit annoyed at wasting my time going all the way out to the library, so I wasn't watching my footing and slipped—what of it? Why are you asking me all these questions? What happened? Obviously something did."

"Thank you for your time, Louise Jane. I might have more questions later, so please don't leave town without checking with me."

"Questions about what?" She threw a look at me. "Has someone stolen the diary? If so, you have to believe it wasn't me."

"Get those tires replaced," Butch said. "First thing tomorrow morning. Or next time I see that van of yours on the road, I'm going to impound it."

Thinking the subject had changed, she visibly relaxed and threw me her customary smirk.

Louise Jane's story was simple enough, and her presence in the vicinity of the library tonight believable, but she'd been jumpy, nervous at answering Watson's questions. She hadn't been wary, I realized, of him, but of me.

"You weren't hoping to find me *in*," I said. "You were hoping to find me *not in*. Which you could have guessed I'd be, as Connor had come to pick me up for dinner." I turned to Watson. "Louise Jane came back after everyone left, thinking we'd all be gone and she could walk right in."

"That's ridiculous," she said, her voice much higher pitched than normal. She coughed. "I mean, how could I do that? The door would be locked."

"You can't. Because we haven't hidden another key outside. You remember, Detective, the spare key an earlier librarian put under a rock on the lawn because she kept forgetting hers."

"I remember," Watson said. "It caused me no end of trouble last summer when I realized anyone who knew about that key could have simply marched in and walked out with the Austen books."

I'd only learned about the existence of the hidden key when Louise Jane used it to let herself in around the time the collection of first edition Jane Austen novels we had on special loan were disappearing. After that, Bertie ensured the key was removed from under its rock, and we'd never tried to find another hiding place.

"Okay. I'll admit the thought had crossed my mind." Louise Jane laughed lightly. "You can be awful absent-minded sometimes, Lucy."

"I'm never anything of the sort."

"Don't let it bother you. Everyone finds it perfectly charming."

I sputtered.

"Although I can't imagine why. I thought it worth a try. I admit it. I checked under a few rocks. No key. So I left."

"Did you try the door?" Watson asked.

"Guilty as charged." Now her secret was out, Louise Jane's confidence had returned. "As I said, Lucy can be forgetful, so I hoped she'd forgotten to lock up."

"I never forget to lock up!"

Another patronizing smile. "If you say so, honey."

"Thank you for your time, Louise Jane," Watson said.

"Are you going to tell me what all this is about?"

"I'm going to tell you something you already know," he said. "Entering someone's home or place of business without their permission is an offense. Even if you happen to find a key where it was not left for you."

"I'll remember that in the future," she said.

Watson turned as if to leave, then he swung back around to face her. "Oh, one more thing. Do you happen to know a man by the name of Jeremy Hughes? I heard he was at the library tonight with the rest of you."

Louise Jane didn't react to the name. "I've met him once or twice. Fancies himself a big man about town. He has family money, or so they say, so he took early retirement from some sort of internet sales company and moved to Nags Head a few years ago to tell us how to best run our town. I can't say I was pleased to see him at the library tonight, not as part of the historical society. His interest in the history of the Outer Banks is about as deep as mine is in the workings of the internet. His other interest—or so they say—is in women. He's known to be quite the ladies' man." She sniffed. "Can't say I found him the least bit appealing, did you, Lucy?"

I suppressed a shudder. "I'll agree with you there."

"Is that so?" Watson said. "Thank you for your time, Louise Jane."

"Get those tires replaced tomorrow morning," Butch growled at her.

We went back to the cruiser. I glanced at the house as we drove away. Louise Jane stood in her living room window, watching us go.

"She was at the library before Jeremy and his killer arrived," I said. "She went up to the door to check if it was locked and didn't notice it smashed almost to bits. That would have been hard to miss."

"Do you believe her story?" Watson asked me.

"I do. Louise Jane has a possessive attitude toward the library. It didn't surprise me in the least to hear she thinks she can walk in after hours as and when she likes."

"You don't think this possessive attitude could turn to murder? If she saw someone damaging the library?"

Butch snorted.

"Is that your professional opinion, Officer?" Watson asked.

"As good as," Butch said. "I know Louise Jane. She'd be more likely to tell anyone she suspected of meaning the library no good that she'd sic one of her invisible friends on him."

"Her what?"

"She believes the library's haunted," I said. "She tells everyone she can commune with the spirits."

"Oh, yeah. That. CeeCee's told me about that. What did you think about the bruising on her face? It looks as though a fight took place in Bertie's office tonight. I didn't see any signs of blows to Hughes's face, and he had gloves on his hands, so I didn't see his knuckles, but I'll ask the autopsy doc to check for any bruising."

"I agree with Butch." I offered my opinion although I hadn't been asked. "The only wrongdoing Louise Jane got up to tonight was to try to sneak into the library because she knew I'd gone out. She was open enough about what happened with her slipping and hurting her face. She didn't seem the least bit defensive about it until you started with the questions. I will admit that she seems to have an animosity toward Jeremy and the historical society. Probably because they don't take her seriously as a historian."

"Animosity can lead to a lot of nasty things, Lucy," Watson said. "Including murder."

"I'm guessing by the questions about people walking on the highway or hitchhiking, you didn't find any other tire prints in the parking lot?"

"Nothing laid down after the rain started, apart from Connor's car and Hughes's. And Louise Jane's. It's entirely possible the person or persons in question left their car on the side of the highway and walked in despite the rain."

"They might have come with Hughes in his car," Butch said.

"If so, how did they get back to town?" Watson muttered to himself as much as to us.

"A boat?" Butch asked.

"Perhaps. But the timeline's tight for someone to be able to arrange alternate transportation, follow Hughes to the library, do the deed, and get away. Lucy, I'll drop you at the library and then pay a call on Curtis Gardner. See if he can tell me anything about Hughes's movements after leaving the meeting at the library."

"It's a long way to go just to take me back," I said. "I'll come with you."

"No," he said.

Curses, foiled again.

Chapter Eight

When at last I let myself into my apartment, cradling a grateful Charles, I was dead beat, but I knew I'd never be able to get to sleep. Far too much was whirling around inside my head.

I put fresh water and food out for Charles, took a shower, and got into my pajamas. I then put the kettle on for hot tea and settled at the kitchen table. I would have loved nothing more than to lie awake in bed, remembering every beautiful detail of my night with Connor. Unfortunately, the beautiful night with Connor had turned into, first, an attempt to decipher the code and, second, wondering what on earth had happened at the library tonight.

Watson might not be so sure, but I believed Louise Jane. She would never have killed Jeremy, or anyone else. *It's entirely possible,* I thought, *if she found him damaging the library or its contents, she'd demand he put a stop to it.* And arguments had a way of turning into fights.

But I couldn't see it. She'd been nervous and edgy when we showed up at her door, but all that ended when she confessed to hoping to find a key, and she returned to her confident self. She hadn't been trying to hide guilt at a murder, and she genuinely didn't seem to understand why Watson wanted to know how she'd hurt her face.

So, if not Louise Jane, then who? And why?

The how was obvious. I hadn't taken much of a look at Jeremy. I hadn't wanted to—a quick glance was more than enough. I'd seen no obvious wounds such as caused by a gunshot or a knife, but the state of Bertie's office looked as though he'd been in a fight. It was likely he'd either been hit on the side of the head or had struck his head when he fell.

I thought over the scene earlier in the day in Bertie's office: everyone excited, arguing about the contents of the tin box. But something had happened before that.

When the group from the historical society arrived, Charlene had ducked her head at the sight of Jeremy and slipped out of the library without a word of greeting to the new arrivals. He'd grinned at her, and he hadn't stopped grinning as she scurried away, as though her actions amused him because he knew her well.

Or knew something about her.

Did Charlene and Jeremy have a history? The moment I met him, he'd triggered my lecherous creep radar, and Louise Jane had said outright that he had a reputation with women.

Until I could ask Charlene about it, I'd keep her reaction to myself, but his behavior might have provided the motive for his murder. Maybe his death didn't have anything to do with the papers in the tin box. Was it possible he'd been at the library after hours for another reason, and his killer had been waiting for an opportunity to get him on his own and do the deed?

Why then, would that person have taken the papers? Because Jeremy was interested in them, and so his killer wanted to see what they were?

I let out a long puff of breath.

I simply didn't know enough about Jeremy, his life, and his acquaintances to speculate.

Besides, I wasn't going to get involved. Not this time.

But I could try to find out what I could about the code page and the map. We didn't have the papers themselves—they'd been stolen—but the images were on my phone. I called them up and sent them to the printer. My own printer wasn't nearly as good quality as the library's, but it would do for tonight. The police were still moving about downstairs, and I could hardly wander down in my shower hair and shorty pajamas.

I poured myself a cup of tea and added a splash of milk and a generous spoonful of sugar. I checked that Charles was comfortably curled up on the pillow-covered bench seat under the apartment's only window, and then I sat back down at the table with my tea, a stack of unused paper to write on, and the printouts of the map and code page.

If it was a code page.

Once again I tried looking for patterns. What was the most common letter? *W.* Did it remain the most common throughout the page? *Yes.* Was there a pattern to the placement of the *W*'s? Not that I could see. I tried some simple substitutions. Nothing became clear. Reading backward didn't make any more sense.

I next searched for anagrams, rearranging the letters. That proved difficult because the words weren't really words. In most cases, there were too many letters between the spaces. At least the printing was clear and legible. Bad handwriting would have created a whole new nightmare in deciphering the text.

When my head started to hurt, I put the code page aside and studied the map. Most of it was recognizable as the Outer Banks, although crudely drawn, but some was not. I didn't know anything about how the land and sea had changed over time, but there were bound to be books in Charlene's collection that could tell me.

I attempted to decipher the meaning of the numbers on the map page. Did they relate to the few numbers scatted among the letters on the code page? I substituted an A for the 1, and a B for the 2, and so on until H. But still, nothing became clear. I did it backwards. No help at all.

I studied the pages of paper on which I'd written my deciphering attempts. All I saw were lines and more lines of absolute gibberish.

Maybe this wasn't a code after all. Maybe it was just the scribblings of an illiterate person copying something they didn't understand and making a mess of it. If anyone got hold of the pages I'd written tonight, they'd search in vain for any rhyme or reason to it.

* * *

I started awake at a simultaneous buzzing and ringing. My head ached, my throat was parched, and I had a crick in my neck.

A cat's paw swatted at my hand, and big blue eyes stared into mine. I blinked.

I'd fallen asleep at the kitchen table. I hadn't pulled the drapes shut, and sunlight streamed in. The fog in my head slowly cleared, and I understood that my phone was buzzing, and the doorbell to the library was ringing.

Charles leapt off the table as I fumbled for the phone and ran for the intercom that would allow me to see who was outside and talk to them. "What? I mean hello?"

"Lucy?" It was Bertie.

I spoke into the phone. "I'm here. What time is it?"

"Eight thirty."

"Sorry—I overslept."

"You have to let me in. I don't have a key for the new lock."

I pushed the button to bring up the security camera. My boss's face appeared in front of me. She held her phone to her ear.

Memories of last night flooded back. *New door. New lock. New keys.*

"Sam phoned me earlier and said we could open the library today. He also said he'd told the locksmith to leave the keys on the circulation desk."

"So you need me to let you in?" I asked. *Maybe I wasn't entirely awake yet.*

"Yes, Lucy, I do."

"Be right there." I dashed down the stairs. The keys were on the desk, as promised. The door was new, and when I pulled it open, I realized it was a good deal more substantial than the one that had previously been here.

"Good morning," I said to Bertie.

"Good morning." She looked fresh and awake, ready for a new day. It was supposed to be another scorching hot day, and she wore a sleeveless pale blue cotton dress that swirled around her calves and sturdy Birkenstock sandals. She glanced around the main room. "Everything seems back to normal. More or less as we left it."

Despite all the comings and goings last night, this morning our beloved library was once again just a library.

"Sam told me I cannot go into my office," she said. "Not even to get my computer or take any papers I might need to work on. So I'll be out here most of the day, getting in everyone's hair. I can help on the desk. Were you up late?"

"Yes, but not because the police were here. I was having a go at deciphering the code. If it is a code."

"I gather you didn't have much luck?"

"Not one bit. I fell asleep over it. If anything came to me in my dreams, I don't remember. Oh, that reminds me. What about the historical society? Are they still coming at nine?"

"I didn't call them to tell them not to," Bertie said. "I had the radio on in the car on my way here. The news mentioned there'd been a death at the library last night, but police were withholding the name of the deceased pending notification of next of kin."

"So they might not know it was Jeremy," I said. "We can watch their reactions when you tell them."

"Detecting again, Lucy?" There might have been a hint of amusement in her tone.

I shook my head vehemently. "No. Absolutely not. I'm curious, that's all. Oh, something else happened that you might want to know about." I filled her in quickly on our visit to Louise Jane.

Bertie threw up her hands. "I can't fault someone for loving our library so much, but sometimes . . ."

"Sometimes," I agreed.

"You don't think Sam's considering Louise Jane to be a suspect, do you? I can't imagine anything more ridiculous. If Louise Jane had fought with anyone to protect library property, she'd be bragging about her role in saving it."

"I don't know what he's thinking. I'll get dressed and be right back." I headed for the stairs.

* * *

I had a quick shower, washed and dried my hair, and was back downstairs at five to nine. Instead of having a toasted bagel or bowl of cereal and yogurt in my apartment as I usually do, I stuffed a granola bar into my pocket to serve as my breakfast. I wanted to be on hand when the members of the Bodie Island Historical Society got here.

The first person to arrive was Detective Sam Watson, accompanied by Officer Holly Rankin and Mayor Connor McNeil, bringing a wave of heat with him. Not yet nine o'clock and the temperature outside was already approaching the nineties. I shouldn't have bothered with my hair. I could practically feel it turning into a ball of frizz in the humidity. Officer Rankin, with her pale skin, red hair, and English heritage, wiped sweat off her brow.

"To what do we owe the honor?" Bertie asked them.

"Last night you mentioned the historical society would be coming in this morning to examine the documents," Watson said. "Did you call to tell them not to bother?"

"No."

"Good. I want to see their reactions."

"And I," Connor said, "don't need an excuse to pop into the library. But if I did, I'd say I'm here to watch your backs."

Watson pointed to a small paper bag Rankin carried. "I'm returning the diary. We fingerprinted it and found nothing at all useable. Not even your prints."

"Charlene made us wear gloves to handle it," Bertie said.

"Hughes was wearing gloves last night. Not proper historian's gloves, but a leather pair that probably belonged to him. Unless you were up to no good, you'd never wear gloves in heat like this, so it's possible whoever was with him last night did so also."

Rankin handed the parcel to Bertie, and my boss clutched it to her chest. "Thank you. I'm going to lock this upstairs in the rare books room. No one is to see it without my express permission. Library employees included."

"Understood," I said.

"Lucy," Watson said, "you might be interested to know that the clerk in the grocery store nearest to Louise Jane's house remembers her coming in around eight. It was raining heavily, and Louise Jane was soaking wet. They're friends, so she asked Louise Jane where she'd been, and Louise Jane replied, 'On a fool's errand.' She didn't notice any cuts or bruising on Louise Jane's face."

"Why do we need to know this?" Connor asked.

"I'm sure all will be revealed," I said. I appreciated Watson telling me. I didn't believe Louise Jane had killed a man in our library, but it was nice to have some confirmation that my instincts were right.

"That's not proof positive," Watson said, "but it does help verify her story."

"Louise Jane needs a story?" Connor said.

"Apparently, she was sneaking around outside last night," Bertie said.

"Really? Did she see anything?"

"She says she was gone before Jeremy or anyone else arrived," Watson said.

"Did you learn anything from Curtis about what Jeremy got up to last night?" Connor asked.

Watson glanced between Bertie, Connor, and me. I tried to look serious. He had no reason to tell us, of course. "No," he said at last. "According to Curtis, he had to drop Diane off at her home after the meeting here, and when he got to the bar, Jeremy was waiting, as arranged. They had a couple of drinks and left, separating in the parking lot. He didn't see if Hughes got into his own car or if he walked or was picked up by someone else. According to Curtis, 'a couple of drinks' means they had one beer each and switched to soda."

"That sounds like Curtis to me," Connor said dryly.

"Right. He wasn't entirely sure of the time. Around nine, he thinks. Jeremy said nothing to him about where he was going, and Curtis went home. Diane Uppiton didn't get home from her family dinner until around ten, and she says Curtis was in bed asleep when she did."

"Do you believe him?" I asked.

"I have no reason not to."

"I don't suppose he showed any physical signs of being in a fist fight?"

"He did not," Watson said. "Not that I could see at any rate."

"Good morning, everyone," Charlene said as she came inside. "Is that a new door? What happened to the old one? Storm damage?"

Watson gave Bertie a slight nod.

"We had a bit of trouble in the night," Bertie said. "Someone broke into the library after we'd all left and . . . died."

"A break-in? Oh my gosh. Was anything stolen? Was he after money, do you think?" She looked at me, her eyes wide. "Lucy! Are you okay? He didn't try to get upstairs, did he?"

"I'm fine," I said. "I wasn't even here at the time."

"We think he was after the notebook," Bertie said.

"The notebook? You mean Mrs. Crawbingham's diary? The one George's crew found? Why on earth? Who would do such a thing?"

"It was Jeremy Hughes," Bertie said.

If I hadn't been watching Charlene closely, I wouldn't have seen it. Shock filled her eyes. She gave her head an almost imperceptible shake, and the expression disappeared as quickly as it had come. She dug in her purse and pulled out her iPhone and the earbuds that would remain attached to her head for the rest of the working day. "Sorry to hear that. I didn't know him. What happened? Was it an accident?" she asked Watson.

"Not an accident, no," he said, "which is why I'm here."

"Is the diary okay?" she asked. "It wasn't damaged, I hope."

"The diary's fine," Bertie said. "But the two enclosed pages were taken."

She gasped. "That's awful." She turned to Watson. "Sorry, Detective. I'm an academic librarian. Sometimes I forget that archives aren't more important than people. Are you saying the notebook and papers might be more valuable than we first thought? They must be, if someone killed to get them."

"I'm working on the assumption," Watson said, "that I'll find the missing pages when I find the killer."

Charlene put the buds in her ears. "I'll be upstairs if anyone needs me." She hurried off, heading for her office.

Bertie hadn't told her that the historical society was coming this morning specifically to work with her. No point, as we didn't have anything for them to work with. Bertie had made it plain that the diary would be kept under lock and key until we knew what was going on.

I couldn't help but think Charlene had shown a surprising lack of curiosity about Jeremy Hughes's final actions. Or that she, who had a passion for old documents, hadn't hung around to ask Watson what he intended to do about finding the pages. I glanced at Bertie. She was watching Charlene go, a worried look on her face.

The door opened again, and Louise Jane marched in. Her lip had swollen overnight. She'd applied makeup in an attempt to cover the dark purple bruise on her left cheekbone, but it wasn't having the desired effect. "I thought I might find you here this morning, Detective Watson. I decided to forgive and forget your insulting visit last night and do whatever I can to help."

Connor studied her face. "Now I'm starting to get it."

"Are you all right, Louise Jane?" Bertie said. "That's a bad cut."

"I'm perfectly fine, thank you for asking, Bertie. I slipped and fell into the kitchen cabinet. You should see the other guy." Her attempt at a joke fell flat.

"Help?" Watson said. "I don't recall asking for your help."

"Not a problem. I'm happy to do what I can. We need to find those pages, and fast. Who knows what damage they might suffer in the hands of an inexperienced person, suddenly exposed to the sunlight and sea air after being protected for decades."

"You're not entirely in the clear, Louise Jane," Watson said. "You getting those bruises on your face last night is quite the coincidence."

"Nevertheless, coincidences do happen, don't they? Pay no attention to him, Bertie. Having a suspicious mind goes with the territory, I guess. Now, I propose we start by searching the black market in historical artifacts. I called my grandmother this morning and asked her to put her ear to the ground."

Watson, I thought, showed enormous restraint by not rolling his eyes.

Bertie stood by the window, caught in a beam of sunlight that threw a halo around her mass of piled silver hair, as though she were the subject of a Renaissance painting. "The first of our guests are arriving."

"Take them into the break room," Watson said. "I'll join you there." He glared at Louise Jane. "Not a word about what happened last night."

"My puffy and cracked lips are sealed," she said.

"See you keep them that way. Did you get the tires on your van fixed?"

"Uh, no. I haven't had a chance yet."

He pulled out his phone. "You were told to have that done first thing. I'll get a tow truck out here. It'll be expensive getting your van into town, and they won't necessarily take it to the cheapest or most convenient garage, but it has to be done."

"Why don't I take care of that now?" she said. "No need to bother you, Sam. I'll be back later, Lucy, and we can put our heads together." She fled, and Watson watched her go. I didn't care for the look on his face. *Surely he wasn't still considering Louise Jane for the killing of Jeremy?*

Louise Jane passed Lynne Feingold, Phil Cahill, and Mabel Eastland on her way out. Lynne wore a sundress with a pattern of big yellow flowers that I thought too young and flirty for her, and she'd drenched herself in an expensive, floral perfume. Phil wiped sweat off his brow and said, "It's going to be another hot one."

"As you seem to have everything in hand here," Connor said. "I'll get back to town. I've a meeting with the financial controller this morning. I'd hoped to have a good excuse to postpone it." He gave me his private smile, and I returned it.

Our new front door was getting a lot of use. Connor left, and Ronald arrived. "Morning all."

"Good morning," we said.

"What happened to the door, and why are the police here?"

"There was an incident last night," Bertie said. "It's been on the news."

"I prefer not to catch up on the news in the morning. Guaranteed to start my day off badly. What sort of incident?"

"We can talk later. In the meantime, I can't keep these people waiting. Will you watch the desk, please, Ronald?" Bertie said. "Lucy and I won't be long."

"I caught the news," Phil said. "Something about someone who died here last night. I have to say, I was worried about what I'd find when I got here, but you all seem hale and hearty and not particularly distraught. What happened? I hope it was no one we know?"

Bertie didn't answer. She led the way out of the main room, and the members of the historical society fell in behind her. "I know no more than you," Mrs. Eastland told Phil. "But quite obviously the police are involved."

Watson, Officer Rankin, and I brought up the rear.

We went into the staff break room, and everyone took seats. Everyone, that is, except for Detective Watson, who stood against the wall, arms crossed over his chest, and Officer Rankin, who stayed by the door. She peeked at Watson, and then also crossed her arms over her chest and tried to look foreboding. Phil Cahill gave Watson nervous glances, but the women of the historical society didn't react.

"We can't start before Jeremy gets here," Lynne said.

"I'm not waiting all day," Phil said. "It's after nine now. Where's Charlene? Where's the book?"

"I called Jeremy this morning to ask if he wanted to get a ride with me," Lynne said.

"I'm sure you did, dear," Mrs. Eastland said.

Lynne threw her a poisonous look. "Just being friendly, Mabel. You should try it sometime. He didn't answer the phone. I thought maybe he'd gone into town for coffee first and would meet us here."

"Did you speak to Mrs. Hughes?" Watson asked.

Lynne studied her freshly manicured nails. "They're not together anymore."

"Is that so?" the detective said.

"They're never together," Mrs. Eastland said, "unless they are. They have a strange marriage."

"She left him," Lynne said. "Walked out. He's finally had enough of her tantrums, and initiated divorce proceedings."

"I wouldn't be so sure about that if I were you." Mrs. Eastland turned in her chair and looked at Watson over her shoulder. "Who are you, and why do you want to know anyway?"

"Detective Sam Watson. Nags Head PD."

Mrs. Eastland sucked in a breath. "The person who died. Here. Last night. Was it . . .?"

"We've identified the deceased as Mr. Jeremy Hughes," Watson said. "That hasn't been made public yet, as we haven't been able to locate his wife to inform her."

Lynne's chair fell back with a crash as she leapt to her feet. "You're lying. Jeremy's not dead. He can't be."

"I'm sorry, Lynne," Bertie said, "but it's true."

Lynne burst into tears and ran for the door. A startled Rankin stepped back and let her pass.

"Go with her, Lucy," Watson said. "Make sure she's okay."

I interpreted that to mean "make sure she doesn't leave the library." I followed and had no trouble locating Lynne. I could hear her sobs from the other end of the hallway. I tapped lightly on the door to the women's restroom. "Are you okay, Lynne?"

"Go 'way."

"I'll go away if you want me to, but I think you need a hug first."

The door opened slowly and Lynne's tear-streaked face peeked out, a dramatic contrast to her cheerful, sunny dress. Her makeup ran in black rivers, and her nose and eyes were turning red. "Is it . . . is it true?"

"Yes. It is. I'm sorry. Were you and Jeremy close?"

"We were"—she swallowed—"planning a life together."

"Oh. That's too bad." Lynne might have been making plans, but I was pretty sure Jeremy wasn't. Not long-term ones. "Why don't you come back to the meeting? Detective Watson will have questions."

"I . . . I can't." Another round of tears. "People didn't understand about Jeremy and my relationship. We had to keep it quiet because of his wife. She was being very difficult over the divorce."

I patted her shoulder. I wanted to get back to the break room and hear what was being said, but I was afraid if I left Lynne alone, she'd walk out. I genuinely did feel sorry for her. The news had come as a terrible shock, and the woman seemed to be genuinely in love with Jeremy. If he wasn't in love with her in return, that wasn't her fault. We've all been there. "Maybe you know something that would help Detective Watson find the killer. Something important."

"I don't know anything," she sobbed. "You think someone murdered him? Who would do such a dreadful thing?"

I sprinkled cold water onto a paper towel and handed it to her. "You never know what might be important. Sometimes all the police need is one little piece of apparently insignificant information to make everything fall into place. Freshen your face, and let's go and join the others."

She wiped at her eyes, leaving raccoon-like black smudges around them. "You think so?"

I took the paper towel out of her hands and used it to dab at the worst of the smeared makeup. "I know so."

"Okay, then. No one wants to see Jeremy's killer found and punished more than I do."

When we got back to the break room, everyone was where we'd left them. Bertie had put a box of tissues on the table, but they weren't needed. Mrs. Eastland was dry-eyed, and Phil looked upset, but nothing more than that. I assumed neither of them had confessed to following Jeremy into Bertie's office and murdering him. I helped Lynne into her chair. She kept her head down. I passed her the box of tissues and took my own seat.

". . . importance cannot be overstated," Phil was saying.

"We don't know that," Bertie said. "If the killer thought the map and so-called code page important, that doesn't mean they are."

"I need to find them," Watson said. "Tell me about Jeremy Hughes."

"I have nothing to tell," Mrs. Eastland said. "He joined the society six, seven months or so ago. He said he was new to the Outer Banks and wanted to get involved in the protection of local history. He was very keen, and we were glad to have him."

"Glad to have his money anyway," Phil said.

"Didn't hurt," Mrs. Eastland said. "He made a considerable donation to the society when he joined. The

Settlers' Day Fair was his idea, and he put up the money to get the process rolling."

"What do you know about his family?" Watson asked.

Mrs. Eastland glanced at Lynne, tearing a tissue into shreds. "He was married. I don't know about any children. He and his wife seemed to spend a lot of time apart."

"She never came to any functions, not even to the Christmas party, as I recall." Phil wiggled his eyebrows at Watson trying to pass on a message.

Just between us men.

"That was the first time I met him," Phil said. "At the Christmas party. We held it in one of the private rooms at Owens." He named a restaurant that was a long-standing Outer Banks institution. "Jeremy made a point of talking to everyone, had a lot to drink. Took a cab home."

"Oh yes, the Christmas party," Mrs. Eastland said. "I remember. He made sure he was the center of attention all night, buying everyone drinks, listening to what people had to say. He made a particular point of talking to the women present."

Lynne blew her nose.

"He could be charming, I'll give him that," Mrs. Eastland said. "Or so some said. I never saw the appeal myself. As for his wife, I tried to get her to help with Settlers' Day. She was polite, but she let me know in no uncertain terms that she wasn't interested."

"I've been told y'all were here, at the library, yesterday between approximately five and six o'clock. Is that correct?" Watson asked.

Three heads nodded.

"What did you do after that? Mrs. Eastland, you go first."

"I went home and made dinner and ate with my husband. We stayed in the rest of the evening and retired around ten, as is our custom."

"Same for me," Phil said. "Except for going to bed at ten. I write after supper most nights. That's when I get my best work done, when the house is quiet. I went to bed around two. My wife can confirm I stayed in all evening, at least until midnight, when she came into the study to say good night."

"Ms. Feingold?" Watson prodded.

Lynne looked up. She twisted the tissue in her hands. "What?"

"What did you do after six o'clock last night?"

"I went home. I had dinner and watched a movie on Netflix. I went to bed around eleven."

"Can anyone vouch for that?" Watson said.

She ducked her head. "I live alone. I saw no one and spoke to no one. I . . . uh . . . well, I wanted to go for a drink with Jeremy and Curtis but . . . he . . . I mean, they wanted a men's night out." She gave a strangled laugh. "Men's talk."

"Please give Officer Rankin your spouses' contact information," Watson said. "We'll want to talk to Mr. Eastland and Mrs. Cahill. Just a matter of form, you understand."

"Happy to be of help." Mrs. Eastland gave him a wide smile.

I studied the three faces, trying not to be too obvious about searching for clues beneath. Only Lynne, chewing her lip and alternately sniffing into her tissue and shredding it in her fingers, appeared to be bothered by the news of Jeremy's death. Phil Cahill didn't care one way or the other, and Mrs. Eastland seemed to be excited at being caught up in a police investigation.

Watson's phone rang, and he glanced at the display. "I need to get this. Thank you for your time. Let me know if you think of anything—anything at all—that might be pertinent. Either about Mr. Hughes or about this diary and its contents." He signaled to Rankin to follow and walked out of the room, saying, "What've you got?"

"As long as we're here," Phil said to Bertie, "we might as well get started on the diary."

"Started doing what?" Bertie asked.

"Examining it, of course. Isn't that why we're here? Is Charlene around? Too bad about the separate pages, but at least the diary itself wasn't taken."

Bertie got to her feet. "Mrs. Crawbingham's diary has been moved to a more secure facility and will remain there until the police know more about what happened last night."

"I for one have no intention of stealing it," Phil said.

"No," Bertie said. "It might turn out that the diary is far more valuable than we thought."

"All the more reason . . ."

"Bertie's right," Mrs. Eastland said. "We can wait until she and the police think it's safe. I only hope this isn't going to interfere with our plans for Settlers' Day."

"No reason it should," Phil said.

"Have some respect." Lynne sniffled into a fresh tissue.

"For Jeremy Hughes?" Mrs. Eastland snorted. "I don't think so."

"Mabel," Phil said in a warning voice.

"We have the money he donated to the Settlers' Day committee, don't we? What else do we need from him?" She pushed her chair back and stood up. "I'm off home. Dreadful disappointment about the map and code page.

You will let us know, Bertie, if you find them, won't you?"

"I will," Bertie said.

"Are you coming, Lynne?" Mrs. Eastland said.

"What?"

"We're leaving now. Pull yourself together, girl. I need to talk to you about the food vendors at Settlers' Day. Have you spoken to Josie O'Malley yet?"

"Josie? Oh yes. Yes, I have. The bakery will have a booth."

"Excellent. Walk with me and fill me in. Come along now, don't dawdle."

The two women left, Mrs. Eastland chattering; Lynne, small and silent at her side.

Bertie shut the door behind them and turned to Phil. "What's the story there?"

"Story?" he said innocently.

"Don't give me that. I've never, ever seen Mabel Eastland be the slightest bit nasty to anyone. She was out-and-out rude to poor Lynne and totally dismissive of Jeremy's death."

He grinned. "Jeremy had a reputation, not entirely a good one, as something of a ladies' man."

"Not to speak ill of the dead," I said, "but he was a dirty old man."

Phil laughed. "Obviously a matter of interpretation. Mabel doesn't suffer fools gladly, and she thought Jeremy was a fool. She thought any woman who fell for his supposed charms was also a fool."

"But they worked together in the historical society?" Bertie asked.

"Not many of us liked the man. I didn't. I thought him far too full of himself. He called himself an 'ideas man.' Meaning he'd throw out impractical suggestions and expect someone else to jump to and implement them. He didn't seem to mind what anyone thought of him and was willing to pay to get along. He pretty much single-handedly fully funded our little group over the last few months. All the seed money for Settlers' Day came from him."

"I wondered why you were able to be so lavish," Bertie said. "You have a couple of quite high-profile speakers coming."

"Now you know."

"If no one liked him," I asked, "did anyone *dislike* him enough to murder him?"

Phil thought about that for a few moments, then he shook his head. "Not anyone I'm aware of. Admittedly, his money helped, but he did have a genuine interest in Outer Banks history. We'll forgive a man a heck of a lot if he loves the things we love."

"True," Bertie said. I guessed she was thinking of Louise Jane.

Watson's head popped into the break room. "Mrs. Hughes has been located. She's in Raleigh and on her way back now."

"Has she been told of her husband's death?" Bertie asked.

"Yes. I'm going into town. I'll be in touch, and remember, no one goes in your office, Bertie. Not even you."

"I'm unlikely to forget."

"I'll walk out with you, Detective," Phil said. "I've been telling Bertie what I know about Jeremy, from the point of view of the historical society. I should fill you in too."

"Let's get back to work," Bertie said to me. "We still have a library to run."

Chapter Nine

M urder in the library always makes for a busy day. Some of our patrons dropped in because they wanted to make sure we, and the library, were okay. Some came because they hoped to get the latest gossip. Some people we'd never seen before arrived, perhaps hoping to be given a tour of the crime scene.

The latter two groups were to be sadly disappointed. For all intents and purposes, it was a normal day at the Bodie Island Lighthouse Library. Not that any day can be called "normal."

Bertie staffed the circulation desk while I helped a regular patron select an assortment of books for her daughter, who'd been confined to bed rest with a difficult pregnancy. The poor thing was being driven out of her mind by boredom, and her mom wanted a variety of books to keep her mind challenged and her spirits up.

I was suggesting the entire Harry Potter series (that would keep her busy for a long time) when George Grimshaw came in, stamping dirt and dust off his construction boots.

"You lost my book!" he bellowed at Bertie.

"What book?"

"The book I found yesterday."

"I did not lose it, and it was not yours," she said. "The library's property was stolen last night."

"I was hoping to put a claim in for half the treasure. My boys dug it up, after all. We coulda snuck it off site when you weren't looking."

Bertie huffed. She'd seen the twinkle in his eye. He lowered his voice. "Bad business, what happened. Book woulda been better left in the ground, if you ask me."

"Maybe it carries a curse." A patron dropped a stack of historical romance novels on the desk. She was an attractive woman in her fifties, well dressed and carefully presented in that way that means plenty of time for the gym and plenty of money for clothes and grooming products. I recognized her as an occasional patron, but we'd never spoken. "Have you thought of that? Maybe it was buried on purpose. It had to be gotten rid of because it was so dangerous."

"I don't think that's a realistic idea, Cheryl." Bertie eyed the covers of the books: shirtless men, all muscles and tattoos; women wearing elaborate, but strategically ripped, dresses.

"I bet that's it," Cheryl said with a shiver of delight. "Whoever stole it doesn't know about the curse. Oh dear." She clutched her books to her chest and left.

Notably she and George Grimshaw had not so much as looked at each other, even though she'd invaded his conversation. "Story there, George?" Bertie asked.

"What?"

"Between you and Cheryl Monaghan."

"Couple of crooks, her and her husband both," he said with a growl. "They asked me to give them a quote on some work at that danged golf resort development project o' theirs."

My ears pricked up. Monaghan. This must be the development Connor was telling me about, the one he had his doubts about.

"Zack and I had a look 'round. Wasn't long before I told Monaghan straight up he was outta his mind if he thought that was a good location for a big fancy hotel. Nice little B&B maybe, boutique hotel with swimming pool and sea views, something like that would be okay, but not what he had in mind. We weren't invited back to complete our quote. I heard they got some company from outta state. Better them than me. I don't need to be caught up in any lawsuits."

"That bad?" Bertie said.

"Don't you be telling anyone I said so. That Rick Monaghan's mighty quick to threaten to take folks to court."

"I won't," she said.

"Not keen to have any part of that project anyway. Everyone knows the land was stolen from Thaddeus Washington way back in the day." He harrumphed and changed the subject. "As for that danged book we found, good thing I didn't try to snatch it. Thief might have done you a favor, Bertie. Taken it off your hands. Maybe I saved your life." He chuckled.

"Pooh," Bertie said. "You might not have work to do today, George, but I do."

He got the hint and headed outside. I followed him.

"George," I called, "have you got a minute?"

He turned with a smile. "For you, pretty lady, anytime."

The heat beat down on my bare head. It was so hot outside, the water beyond the marsh shimmered. Dust from the construction site filled the air, equipment roared, and men shouted at one another. Zack gave me a wave as he trotted past with his ever-present iPad.

"I'm curious as to what you and Bertie were talking about just now. The land development I mean. Sounds like there's an interesting history behind it. You said the land was originally stolen?"

"Story's been told and retold," he said. "Things change over the years, but what I heard from my own grandpappy is that Zebadiah Monaghan out and out stole part of that patch o' land o' his from the Washington family."

"When was this?" I asked.

"After the war."

"What war?"

"War Between the States, of course. Land was left by Ethan Monaghan to a free black man name of Thaddeus Washington in return for some favor or another, sometime in the years when Washington was a leader of the Freedmen's Colony over by Roanoke. Ethan's son, Zebadiah, used his political connections to have the will overturned. Washington himself died around the same time as the old man, and his family couldn't prove it was intended for him, so they lost it."

"That's a long time ago," I said. "Do people still care?"

"Bankers have long memories."

"So I've been told."

"Zebadiah's son, Nathanial, was another kettle of fish altogether. When he inherited on his father's death, he kept the land as it was. Lived in the house he'd been born in for almost eighty years, turned away anyone who wanted to buy some of his property."

"But he didn't try to reimburse this Washington or his family?"

"Nathanial Monaghan might have cared about the Outer Banks, Lucy, but he was a man of his time. He didn't give land away and certainly not to any folks who didn't have the money to fight him in the courts. He lived out his life in his parents' house and walked the land he thought was his every morning until the day he died. But what goes around comes around, and his son Rick has it now, and Rick's got mighty big plans."

"Washington. That wouldn't be Janelle and Neil Washington would it?"

"Might be. Far as I know that family stayed on when the Freedmen's Colony was broken up. I know Neil. Used to work for me." He shook his head. "He was a darn good worker. After he hurt his back so bad, I tried to give him some office work so as to keep him on, but even that got too much. How they doin'?"

"Janelle comes to the library regularly and brings her twin girls. She's an assistant at a real estate office, so I think they're managing okay. The girls are lovely—polite and well-mannered, although pretty much of a handful. They're always nicely dressed and look healthy and happy."

"Glad to hear it," he said. "It's hard, though, when the man of the family can't put bread on the table." He turned at a shout from one of his crew. "Better get back at it."

"Thanks, George," I said. "That was interesting."

*   *   *

"I need to talk to Charlene for a moment," I said to Bertie. "Be right back."

Bertie waved a hand at me from behind the circulation desk.

I climbed the stairs to the third floor. The door to Charlene's office was open, and she was at her computer, typing away, earbuds in place. The powerful lamp on her desk threw a circle of light around her. Her office was small—just enough room for the desk and one chair—made even smaller and darker by the rows upon rows of shelves bulging with books. All the books in here were reference materials. The rare books themselves, of which we had a good number, were kept in their own secure space.

"Hi," I said. "Got a minute?"

She pushed her chair back, stretched her shoulders, and pulled out the earpieces. The driving sound of rap music leaked from the buds. "Happily. I've been asked to provide some advice on costumes for Settlers' Day. I'm happy to do so, but I'm getting tired of telling people that women who crossed the sea from England in the sixteenth century did not dress in silk and lace and jewels. And it's unlikely many of the men looked like this." She pointed to the computer to show me a photo of Johnny Depp as Captain Jack Sparrow.

"Realism in historical reenactment only goes so far," I said. "Not many people are going to wear their costume every day for a year without washing it, to get the scent authentic."

Charlene chucked. "And thank heavens for that. What's up?"

With Charlene it was always best to get straight to the point. I did so. "Jeremy Hughes."

She rubbed a hand across her eyes. The track on her music changed, and a woman began to sing. Or shout. Sometimes I can't tell the difference. "What about him?"

"What's the story there?"

"You think there is a story?"

"You left mighty quickly when he arrived Monday night. Couldn't wait to be out the door, I thought."

"I didn't know he'd joined the historical society. All the people I've been dealing with for Settlers' Day have been women or Phil."

"Is there a reason you should have known?"

"Yes," she said. "So I'd keep myself well out of it."

"I know it's none of my business. Except that—"

"The man died here. In our library. That makes it our business."

"Much to Detective Watson's dismay, it does." I studied her face. She didn't look particularly upset.

"Do we know what he was doing in the library last night?" she asked.

"We can guess he was after the diary and papers. Why he couldn't wait until this morning, and who was with him, are questions the police have to find answers for."

"I didn't come back after Mom was asleep to meet Jeremy Hughes, or anyone else, in order to conduct some sort of assignation, if that's what you're asking."

"It is not. You don't have to tell me anything if you don't want to, but I get a strong feeling there's some history between you two."

"*History.* That's the right word. He and I had a . . . fling, I guess you'd call it. It's totally over and done with, and has been for a long time."

I'd been expecting something like that, but it still came as a shock. The notoriously lecherous Jeremy and the practical, down-to-earth Charlene? I couldn't see it. I said nothing.

She let out a long sigh. "What can I say? It was a mistake. A bad one. It happened two years ago. I'd just returned from England and moved in with my mom. I love my mother very much, Lucy, and I had no problem coming back to Nags Head when she needed me. My dad died when I was five years old—cancer—and she was left with pretty much nothing except his hospital bills and me. She worked darn hard and went without a lot of things to make sure I got a good education. I remember my rebellious teenage years, when she just said over and over and over that I was going to college and that was that. She was nothing but delighted for me when I was offered my dream job at Oxford, and she insisted I go to England. 'We'll have plenty of years together, Char,' she said when I told her about it. 'It's your time now. You follow your dream.'"

She paused and ran her hand over the book on her desk, *Costuming in the Seventeenth Century*. There's no window in this room, and shadows filled the corners.

"I've no excuses, not really, but I was adrift when I got back. Most of my friends had moved on, and my mom was in a bad way. I landed this job and was darn lucky to get it, so with that and her small savings, I could hire a good caregiver for Mom. In the back of my mind, I was angry and resentful. And so guilty for feeling that way."

"That's natural enough," I said.

"I was easy pickings for a slimeball like Jeremy Hughes. I must have been out of my mind to find him attractive, but he turned on the charm and the flattery. And, I have to say, he spent money on me. Fancy restaurants, nice presents. He paid for a sitter for Mom so I could go out in the evenings and bought her little gifts. I knew he was married—more fool, me—but he fed me the same old story. They were soon to be divorced, and his wife didn't care what he got up to."

I thought of Lynne before asking, "I'm guessing the wife did care."

Charlene laughed without humor. "Funny thing is, that, at least, was true. She didn't care what he got up to. Not one bit. Most of the time. She tracked me down, came to my house one day, and told me there was no pending divorce, and I was but the latest in a long line of foolish girls hoping to snag a rich man."

"Why would she do that if she didn't care if he was having affairs?"

"He gave me a ring. Not an engagement ring—he never said it was that—but it was nice, a ruby. It belonged to her, so she said, and she wanted it back."

I was horrified. "Oh my gosh, Charlene. How terrible for you."

"The words 'total and complete humiliation' come to mind. I didn't think—not for a moment—to believe she wasn't telling me the truth. When I thought about it after, I realized all the signs were there. She must have told him she'd been to see me, because he never called me. I literally never spoke to him again. Nags Head's a small town, but not that small. Our paths never crossed. I soon forgot all about him and settled down to enjoy my life. My job, my friends." She smiled at me. "My coworkers. I still have my mom. She might not be able to get around anymore, but she's as fun and witty and loving as she ever was. The way I look at it, I had a lucky escape. Jeremy and I only dated for a few months."

"Bertie was going to ask you to work with him on the diary. It would have been awkward for you to be around him."

"Nah," she said. "It was a shock to see him here at the library, in my safe place—that's all. I'm totally over it." The smile she gave me was forced, and I wasn't sure I believed her, but I changed the subject. "Are you any good at word puzzles?"

"Not in the least. You want me to look at this code page I've been hearing about?"

I'd printed several more copies this morning, and I handed her one. She reached up and tilted her desk lamp so the light fell fully onto the page. "I suppose there's a pattern in there somewhere, but I don't see it. I'm great at reading unintelligible handwriting and minuscule print faded almost to nothing, but not something like this. Sorry. Can I keep this?"

"I've made copies."

"If something occurs to me, I'll let you know, but I don't expect anything will. I can only wish some of the historical documents I come across have writing as neat as this. I'd love to know what it says, from a historical perspective."

"The latest rumor's that the diary's cursed and it was buried deliberately, sort of like the North American version of a mummy's tomb. The curse is what got Jeremy."

"No ancient Egyptian curse killed Jeremy Hughes," Charlene said, and I caught a glimpse of something deep and dark behind her eyes. "But a woman scorned might well have."

Chapter Ten

I went downstairs full of thought. "Can I have a few minutes?" I asked Bertie. "I have something I need to tell Detective Watson."

"What about?"

"I've only met Jeremy Hughes once, but I do have some impressions of the man I'd like to share."

"I haven't met anyone who didn't have an opinion about him," said Bertie. "One way or the other. Take what time you need." She checked her watch. "It's coming up to noon. Why don't you go into town, talk to Sam, and then pick up lunch for me at Josie's? And get something for yourself. My treat. Come to think of it, get sandwiches, drinks, and some sort of dessert for us all. I'd tell you to dip into petty cash, but that's in my office, and I'm still forbidden from entering. If you pay, I'll reimburse you later. I'll expense it to the library budget. We deserve a treat after what happened here last night. You most of all."

"I won't argue with that," I said.

I ran upstairs for my purse and car keys. Cell phone reception within the thick stone walls of the library is poor at the best of times and nonexistent at others, so I waited until I was outside before calling the good detective.

Despite the heat, the children's construction site was busy, and two volunteer parents chatted in the shade of the umbrellas while keeping a close eye on the goings on. Kids filled the back of trucks with sand and pushed them a few feet before dumping them out, while other children reloaded the trucks and drove the sand back. One guy was building a road, patting down and smoothing out the sand, while a little girl, so cute in a pink construction hat, played with a toy jackhammer, her body jerking to a rhythm only she could hear.

At least her jackhammer was silent. The one at the real site hadn't been used today, thank heavens, but when it was, the noise rattled the very walls of the lighthouse, not to mention my back teeth. To the east side of the lighthouse tower, George and his crew were hard at work. The lawn was completely torn up, and the tracks of heavy equipment churned through the earth. Most of the work was being done underground, giving me not a hint of how they were progressing, but as far as I knew, George hadn't been into Bertie's office to complain lately. They wouldn't be finished before Sunday, Settlers' Day, but the construction area was safely marked off by the wire fence, and plenty of open space remained to accommodate all the day's participants and guests.

Thank heavens, George's crew hadn't found a dead body or a skeleton in the excavations. That would have brought work to a screeching halt. Zack saw me watching and sauntered over. He politely touched the brim of his bright yellow construction hat.

"How's it going?" I asked.

"Good," he said. If the job were proving to be a total and complete disaster, Zack would still say, "Good."

"I'm going into town. Do you want me to bring you anything? A sandwich or a soda?"

"Brought lunch," he said.

"Zackary! What do you think you're doing?" George bellowed. "Get over here! Son of mine or not, I'm not paying you to flirt with pretty young women."

Zack touched his hat once more, slowly turned around, and sauntered back to work. He might seem to move at a snail's pace and not react to much at all, but I'd soon learned Zack had a mind that moved like lightening. He did many of the measurements and calculations for his dad's construction jobs in his head and only used his ever-present iPad as a backup.

I placed my phone call, feeling strangely pleased at being called a "pretty young woman."

Sam Watson answered immediately. "Lucy, what's up?"

"I want to talk to you about Jeremy Hughes," I said.

"Do you know who killed him?" Watson rarely beat around the bush.

"Uh, no. Sorry. I've made some observations you might not have."

"Why wouldn't I?"

"'Cause you're not a woman."

"So my wife tells me. About observations, I mean. I'm in my office—come on in."

"How about if I make a stop at Josie's on my way? Can I bring you a coffee and a cookie?"

"I never say no to Josie's." He hung up.

My cousin Josie O'Malley owns Josie's Cozy Bakery in town, not far from the police station. As well as Sam Watson's favorite lunch spot, Josie's is rapidly becoming the in spot in Nags Head for coffee, sandwiches, and pastries.

It was quarter to twelve when I pulled out of the library parking lot. I would have suggested Watson and I meet at the café and grab something for lunch, but at this time of year, in the height of tourist season, it could be almost impossible to get a seat in the small, hugely popular bakery. Traffic heading both north and south on Highway 12 was heavy, and it got worse when I passed through Whalebone Junction and headed into town. Half the cars I saw were from out of state, and many were piled high with camping equipment or beach paraphernalia. I joined the slow crawl along South Virginia Dare Trail, and soon Josie's place came into sight. I'd been right: a line stretched out the door, and every parking space in the small strip mall where the bakery was located was taken. I parked on the street and approached the bakery. Earlier this season Josie had installed an express line, so those wanting a cup of plain coffee or glass of tea or soda with a baked item could move through faster than people in search of fancy drinks, full lunches, and seats.

The bakery was not far from the police station, so I could leave my car here and come back for the library lunch order after meeting with Sam.

The express line moved quickly, and I soon had a plain coffee, which I knew he took black, for Watson and an iced tea for me. I also carried a white paper bag containing a handful of assorted cookies.

Watson came out of the back of the police station to meet me as soon as he was told I'd arrived. We walked through the busy open office—people yelling into phones, people yelling at one another, computer keys clicking, printers spitting out paper, a radio somewhere playing hard rock—to the quiet (comparatively) corner where Sam had his desk. He cleared off a stack of papers by simply dumping them on the floor so I could put down the drinks and bag of treats.

He gestured to me to take a seat, pulled out his wallet, handed me a ten-dollar bill, and took the lid off his coffee. I'd long ago given up offering to pay. Maybe he was afraid I was trying to bribe him with a cup of Josie's coffee.

And cookies. Mustn't forget the cookies. Josie's pecan peanut butter and lime shortbread cookies were so rich and intense they *were* almost illegal.

Watson took a seat in his own chair. "Hughes."

"You heard him referred to as a ladies' man by Louise Jane and then again in our staff break room this morning?"

"Yes."

"You're a . . . bit older than me . . ."

"Meaning I'm an old fogey, yes."

"I didn't quite mean that. But you are of an earlier generation and you're not a woman, so you might not realize that referring to someone as a ladies' man is no longer meant as a good thing. It doesn't, to a lot of younger women anyway, mean a harmless flirt. It means a dirty old man."

"Do you have a personal reason to know this?"

"Yes, I do. I'd never even met Jeremy Hughes before yesterday, and he made a determined effort to oh-so-casually brush up against me. Several times. It wasn't comfortable."

"Understandably."

"On the other hand, you might have noticed that Lynne Feingold was completely overcome by news of his death."

"It hadn't escaped my notice, Lucy. You and she talked after she ran out of the break room."

"She told me she and Jeremy were having an affair, although she didn't use that word. She said they were, quote, planning a life together. She said Jeremy and his wife were in the process of getting a divorce. Another woman of my acquaintance—and I won't tell you who so don't ask—says he told her the same thing, but she soon realized no divorce was pending. They—he and my friend—broke up once she realized the situation. This happened, so I've been told, a couple of years ago. Sounds to me like there's a pattern there."

"So it does. Officer Rankin went around to Ms. Feingold's house earlier to have another chat. I thought she'd be more open away from the rest of the historical society. She doesn't deny what you said; in fact she confirms it. She was expecting Hughes to leave his wife and marry her. I wasn't aware, so thank you for telling me, that this is a pattern of behavior with him. I therefore have to ask if Ms. Feingold knew he planned to betray her."

"She doesn't have an alibi for last night."

Watson sipped at his coffee. His expression never gave anything away. "She said she was at home alone. And before you read anything into that, plenty of people who live on their own, as she does, spend their evenings alone at home. Phil Cahill's wife and Mabel Eastland's husband confirm they were home all evening, although Mrs. Cahill says she went to bed before her husband did. Again, I'll caution you that that means nothing. It's their normal pattern, according to her."

He pulled a scrap of paper toward him, picked up a pen, and jotted a note. I strained my neck, trying not to be too obvious about it, trying to read what he'd written. He flipped the paper over. I might have seen a grin tug at the corners of his mouth.

"You've given me something to think about, Lucy. I've had my officers looking into Hughes's relationships, if he has any, with collectors, shady and otherwise, of historical documents. That he was at the library last night to steal the contents of the tin box is almost certainly the case. Doesn't mean his killer had the same object in mind." His desk phone buzzed, and he picked it up.

"Show her to interview room one." He put down the phone and stood up. "Mrs. Hughes is here. I know you'd like to hear what she has to say . . ."

My hopes soared. *Was he going to invite me to take part in the interview?*

"But you can't," he said. My hopes deflated. "Thanks for coming in, Lucy. You can see yourself out."

"Uh, okay."

Watson tossed the last of his peanut butter cookie into his mouth and slipped the bag into a drawer, no doubt intending to finish the rest of them later. He headed toward a back hallway, clutching his coffee cup.

I went in the other direction, through the main room, heading for the exit. As I reached the door to the reception area, Officer Holly Rankin was coming through it, accompanied by an older woman. She was in her mid-fifties, dressed in blue boat shoes, blindingly white capris, a white-and-blue-striped T-shirt, and a blue linen jacket crumpled around the back, indicating she'd spent a lot of time sitting down since putting the jacket on. Perfectly sculpted waves of golden hair framed her face, and thick bangs fell over her forehead. Her makeup had been applied with a trowel, albeit an expensive trowel. Diamond studs were in her ears, and a diamond and white gold tennis bracelet was wrapped around her wrist. My mother was fond of jewelry like that, and when my parents had been having marital problems (hopefully now resolved), my dad bought her a bracelet much like this one. It cost in the five-thousand-dollar range. I knew that because Mom had told me.

It wasn't hard for me to guess who this woman was.

"Hi, Officer Rankin," I said in my friendliest voice. "How are you today?"

"Okay, thanks. Uh . . ."

"I'm Lucy, remember? We met yesterday at the library?"

"Oh, right," the young officer said. "What are you doing here?"

"Helping Detective Watson," I replied. I turned to the woman next to her. "Hello."

"Hi," she said.

Officer Rankin was young and new and trying to make a good impression. She was also a Southern woman. Of course she introduced us. "Maya Hughes, this is Lucy Richardson."

I thrust out my hand, and Maya took it in hers. The sapphire on her right hand dug into my fingers. The square-cut diamond on her left hand could be used to send signals to space.

"Nice meeting you," I said as I slipped away.

* * *

I wasn't getting involved. Not this time.

I'd told Detective Watson what I knew about the deceased, but that wasn't "getting involved." It was being a responsible citizen.

I wasn't getting involved. But I did know people, and I thought it couldn't hurt to put the word out.

As I walked back to Josie's I called Theodore Kowalski.

"TK Rare Books," said a deep, distinguished English voice that put me in mind of a member of the royal family. "How may I be of assistance?"

"Hi, Theodore. It's Lucy."

"Oh, hi, Lucy," said a young voice with a North Carolina accent. "What's up?"

"You heard what happened at the library last night?"

"Yes, I did. It's been on the news. Jeremy Hughes died. They aren't saying it was deliberate, but I can put two and two together. The report said he was alone in the building when he was found. Which seemed rather odd to me."

"It was odd. He broke in after hours, almost certainly either to steal the diary George's crew found or to have a private peek at it."

"And the diary?"

"It wasn't taken. But the two separate pages were. Presumably by whoever killed Jeremy."

"That is most unfortunate. Those were rare and potentially significant items." Theodore sounded more distressed over the loss of the pages than the man. "As I told you I would, I asked my mother what she knows about the Crawbingham family. I'm sorry to report that she's never heard of them."

"Did you know him? Jeremy Hughes?"

"Not personally. I knew of him. I've seen him around, but that's all. He isn't . . . wasn't a book collector."

"Speaking of collecting, if something like that diary or the separate pages came up for sale, would they be of interest to you?"

"It's not my field, Lucy, but a dealer is always on the lookout for a potential deal. I know people who know people who collect private letters and the like. A personal record written in the year or two prior to the war would be of interest. A hand-drawn map, probably even more so."

The hot noon sun poured down on my head; waves of heat radiated up from the pavement beneath my sandal-shod feet; and passing cars spat out hot exhaust fumes. With my free hand, I unobtrusively shook at my skirt, trying to get some air moving. Beads of sweat dripped from my hairline. I could see Josie's up ahead. Lovely, cool, air-conditioned Josie's. The lineup was fractionally less than it had been earlier.

But I didn't want anyone overhearing this conversation, so I didn't hurry to take my place. Instead, I stood on the sidewalk and slowly, steadily melted. "Can you keep your ear to the ground, maybe try to find out if anything like that's coming onto the market?"

"If the pages were stolen, which they seem to have been, then, unless our thief is a total amateur, they're unlikely to be advertised in the more respectable forums." He coughed modestly. "Fortunately, I know some of the less respectable ones, and I'm happy to be of help. I'll let you know if I hear anything."

"Not me. Tell Detective Watson. I'm not getting involved."

"Whatever you say, Lucy."

"Bye, Teddy. Oh, are you coming to book club on Wednesday?"

"Wouldn't miss it," he said. "Mr. Verne always takes me back to my childhood. My father loved the classic tales of adventure."

* * *

The lineup at Josie's moved slowly but steadily, and before too long I was through the doors, gratefully wrapped in cool air. A sign had been stuck to the front window, featuring a silhouette of a couple—her in long dress and bonnet, him carrying a musket—advertising Sunday's Settlers' Day festivities. Inside, every table was taken, and the staff ran to and fro, delivering orders and clearing off tables.

"Hey, Lucy. Nice to see you," Alison said when it was my turn to be served. "What can I get you?"

I asked for a roast beef sandwich on rye, chicken salad on a croissant, ham and cheese on wheat bread, and an heirloom tomato with arugula on a baguette. I dithered over the dessert selection. Josie's pies, tarts, cakes, and cookies were simply the best I'd ever eaten.

Conscious of the restless line behind me, I finally said, "I'll have four of whatever you want to give me."

Alison rang up the bill. I paid and went to stand at the end of the counter while my sandwiches were being prepared.

The head baker herself came out of the back, wiping floury hands on her apron. My cousin wrapped me in a hug. She smelled of cinnamon and pure vanilla. "Thought I heard your voice," Josie said.

"Bertie decided we needed a treat after last night. She keeps feeding us to keep us from quitting. Your food is the only reason we're still in business."

Her cornflower blue eyes sparked. "Glad to be of service." Josie and Jake Greenblatt, brother of Butch, had been married over the winter. I never had to ask how marriage was treating her. My cousin had always been a beautiful woman, but since the wedding she shone with an extra glow that seemed to light her up from inside. The sparkle faded fractionally, and she lowered her voice. "Yeah, I heard about what happened last night. You had an intruder and he died. Butch told Jake you weren't there when the guy broke in, thank heavens. This isn't the place to talk." She indicated the busy bakery with a nod of her head. "You can tell me all about it on Wednesday. That's if book club's still on?"

"It is."

"Great. I'm enjoying the book, and I appreciate how short it is. I don't have a lot of time to read over the summer."

"No kidding," I said.

"I like to read a couple of chapters in bed every night. It helps calm my mind and get me to sleep."

I didn't make a silly joke about not needing her new husband to help her get to sleep. Josie owned a bakery, so she got up extremely early and worked full out until late afternoon. Jake ran a successful restaurant, meaning he started work in late morning and rarely got home until after midnight.

Their schedules might not match, but they were the two hardest-working people I knew, and they made it work for them.

"Hey, Josie!" a voice yelled from the back. "Where'd you put that bag of coconut?"

"No rest for the wicked," she said to me. "You take care, sweetie. I don't like to hear about people creeping around in the night and getting themselves killed."

"Who got themselves killed?" the sandwich maker asked as he handed me two bulging bags.

"Figure of speech," I said. "Say hi to Jake for me."

"Will do," Josie said.

I stepped outside into the searing heat and headed for my car. We didn't often get this sort of relentlessly hot and humid weather in the Outer Banks, as the lovely ocean breezes normally play a moderating role. I spotted someone

I knew standing patiently in the line, waving at me, and made a quick detour to say hi.

"Sure is hot." Janelle Washington looked lovely and cool in a red and white sleeveless dress that showed off her dark, well-toned arms.

"You can say that again," I said. "That's a pretty dress."

"Thanks." Her face twisted, and I guessed that she hadn't been flattered by the compliment, although it had been sincerely meant.

"Something wrong?" I asked.

"No. I'll agree that this dress fits me well and looks nice, but I have to say, I don't like it."

"Why do you wear it then?"

She glanced around, checking that no one was listening to us, and lowered her voice. Instinctively I leaned closer. "One of the realtors in my office gave it to me. She told me it didn't fit her any more as she'd lost weight. As if. She always makes a big show of extending charity to me, and I'm supposed to be *so* grateful for Her Ladyship's bounty."

As she talked, we kept an eye on the progress of the line and edged steadily toward the door. Every time someone entered or left, the people at the front sighed happily as they were hit by a wave of cool air.

"I'll admit things have been tough since Neil's injury put him out of work," Janelle said. "But we manage. I only hope I don't have to wait until the end of the month to be reimbursed for this lunch."

"What do you mean?"

"She sent me to get lunch for the office. 'Too hot to go out,' she said. Not too hot for me to go out, apparently. Sandwiches, drinks, desserts—the works for ten people. When she went to get her purse—guess what? She'd left her pocketbook at home. How silly of her. She promised to pay me back tomorrow. So now I'll spend the rest of the week trying to remind her without sounding as though I'm desperate." Janelle forced out a smile. "I'm so sorry, Lucy. I don't mean to complain, and I hardly know you. I guess you were just here at the right time—the wrong time for you—when I felt like dumping on someone. Forgive me?"

"Nothing to forgive," I said. "We all need to vent now and again."

It was our turn, and we stepped into the bakery. Janelle pointed to the sign in the window. "I'm planning on bringing the girls to that. They're excited about it. Are you going to be there?"

"I am. My mother's family came to the Outer Banks sometime in the mid-nineteenth century. The men fished, the women worked in the fish plants."

"Life was hard here," Janelle said, "for most of our ancestors. Despite that, I hope they got pleasure out of it in the way we do. The beach, the ocean."

Alison stepped up to the blackboard behind the counter that advertised today's specials and put a thick line through lime shortbread cookies. Half the people in the place groaned.

I was about to say goodbye to Janelle when I had a thought. "What's the name of this woman in your office?"

"Cheryl Monaghan. She's one of our lesser-selling realtors, so I don't know how she manages to get away with acting like the queen of the roost, but she does. The influence of her husband's family name, probably. The Monaghans have been in the Outer Banks for a long time. As long as the Washingtons, come to think of it, but no one seems to consider us OBX royalty." She shook her head and gave me a wry grin. "I'm sorry, Lucy, really I am. I'm still complaining; I should know better than to let her get to me. You won't tell anyone I said things about her, will you? It could jeopardize my working there, and I really need this job. At least until Neil gets back on his feet."

"Of course I won't. What you've said ties into something I heard earlier today. A local family named Washington claimed to have been given land by the Monaghan family a long time ago. Was that your husband's family?"

"Yes, it was. His name was Thaddeus, and he made a good living as a boat builder. People still talk about that. Bankers have long memories."

"So I've been told."

"Every once in a while, Cheryl reminds everyone that her husband's family has owned some of the best land in the Outer Banks for generations. She pretends she's being nonchalant about it, but she peeks out of the corner of her eyes at me, hoping for a reaction. It's all water under the bridge to Neil's family. Happened so long ago. His wasn't the first black family to have been cheated out of what was rightfully theirs. It happened to everyone at the Freedmen's Colony."

Janelle was next to be served, and I needed to get back to work. I knew a little about the Freedmen's Colony, a community on Roanoke Island established by escaped and freed slaves during the Civil War years, and decided I'd like to learn more. "Did your husband or his family ever talk about someone named Crawbingham?"

"Not that I remember, and surely I would have. That's quite the name."

"What can I get you?" Alison asked. Janelle pulled a list out of her bag, and I said, "I have to be going. The construction playground will be up for at least another two weeks, so bring the girls around."

"I'll do that. Thanks for being a good listener, Lucy."

Chapter Eleven

When I got back to the library, Bertie told me she'd asked Charlene to read through the diary, to see if she could find any clues relating to the code page or the meaning of the map. I trotted upstairs to see if Charlene needed anything. I met her locking the door of the rare books room behind her. Her earbuds were draped around her neck, the thin white cord trailing into her pocket, but the sound had been turned off.

"Any luck?" I asked.

"No. Bertie was hoping for a line saying something like, 'To solve the code do this and that, and then apply that and this to the map.' But it's nothing but an account of the weather and the tides. Not even a mention of what's for dinner. The last entry is dated November 1870, and the following pages are all blank. The last page is ripped out. I suspect that's the one that was used to write the code."

"Although the map page wasn't taken from that book, which is interesting. Can you tell if the diary was written in the Outer Banks?"

"I don't think so. Not at the beginning anyway. I haven't had much of a chance to compare weather records."

"The historical society was going to try to do that, but now Bertie won't let them see the diary."

"On one day when I know there was a heavy rain storm here, Mrs. Crawbingham just says, 'Cloudy with threat of rain.' When I have the time I can do a proper comparison. I don't know that it matters, though."

"Perhaps not. Lunch is laid out downstairs. Bertie sent me into town for a run to Josie's."

"Thanks. That was nice of her. And of you."

"I had to go to the police station anyway. I wanted to talk to Sam Watson."

"Getting involved again, Lucy?"

"Not at all," I said firmly.

* * *

The library wasn't particularly busy that afternoon. The hot weather had everyone who didn't have work to do heading for the beach.

"The forecast for the weekend is promising," Bertie said to me. "Temperatures dropping to reasonable levels and no rain. Fingers crossed."

"Fingers and toes," I said. Rain on Sunday would not be a good thing as the Settlers' Day festivities were going to be held outside. "I saw signs advertising the event when I was in town. The historical society's going all out. No one thinks it's a bit tasteless after Jeremy died? And here, so close to where it happened?"

"Mabel called me earlier. They're calling the event a tribute to Jeremy. She said he would have wanted it to go ahead. I think it's more that no one particularly liked him, so they don't much care what he would have thought."

"Isn't that a bit harsh, Bertie?"

"I've been hearing things," she said. "It's interesting sitting at the circulation desk. I need to spend more time here. This spot is Nags Head Gossip Central."

"It can be that, all right," I said.

Bertie checked her watch, noticed that it was almost six o'clock, and called out. "Five minutes to closing, people."

The handful of patrons waved at her and began gathering up their books. I had no plans for tonight—Connor had a business dinner—and I was looking forward to finishing *Journey to the Center of the Earth* and having an early night. My lunchtime sandwich had been so enormous, and I'd indulged in a coconut cupcake (my fave!) on my afternoon break, so I wanted nothing more substantial than a bowl of soup for dinner. But first, I planned to head to Coquina Beach for a dip in the cool waters and a nice long, head-clearing walk in the surf.

Patrons lined up at the desk, and Bertie checked out their books. Ronald had left at four, after wrapping yellow barricade tape around the children's construction site.

"I'm looking forward to Settlers' Day," one of the patrons said as she hoisted her stack of cookbooks. "Is Louise Jane going to be telling stories?"

"I don't think so," Bertie replied. "The historical society has arranged for several speakers, including a college history professor."

"I hope he or she is better than other speakers they've had. I went to a lecture at the society a couple of months ago. That's an hour and a half of my life I'll never get back. Driest bunch of facts I ever have heard."

"The history of the Outer Banks is exciting," her friend said. "That speaker made it sound so deadly boring I fell asleep."

"Then again," the first woman said with a laugh, "you fell asleep in *Mamma Mia*."

"I'd had a rough few nights before that."

"Regardless of the speakers," Bertie said, "it's going to be a fun day."

The two women left, chattering about what they were going to wear on Sunday. I heard, "Probably too hot for a bustle."

"Is Ronald going to open the children's construction area on Sunday?" I asked Bertie when the last of the patrons had left.

"He says better to have it available and someone keeping an eye on it than tempting kids to crawl under the tape."

"Not exactly historically accurate for Settlers' Day." Charlene's expression was disapproving as she headed for the door, briefcase in hand. "Dump trucks? Earthmoving equipment? Hard hats?"

"Happy and occupied children," I said.

"Worth having some historical inaccuracies then," she replied.

Louise Jane liked to make a dramatic gesture on arrival, throwing the door open and posing in the entrance, but our new door was heavy enough that she had to tug at it, which spoiled the impact considerably. "I can't believe it took all day to get a set of tires replaced," she said when she eventually made it in. "Take my advice: don't go to Fitzroy's Garage. He wouldn't take me first, said he had people who'd made appointments to see to. Imagine the cheek! His mother was a second cousin of my uncle Albert, the one we always called Bertie—like you Bertie, I'd forgotten that until now—and rumor says he—Uncle Bertie—wanted to marry Lydia Fitzroy, but her family put a stop to it because she was too young."

I didn't bother to try to figure out the degrees of relation between Uncle Bertie and Lydia Fitzroy and Louise Jane.

"You'd think close family would get some sort of privileged service, wouldn't you? It's not as if I was expecting a discount or anything. Although that would have been an awful nice gesture. I told him I had an important meeting to get to, but oh no, I had to take a number and wait. I sat there all day. I would have gotten up and taken my car someplace else, but I was afraid the cops had been told to be on the lookout for me and I'd get pulled over.

"Now, where were we? Oh yes, Jeremy Hughes. No loss to anyone, but the theft of the map and code page certainly are. What have you done about finding them, Lucy?"

"Me? What makes you think I've been looking for them? The police are investigating."

"They're investigating Jeremy's murder. Probably not looking awful hard for the stolen items. Okay, if I must. Let me see that code page. I trust you were sensible enough to make a copy of it."

"Well, yes, but . . ." I threw a questioning look to Bertie, but she wasn't looking at me. The door opened, and a bright smile leapt into my boss's eyes.

"Good afternoon, everyone," said Professor Edward McClanahan.

Bertie jumped to her feet. "Eddie! This is a surprise. What brings you here?"

"Skullduggery of the darkest order, my dear." He came around the desk and gave Bertie a peck on the cheek. She turned various shades of pink and red.

Bertie and Eddie had been a couple way back in their college years. That ended largely because he was almost the movie definition of an absent-minded professor. He even looked the part, with his mane of curly white hair; salt and pepper mustache, curling at the ends;

rimless glasses with thick lenses; and tall, thin, stooping frame.

He and Bertie had reconnected last October when she and I had gone to Blacklock College, where he taught ancient Greek and Latin, in search of gossip—I mean important information—about Professors McArthur and Hoskins.

"Hi," Louise Jane said.

"Nice to see you, Professor," Charlene said.

He nodded politely to Louise Jane and Charlene, clearly not remembering where he'd met them, which had been at Jake and Josie's wedding.

"What sort of skullduggery?" Bertie asked.

The professor glanced at Louise Jane, Charlene, and me.

"It's okay," Louise Jane said. "You can talk freely in front of us. No secrets are kept from me in this building. Right, Bertie? I said, isn't that right, Bertie?"

"Uh, right," Bertie said.

"I assume you mean Lizzie and Norm are up to something," I guessed.

"I do," he said. "As you know, their positions at the college are tenuous, to say the least." At the time of the death of Jay Ruddle, North Carolina History—that is, Professors Elizabeth McArthur and Norman Hoskins—had been in danger of being eliminated from the curriculum so Blacklock College could concentrate on their main focus, which is ancient and modern languages. The Ruddle collection would have been an invaluable boost to the professors' efforts to keep the North Carolina History Department—and their jobs—alive. They hadn't secured the collection, nor had we, and they would be on the lookout for another way of proving their importance to the college.

Our mysterious little diary might well be it.

"What's happened now?" Bertie asked.

"I took the liberty of printing off an article that was published this morning in the college's online newspaper." The professor fumbled in the pockets of his seersucker jacket. Out came a set of keys; a cigarette lighter, although he didn't smoke; a packet of tissues; two pens; a pencil nibbled down to the stub; a worn brown leather wallet, bulging with scraps of paper; a flat black rock; another rock, this one round and white; a pair of reading glasses; and a pocket Greek–English dictionary. "Now," he muttered to himself, "where did I put it?"

"Maybe tucked in that little book?" Bertie suggested.

He checked and proudly produced a computer print-out. "Ta-da."

Bertie smiled at him.

He unfolded the paper and said, "I won't bore you with the tedious overly formal language and barely disguised slander. Or is it libel? I always forget."

"Libel is something in print. Slander is spoken words," Charlene said.

"Yes. Libel. The gist of this piece is that Lizzie and Norm are accusing you—the unnamed director of this library—of staging the stealing of pages of the diary in order to keep them from—and I quote—'undergoing an unbiased, independent, professional examination.'"

"Phooey to them," Bertie said. "No one cares what those two have to say."

"I think you should take this seriously, Bee. I chose to confront them upon reading this, and they told me they'd been in contact with the police."

"That's ridiculous," I said.

"Because," the professor added ominously, "whoever stole the pages is likely to be the same person who killed this Mr. Hughes."

Bertie sputtered. "No one, least of all Sam Watson, is going to think I broke down the front door of my own library and smashed the lock on my own desk in order to sneak something out of it that I'd put there myself, and then murdered some innocent passerby who just happened to wander through the building after closing."

"Put like that," Charlene said, "it does sound pretty stupid."

"It sounds ludicrous," I said.

"The police will have to take their observation into consideration," Professor McClanahan said.

"First the cops accused me, and now you, Bertie," Louise Jane said. "This is getting too close to home."

"They accused you of killing Jeremy?" Charlene said. "I didn't know that. Why?"

"No reason."

"There has to have been a reason."

"Let me rephrase that," Louise Jane said. "No reason that is any of your business."

"I'd say whatever happened here that night—any night—is the business of us all," Charlene replied. "How did you get that bruise on your face anyway? It's a bad one."

"Not in a fight to the death, I can assure you of that."

"Let's not squabble," Bertie said. "None of us did it, and we'd all be more than happy to see the pages returned. In that, Eddie, you might be able to help us."

"Happy to, my dear. How?"

She patted her hips. At work, Bertie usually wore long colorful dresses with voluminous pockets stuffed with everything she might need in a day. Those pockets, I thought with a hidden smile, were somewhat like the professor's. She found what she was looking for and produced her copy of the code page. "Fortunately, Lucy had the brilliant idea of taking a photograph of the page that seems to be written in code and the map. We have that at least."

"I have to get off home," Charlene said. "Good luck with it, everyone."

"See you tomorrow," I said.

Bertie handed the printout to Professor McClanahan. Louise Jane leaned over his shoulder. "It's in code," he said.

"Really, Eddie, is that all you can say?" Bertie said. "We know it's in code."

"We're *guessing* it's in code," I said. "It might be the ramblings of someone who can't read or write."

"Unlikely, with handwriting this precise," he said.

We were quiet for a long time. I pulled out my own copy and once again tried to find a recognizable pattern.

"Is it in English, do you think?" Bertie asked.

"One of the modern Western European languages, I'd say," the professor replied. "There appear to be no accents on the letters, or tildes."

"Which means it's probably in English, right?" I said.

"Not necessarily. The substitution might be replacing accented letters with different ones."

"Meaning an *e* with an accent is being replaced by a different letter than an *e* without?" I asked.

"Yes."

"Oh good." I threw up my hands. "More complications."

"We need the key," he said.

"That's the problem," I said. "We don't have the key, and we don't have the slightest idea where to find it or what it might be. If there even is one."

"It's probably lost," Louise Jane said. "Lost forever, as it was known only to the coder and the person the message was intended for."

"May I take this with me?" the professor asked. "I might be able to find some sort of pattern if I spend some time with it. I was rather good at word puzzles when I was younger."

"Please do," Bertie said.

"Make a copy for me too, Lucy," Louise Jane said. "If there's some reference in there to Outer Banks people or locations, I might be able to figure it out."

I glanced at Bertie, who gave me a nod. "The more the merrier," she said. "We're getting nowhere, and fast. Louise Jane, I'll let you have a copy, but only on condition that you don't share it with anyone."

Louise Jane put on her innocent face and crossed her chest. "Promise."

"I do not want word getting around, more than it is anyway, that we have a guide to buried treasure. People won't wait for the clue to be deciphered before descending from far and wide and digging up the lawn."

"That's not what that mess outside is?" Professor McClanahan asked. "If not, you have very big moles around here."

Bertie shut down the computer and said, "Louise Jane, good night. We're locking up. Now. Lucy, I'll see you tomorrow. Eddie, as long as you're in town, you may take me out to dinner."

He bowed deeply. "It will be my pleasure."

* * *

I nipped upstairs, changed into my bathing suit and a beach wrap and flip-flops, grabbed a towel and my book, and jumped into my car. I was turning into the parking lot at Coquina Beach when my phone rang. I answered it, using Bluetooth, while I found a parking space. It was late in the day, but the intense heat lingered, and plenty of people were out taking advantage of the slight wind coming off the sea. "Hi, Charlene."

She didn't bother with pleasantries. "How could you do that to me, Lucy?"

"Do what?" I switched off the engine. The air-conditioning died, and sticky heat instantly began filling the car.

"I told you about Jeremy Hughes and me in the strictest of confidence." She spoke rapidly, almost biting into each word. "I thought you, of all people, would have understood that."

"Charlene, I don't know what you're talking about. Honestly, I don't."

"You told Detective Watson. You went to the police station earlier today, and you told him. I never thought you could be so mean as to betray a confidence."

"But I didn't. Your name didn't even come up when I was there. What's happened?"

She let out a long breath. "You didn't mention it?"

"No. I didn't. Not to Watson, and not to anyone else. Please believe me."

"Then I'm sorry. I guess I'm just upset. Bye."

"Wait! Wait. What's going on?"

"He's on his way here. Watson. To my house. He sent an officer around to pick me up, to bring me to the police station. I can't go; I can't leave Mom alone, and the neighbor who helps out in an emergency isn't at home. So he's coming here."

"He probably wants to talk to you about security at the library on Monday night," I said. "I'm sure that's it. He'll ask if you know about a spare key or anything." I wiped sweat off my forehead.

"He said he wants to discuss my relationship with Jeremy," Charlene said.

"Oh. How about if I come over? I'll stay with your mom if . . . if he wants you to leave with him. I can be there to run interference if you need." I switched the engine back on and checked my mirrors and backup camera. A family laden with beach chairs, umbrellas, coolers, water toys, and sand-covered kids with red faces, lumbered slowly behind me. "Watson and I have an understanding." What sort of understanding I didn't know. Sometimes he didn't seem to mind—too much— when I got involved in his cases. Sometimes he got down-right angry. He would not be happy to see me pop up at Charlene's.

Too bad.

The family passed, the dad giving me a weary wave of thanks, and I backed out. "I won't be long," I said. "I'm halfway to your place already. How long ago did you speak to him?"

"I called you as soon as I hung up. The police offi-cer who's here didn't want me phoning you, but she had no authority to take my phone away. I'm hiding in the bathroom. Fortunately, Mom's taking a nap before dinner."

"I might beat him then. I'll be there in a couple of minutes. If not less." I disconnected the call as I turned right onto Highway 12 and sped toward town. Traffic was heavy with people returning to their hotels or vaca-tion homes for dinner, but I didn't have to go all the way into town. I turned right into South Old Oregon Inlet

Road, heading for the small collection of streets and houses located south of Whalebone Junction and the bridge to Roanoke. If traffic was bad in town, and it likely was at this hour, I had a good chance of getting to Charlene's before Watson.

Instead, I arrived at the same time. We parked nose to tail on the sidewalk outside Charlene's house. A police cruiser filled the narrow driveway. Watson got out of his car and stared at me. I almost said, "We can't go on meeting like this," but decided discretion was the better part of valor and held my tongue. I felt rather exposed in flip-flops and a wide-brimmed straw hat, wearing nothing but a red tankini under a loose black beach wrap.

"What brings you here, Lucy?" he asked.

I tugged the wrap tightly around me. "Charlene called me. She needs emotional support as well as assistance with her mother. You know her mother's housebound, don't you?"

"I am aware of that, thank you, Lucy." He threw up his hands. "What the heck. You might as well come in now that you're here."

We walked up the front path together and climbed the long wheelchair ramp to the veranda. This close to the sea, the house was built on stilts, with an open carport tucked under the building, containing Charlene's small car and an assortment of garden supplies and the usual junk everyone has. Officer Holly Rankin opened the door before Watson could knock, and she threw me a questioning look. "I'm here as Charlene's friend," I said.

She stepped back and we walked into Mrs. Clayton's sitting room. The blinds were open to a view of the small backyard, and the house was comfortably cool. At the same time the wheelchair ramp had been installed, the inside of the house had been renovated to accommodate Mrs. Clayton's needs. The living and dining rooms were moved upstairs, and most of the main level was converted into a bedroom and TV room. A large, comfortable medical chair sat in front of the huge flat screen TV. A cabinet in the far corner held neatly organized medical equipment, and pictures of Charlene and her mother through the years filled the tabletops and the walls. I glanced at what was almost certainly Mr. and Mrs. Clayton's wedding photo: she, glowingly beautiful in a white lace dress; he, standing tall, handsome, and proud at her side. Charlene saw me looking and gave me a smile.

I was glad of it. I was afraid that, despite my protestations of innocence, she might still suspect I'd told Watson what she'd revealed to me in confidence.

The room was spotlessly clean, the tabletops and photo frames dusted, the glass in the windows sparkling, the beige paint on the walls and baseboards unmarked. A big bouquet of fresh flowers sat on the center table, but the air of long-term illness and medicinal intervention hung over everything. Almost everything: I smelled something delicious coming from the kitchen. A beef stew, I guessed.

Charlene had changed out of her work clothes into shorts and a T-shirt. She gave me a nod of welcome but spoke to Detective Watson. "My mother's resting in her room. We'll talk upstairs so as not to disturb her." She led the way, and we followed. She gestured for us to take a seat, and Watson and I did so. Rankin leaned up against a wall, her arms crossed over her chest. Charlene perched on the edge of the sofa, holding her hands so tightly together the knuckles turned white. Her face was very pale, and I could tell she was frightened.

Watson got straight to the point and asked Charlene about her relationship with Jeremy Hughes. Calmly, she told him what she'd told me. A brief, highly regrettable affair that hadn't lasted for long. It ended when she realized he was married and had no intention of leaving his wife. She hadn't seen nor spoken to him for almost two years.

"I wasn't aware Jeremy had joined the historical society. I'll admit it came as a surprise to see him at the library yesterday evening, but it shouldn't have been. It's only by chance we never ran into each other since our relationship ended. I didn't want to talk to him—I have nothing to say—and so I left. If I'd been asked to help them with the diary, I would have readily agreed. That is, after all, an important part of my job."

Watson tried to suggest that Charlene had invited Jeremy to return to the library on Monday night to meet with her, but his heart didn't truly seem to be in what he was saying. She didn't have an alibi for the estimated time of his death. She'd gotten home from work shortly after five and relieved her mother's occasional caregiver. She fixed dinner and ate with her mother while they watched TV. Mrs. Clayton went to bed at her regular time of eight o'clock. Charlene read until ten before she also turned in.

"Before you ask," Charlene said, "My mother takes a sleeping pill every night. You can check with her doctor if you don't believe me. If I'd snuck out, she wouldn't have heard me go."

Watson got to his feet. Officer Rankin pushed herself away from the wall. "I know this was difficult for you, Charlene," he said. "I hope you appreciate that I have to follow every line of inquiry."

"Of course," she said. "I can't help but wonder who told you Jeremy and I had once been involved. It was a long time ago, and even at the time it wasn't exactly common knowledge."

He just smiled at her and turned to go. "Coming, Lucy?"

"I'll stay for a bit. I don't feel like going to the beach any more."

Charlene and I walked the police to the door. When it shut behind them, she turned and leaned against it. "I am totally innocent, but that was still so unbelievably stressful. I know Sam Watson, and I know he's a good cop, and a good man, but I kept expecting him to leap to his feet and tell me I was under arrest."

"Charlene," a voice called. "Are they gone?"

"Yes, Mom, they are. Give me a sec and I'll be in. Dinner's almost ready."

"Is that beef ragu I smell?"

"It is."

"Yummy," Mrs. Clayton said. "Why don't you invite your friend to join us for dinner?"

Charlene turned to me. "Will you stay? You'd be very welcome."

"Thanks, but I think not. I have a call to make. Do you know Jeremy's address?"

"No. I never went to his house, but I'm pretty sure he lived in Nags Head. Why do you want to know?"

"I didn't tell the police you and he had been in a relationship. Obviously someone did. Maya Hughes was interviewed at the police station earlier this afternoon. I saw her there myself. I'm thinking I might pay a call on her and ask her what she had to say. You told me she confronted you over her husband. Maybe she wasn't as blasé about his affairs as you thought, and she's happy to have the chance to get you in trouble." I glanced down at my bare toes. "If I expect her to take me seriously, I need to go home and change first."

* * *

Before I drove away, I checked 411.com for Jeremy Hughes's address. He lived, so I found, east of Virginia Dare Trail, close to the sea. I didn't want to phone ahead and alert Maya Hughes to my desire to talk to her, so I'd have to take a chance on finding her at home. I drove back to the lighthouse and let myself in. Charles greeted me at the door, and then he led the way up the spiral iron staircase to the fourth floor, his fluffy tail held high. I put food and water into his bowls before changing into black ankle boots, gray slacks, a crisp white blouse, and a dark green linen jacket, appropriate attire for pretending to be a police officer.

Not that I was planning on pretending to be an officer of the law. Not at all. Maya Hughes had met me in the police station, and we'd been introduced by Holly Rankin, who'd said nothing about who I was or why I was there. I'd said, completely truthfully, that I was assisting Detective Watson. If Maya Hughes wanted to assume I was a cop, who was I to dissuade her?

Watson might not look at it quite the same way, but hopefully he'd never find out.

* * *

Jeremy and Maya Hughes's home was a typical Outer Banks beach house in a network of small streets dead-ending at the beach. By typical, I mean with five or six bedrooms and worth a couple of million bucks. The house was narrow and four stories tall, the bottom one of which served as the garage and storage areas. That design afforded the upper levels spectacular views over the dunes, to the beach, and out to sea.

I parked on the street. No cars were in the driveway, but the double garage doors were closed. I adjusted my sunglasses on my face, took a deep breath, and walked with (I hoped) confident strides up to the front door, which wasn't easy as I felt like I was on the point of bursting into flames in my long pants and jacket. I couldn't begin to imagine how cops stayed cool in this sort of heat in their dark uniforms and bulletproof vests. I rang the bell and waited.

I didn't have to wait long before the door swung open, and Maya Hughes peeked out. She was, I was thrilled to discover, accompanied by a blast of air-conditioned air.

"Good evening," I said. "I was hoping we could have a quick word. I'm Lucy Richardson. We met earlier today at the police station."

"I remember." She held the door open. "Please, come in."

I did so. Without my having to ask, she led the way up the stairs to the main level. I've been in some nice homes on the Outer Banks, and this one was right up there in terms of up-to-date style and money spent. The main floor was fully open plan. The paint on the walls and ceiling was white, the floors light gray concrete, the lamp stands and shades white. The sectional sofa and damask wingback chairs were covered in a deep red fabric, the tables clear glass mounted on chrome frames. A small kitchen—chrome appliances, gray granite countertop, red bar stools—was off to one side. This wasn't the main living room; it would mostly be used for casual winter entertaining. Spacious decks, with views out to sea and stairs to the pool area, would be on the third and fourth levels. A fireplace, now thankfully unlit, filled most of the wall opposite the mini-kitchen. The art was modern, red and white mostly, with wide brush strokes and thick slashes of paint.

Maya turned and faced me. Her smile was pinched, showing the network of fine lines around her mouth and unsmiling eyes. She wore a sleeveless beige silk blouse and skinny white jeans, fashionably shredded at the knees. A glass of white wine sat on the coffee table, next to an ice bucket and a pile of fashion magazines. Music came from invisible speakers. A playlist, I guessed, as I recognized the movie theme music. "Have you learned any more about my husband's death?" she asked.

She *had* mistaken me for a cop. As long as she didn't ask me directly or put me in a position where I'd have to confess or lie, I wouldn't tell her I was nothing more than a nosy librarian.

Gathering my thoughts, trying to look casual, as though I interviewed suspects every day, I walked toward the French doors that opened onto the swimming pool area—sparking blue water, comfortable lounge chairs, brilliant flowers and lush grasses in terracotta and concrete pots.

I admired the view for a moment and then turned to face into the room. I glanced at one of the wingback chairs.

"Please," Maya said, right on cue, "have a seat."

I sat. She dropped onto the couch and tucked her feet underneath her. She picked up her wine glass and was about to take a sip, when she remembered the rest of her manners. "Can I offer you a drink?"

"No, thank you. I won't stay long."

Her lips didn't say, "Thank heavens for that," but her expression did. She leaned back and took far more than a sip. More like a glug.

"Detective Watson interviewed Charlene Clayton earlier this evening," I said.

Maya nodded. "I told him about her."

"She says her relationship with your husband ended two years ago. Do you have reason to believe otherwise?"

She studied me through clear, narrow eyes, heavily outlined in black liner, the lashes thick with mascara. This woman had not been crying recently. "He died at the library, didn't he? I know she works there. Why on earth else would Jeremy be in a library, of all places, other than to meet up with her?" I could think of plenty of reasons a person would want to be in a library, and very few of them had to do with illicit assignations.

"He'd been there earlier with members of the historical society."

She waved a freshly manicured hand. The deep red polish matched not only her toes but the furniture. "Oh, that. Whatever."

"How do know Ms. Clayton works at the library?"

"I keep tabs on all Jeremy's . . . friends. Past and present."

"He had a lot of . . . friends?"

"Over the years."

"That didn't bother you?"

"Why are you asking me all this? I told Detective Watson Jeremy and I had a completely open marriage. He did his thing, and I did mine."

"Yet you kept tabs on his girlfriends."

"If you want to call them that." A smile touched the corners of her mouth. The smile was so cold I almost shivered. "He can do . . . could do . . . whatever he liked, but I needed to know if anything threatened to become serious, so I could do something about it in time. Nip it in the bud, so to speak."

"Like you did with Char—Ms. Clayton?"

She shrugged. "He gave her his maternal grand-mother's ring. He'd never done anything like that before. I had to make sure it didn't happen again."

"You told her it was your ring."

"Did I? I suppose I did. Better to make it sound like he was a thief rather than an infatuated little boy making a romantic gesture."

I stared at her. This woman was so cold and calculat-ing it scared me.

She realized she'd shocked me and she grinned, pleased with herself. Her eyes studied me over the rim of her wine glass. "And so the pattern continued. Just between you and me, dear, I was surprised when I checked the web page for the historical society shortly after he joined. I assumed he was interested in a woman there, and then I saw pictures of the other members." She laughed. "Everyone of them middle-aged and up. Way up. Positively geriatric. Not a pretty young woman in the lot. Poor Jeremy, getting old, I suppose, and times are changing. Young women these days aren't quite as naïve as they used to be, are they?"

I thought of Lynne Feingold. Not even worthy of Maya Hughes's scorn.

"Do you yourself have many . . . friends?" I asked her. *What a shockingly personal question.* This pretending (without actually pretending) to be a detective was mak-ing me bold. I could imagine my mother, a Boston Brah-min matron to the core, gasping in horror at my impudence. Which isn't to say my mother didn't like gossip—she and the rest of her social set lived for it; she just thought one should approach the important business of the gathering of gossip with some delicacy.

Maya didn't seem to mind. She wiggled a well-plucked eyebrow at me. "I might. I might not. That's absolutely none of your business, but I'll tell you what I told your boss . . ."

I almost asked when she'd spoken to Bertie, but at the last minute I realized she must be talking about Sam Watson. "When Jeremy died, I was at the Calming Waters Spa near Raleigh for a few days of pampering. I try to go there several times a year. I wish I could produce a handsome young lover to be my alibi, but sadly I was alone that evening. I had a Swedish massage from three until ten to four and then retired to my cabin for some much-needed peace and quiet. I watched TV for a while, decided not to go to dinner—I worry that the quality of guest they're attracting lately is deteriorating—and went to bed early. Alone. That is the purpose of a spa stay after all, dear. To be alone."

A lot of rich and not-so-rich women went to spas for the stated purpose—rejuvenation and relaxation. Some of them went to dry out. Others went because they needed an escape from a failing marriage and a cheating husband, another thing I knew from when my parents' marriage wasn't doing so well. "Your husband's affairs didn't bother you?"

Once again she waved a hand in the air, and her diamonds flashed. "Not in the least. He could do what he wanted. To be honest, I couldn't stand the blasted man, and the less time I had to spend in his company, the better. There, I said it. Are you shocked? Your boss certainly was. I considered playing the grieving widow but decided not to bother. You police have ways of finding things out, don't you? Any of my friends, my so-called girlfriends that is, would be more than happy to tell you all the salacious details." She plucked the wine bottle out of the cooler and refilled her glass. About a quarter inch of wine dribbled out, and she gave it a shake to get the last few drops.

"Then why," I asked boldly, "did you and your husband stay together?"

"Money, why else? Jeremy's mother is still alive. Miserable old woman. Almost as miserable as her son. She clings to some rather old-fashioned ideas about marriage. She has . . . had . . . three sons, and her estate is to be divided equally among them when she finally does us all a favor and goes to her vastly undeserved reward. If any of the sons get divorced, the money will go to the others. If they all divorce, a home for wayward cats gets the lot. Controlling shrew."

If Jeremy's mother had been murdered, I knew who my prime suspect would be.

I wondered about the conditions of this will. Was Maya now in line to inherit Jeremy's share?

I was feeling bold, but not that bold. I simply couldn't ask. It was possible, likely even, Maya didn't know the other conditions of the will.

She threw back the last of her wine and got to her feet. "If you don't mind, I have dinner plans."

I stood up also. "Okay. Thanks for your time. Did Detective Watson ask you not to leave town?"

"Yes, he did. I might have objected, just on principal, but why bother? I've no plans to go anywhere. I gave your boss the contact details for Mrs. Hughes and Jeremy's brothers. He said he'd let them know when the body"—she giggled "—is ready to be released. Let them handle it. They can stick him in that big family plot on

Long Island next to his father and grandparents." She laughed. "You should see your face. I've shocked you again. You are an innocent little thing, aren't you?"

I tried to look non-shocked and non-innocent.

"My husband was not a nice man, and I see no reason to pretend to care about him now he's dead." She headed for the stairs leading to the street level, and I followed.

"Uh, thanks for your time," I said, opening the door to the sticky heat.

"I'm having a little party tomorrow evening. Drinks by the pool at five. Come if you're free. Bring your dishy boss."

She shut the door, and I was left standing on the hot pavement.

Was Sam Watson dishy? I'd never thought so.

Chapter Twelve

I didn't feel like driving back home to get my bathing suit, but I needed some beach time. I drove to Coquina Beach, where I threw my jacket into the back seat and rolled my pants up to my knees. I unbuttoned the blouse as much as I dared and folded the sleeves back. It was coming up to eight o'clock, and the sun hung low in the western sky. A light, salty wind ruffled the tops of the beach grasses and sea oats.

I slipped off my shoes at the bottom of the beach path and dangled them from my fingers. I walked for a long time, making tracks in the wet sand before the surf washed around my feet, removing all traces of my passing. The swimmers and sunbathers had gone home, but a few family groups were gathered around picnic baskets or bonfires, and the scent of roasting meat and the sound of laughter filled the air. Fishermen lounged comfortably in their beach chairs, an open beverage can in hand and a cooler, optimistically waiting to receive the catch, resting at their feet while their long poles arched over the sand into the water.

As I walked, I tried to push aside my jumble of thoughts and enjoy the feeling of the world settling down for the night.

My jumble of thoughts won out. They would not be pushed.

Maya said she saw no point in pretending to be grieving for Jeremy. Just as well—I doubt she could have pulled it off. Her spite and sheer viciousness was so strong it was almost physical.

I had no problem seeing Maya as the killer. She didn't have much of an alibi. Raleigh was a three-hour drive from here. If the last time she'd been seen was when her massage finished at four, she would have had time to drive to the Outer Banks and arrive around seven. If she'd followed her husband to the library, killed him, and driven back to her spa, no one would have been the wiser. Watson might be able to find out if her car had been in the spa's parking lot all night, but I didn't expect him to share that information with me. Even if she hadn't taken her car out, there are other ways of getting around. *Other ways of getting around.* As far as I knew, Watson still hadn't found out how the person who killed Jeremy had gotten away from the library area without laying down tire tracks in the mud. Was it possible that person had arrived by helicopter? I dismissed that thought almost immediately. I didn't know much about helicopters, but I didn't think they could fly in the sort of heavy rain and high winds we'd had that night.

The police had been asking anyone who'd been at the library or passing by at the time in question to get in touch with them. I'd assume a respectable helicopter pilot would have done so.

Then again, there were less-than-respectable ones, weren't there?

How much did it cost to hire a helicopter and a pilot willing to operate under the radar? Probably a heck of a lot.

The idea, I realized, was silly. A helicopter would have left a pretty big mark behind to show where it had landed.

Had Maya thought Jeremy really was going to the library late at night for an assignation with Charlene, and decided to finally get rid of him? I thought it unlikely. No one in their right mind—and I had no doubt Maya was that—would plan to kill someone if a witness was going to be on hand. More likely, if she'd followed him and killed him, she'd been intending to do so for a while and took advantage of the opportunity when it presented itself.

How would she, if she was away in Raleigh, have known he was planning to go to the library that night? Even he didn't know that until around six, when he was told to come back tomorrow to see the diary.

Then again, maybe she was simply following him, saw him go to the library, and took her chance. Which, of course, precludes the use of a boat or climbing a rope ladder into a helicopter to make her escape.

As for why, finding a motive would be the least of my (I mean *the police*'s) problems. Maybe Maya was in line to inherit Jeremy's share of his mother's money if he was dead. If the elder Mrs. Hughes was such a believer in the sanctity of marriage, it was possible. Maybe Maya wasn't prepared to stay in a sham marriage in expectation of money she might not get for years, but wanted to inherit from Jeremy himself right now. They had to have some money of their own. That house was worth a bundle, and Maya didn't appear to live or dress cheaply.

Then again, what did I know about their finances? They might be in debt up to their eyeballs.

Which made me think about life insurance. Did Maya need to get rid of Jeremy sooner rather than later so as to grab the insurance payout before their debt overwhelmed the miserable couple?

I needed to know the contents of Jeremy's will, the condition of the couple's bank accounts, and the state of their life insurance policies.

Highly unlikely I could persuade a bank or insurance company to talk to me on the pretext I was helping the police.

I'd found myself getting involved, despite my determination not to, when first Louise Jane and then Charlene had come under suspicion. But those suspicions, thankfully, had led nowhere.

Time to leave this with Watson. He had access to all the necessary information, and he'd met Maya Hughes. He'd arrive at the same conclusions I had. If she'd killed her husband, for whatever reason, Watson would find the proof he needed and charge her.

Although . . . If Maya had followed Jeremy to the library and killed him, for whatever reason, what happened to the papers from the diary? Jeremy might have broken into Bertie's desk and taken them out, but I couldn't see Maya stopping to pick them up after killing him. She wouldn't have had any interest in their historical value, and on first glance they were nothing but some old papers. They didn't look as though they had any monetary worth.

If the theft of the papers was directly related to the death of Jeremy Hughes, then it was unlikely Maya was the killer.

I suppose it was possible Maya killed Jeremy, and after she left, someone else just happened to be passing, saw the open door, and went directly to Bertie's office to grab the diary.

Unlikely to the point of improbable. But not impossible.

I turned around and retraced my steps to my car. Thinking about the diary made me want to have another try at decoding it.

That was the thing about puzzles: I simply couldn't admit defeat.

Chapter Thirteen

"It's unfortunate what happened," Phil Cahill said, "but we can't let that interfere with our plans. We've gone to so much work already."

"Unfortunate," Lynne Feingold sniffed. "You mean it's unfortunate that a man, your friend and colleague, died."

"I wouldn't call Jeremy either a friend or a colleague. I barely knew the fellow, and he had yet to prove himself to the society as anything other than a good source of funds."

"How can you say something so rude?" Lynne said. "Without his ideas, Settlers' Day would be just another of our little picnics in the park."

"Stop squabbling," Mrs. Eastland said. "I declare, it's like dealing with a pack of unruly children. If you two can't behave, I'll send you outside to the play area."

"Tea?" I asked. "I made a fresh jug this morning."

"That would be lovely, thank you, dear," Mrs. Eastland said.

I poured the drinks and was serving the icy glasses when Bertie came into the break room. "Sorry. I was on the phone to one of my colleagues at another library and simply couldn't get off the line."

Watson had told Bertie she could use her office again, and on Wednesday morning she returned to her staff reports, budget spreadsheets, and board meeting minutes, muttering about the weighty responsibilities of management and how she preferred sitting at "gossip central."

"We've been saying how much we're going to miss Jeremy's input," Lynne said.

"We were?" Phil said.

Mrs. Eastland's glare was positively poisonous.

"Oh yes," he said. "So we were. Invaluable."

The group from the Bodie Island Historical Society was here to finalize plans for Sunday's Settlers' Day Fair, and I'd been asked to sit in to take notes. I'd known they were expecting a lot of people to come, but hadn't realized what a big deal it was turning out to be. A podium and a scattering of chairs would be set up on the lawn for the three lectures. A representative of the Elizabethan Gardens in Manteo would give a talk about farming techniques and what crops and garden produce would have been known to the first European settlers. A university professor was going to discuss the changing landscape of barrier islands, and a historical author would give a talk on both the Lost Colony of 1585 and the Freedmen's Colony. After my chat yesterday with Janelle, I was looking forward to learning more about the latter.

Phil Cahill planned to sell his own books and give a talk aimed for preteens at his booth. Shops from town and local artisans and crafters would have booths in which to display all manner of goods. The Elizabethan Gardens were going to sell plants and garden features; a food truck would be serving pulled pork sandwiches and coleslaw; a street vendor grilling hamburgers and hot dogs out of his cart; and Josie's Cozy Bakery would be on hand with plenty of marvelous baked goods. Volunteers were coming in historical costume, and attendees were encouraged to do so also. There would be period-appropriate games for the children and a contest for best costume in three categories: children, adult female, and adult male.

"We're hoping for several hundred people over the course of the afternoon," Lynne said. "Jeremy would be so pleased!"

Phil rolled his eyes.

"You will pay tribute to Jeremy, won't you, Mabel?" Lynne said. "He won't be with us in person, but I know he'll be here in spirit."

Phil swallowed a mouthful of tea too quickly and burst into a bout of coughing. I tried hard not to glance at the wall between the break room and Bertie's office. The spirit of Jeremy Hughes was not something I wanted hanging around the lighthouse.

"Bertie will welcome us to the library, and then I'll open the festivities," Mrs. Eastland said. "I'll mention Jeremy, yes."

"Lucy," Bertie asked, "is the mayor coming?"

"Connor's coming," I said, "but I don't know if he's doing so officially. He might not want to be formally introduced."

"Imagine, a politician who doesn't want to stand up on a stage," Phil said. "Will wonders never cease."

"This isn't an official town function," I said. "Connor doesn't think he should be welcoming people."

"That's why I voted for the guy," Phil said. "Most of them would trample their grandmother to get up there, and they'll make a speech at the opening of an envelope."

"I voted for him because he's so handsome," Lynne said.

Bertie threw a look at me, and I smothered a laugh. "Everything seems to be well in hand," she said. "We have some experience here with large outdoor events, and I don't anticipate any problems."

"It's the problems we don't anticipate that are the worst," Mrs. Eastland said.

"True enough," Bertie replied.

Lynne rummaged inside her giant tote bag. "Do you have a space to display this?" She unrolled a larger version of the poster I'd seen earlier around town, advertising the day.

I leaned across the table and took it from her. "I'll stick it on a whiteboard and put it up next to the circulation desk."

"Thank you," she said.

"Now that's over, what's happening about the missing pages?" Phil asked.

"I don't know," Bertie said. "The police are investigating the murder of Jeremy, and we're hoping that when they find the person responsible, they'll find the pages as well."

"If only you'd let us study the diary that night, like we wanted to," Phil said, "instead of waiting until the morning, we might have been able to figure it all out."

"You can hardly blame me for not foreseeing that a thief was going to break in," Bertie replied sharply. The diary and its pages, I knew, were starting to get on her nerves. The other night at dinner, Professor McClanahan had scarcely said a word; instead, he spent the entire meal poring over the printouts. She'd encountered me, more than once, sneaking into the break room to give them one more look, and had come up behind Ronald, when he was working on the computer, to ask him about children's programming for the fall, and found him on a cryptography website. Louise Jane had taken out every English-to-foreign-language dictionary we had, trying to identify word patterns, and asked Bertie to order a Welsh-English dictionary. A number of people from Wales had settled in North Carolina in the early eighteenth century, she explained. Bertie had gone down the hall to her office without a word. We heard a door slam, and Louise Jane said, "I wonder what's gotten into her?"

"Unfortunately," Phil said, "I was not gifted with a photographic memory. I saw the diary and the separate pages, but I simply can't remember the details well enough to try to make sense of them."

Bertie and I kept our faces impassive. I'd been surprised that word hadn't leaked out that a picture had been taken before the pages were stolen. The library staff could be counted on to keep mum—it was after all, library business—as could Connor and Professor McClanahan. But even Louise Jane hadn't breathed a word. I wondered if she kept the piles of dictionaries she'd lugged off to her house out of sight or if visitors thought she was planning an extensive European trip.

Bertie got to her feet. "I think we're done here. See you all Sunday morning."

"Oh, I can't believe I forgot." Lynne slapped her hands to her face. "Those lovely people from Blacklock College have agreed to give a small lecture."

"They've what?" Bertie said.

"Isn't that nice of them? I met them on Monday, when we were all here, and she—Professor McArthur—called me the next day. She offered to speak at our fair. Her topic will be the industrialization of North Carolina."

Bertie's mouth flapped open.

"Is that wise, Lynne?" Mrs. Eastland said. "The subject doesn't exactly sound thrilling, and university professors aren't always known for their public speaking skills. They can be rather dry in their areas of expertise, and we want to appeal to the general public, including children. The sort of people with not much more than a vague idea of history, but a desire to learn more."

"Not even that," Phil added. "Most of them want to get the kids out of the house for a day and have a chance to eat as much of Josie's pecan squares as they can handle."

"*I* think it's very wise," Lynne replied. "Which is why I invited them to come and speak. You can't un-invite them."

"I certainly can," Mrs. Eastland replied. "We have three lectures scheduled. Four is too much."

"No it isn't," Lynne said. "The fair runs from one until six. That's five hours. Plenty of time. We can slot her in third, so the day closes with the talk on the Lost Colony and the Freedmen's Colony, as planned."

"I suppose it'll be all right," Bertie said, albeit reluctantly. "No one will be forced to sit and listen to them. We agreed to keep the booths open while the speakers are at the podium, so as to have the activities constantly moving."

"Moving in my direction, I hope." Phil got to his feet. "I've ordered a lot of books I intend to unload. I mean offer to eager buyers."

After walking our guests to the door I pulled a white-board mounted on a three-legged stand out of the storage closet, stuck the poster to it, and placed it close to the magazine rack, where everyone could see it. I then went back to the break room to put the tea jug away and wash up the glasses. I found Bertie still in her chair, jotting notes on a pad of paper. "I think that went well," I said.

"It should be a good day. The society's donating handsomely to the library for the use of our grounds and doing most of the work." She lifted her head from the papers in front of her. "Lucy, have you considered Lynne for killing Jeremy?"

"Lynne? No. The thought never crossed my mind. She seems so . . . mild mannered. Do you think we should have?"

"Perhaps. It's obvious she was infatuated with the man. I didn't get the impression he returned her feelings."

"That's no reason to kill him."

"Not to you and me perhaps, but humiliation can be a powerful motive."

"Do you know her well?"

"She comes to my yoga classes." Bertie was a part owner and instructor in a yoga studio in Nags Head. "Not regularly, but on occasion. She was married at one time and has two, or maybe three, adult children. The children moved away and don't visit often. Her husband left her a year or so ago, after thirty-five years of marriage, for another woman."

"Humiliating," I said.

"Yes. I've heard she didn't take the divorce well and has thrown herself into local activities, such as the historical society, to give herself something to do. She hasn't, as far as I know, murdered her ex-husband, so maybe I'm reaching here . . ."

"Then again, you think it's possible the second round of humiliation became too much for her to bear?"

"Something to think about," Bertie said.

"I've been wondering how the disappearance of the diary pages ties into the murder. Did the killer know what they were? Why take the separate pages and not the main book? Did he, or she, intend to take it all, but had to flee suddenly for some reason? Was taking the diary their main aim that night, and Jeremy got in the way? Or was the theft an accidental byproduct of the murder? How likely is it Lynne stole the pages for her own ends?"

"Highly unlikely, I'd say. Her interest isn't so much in history itself, but belonging to the society gives her a purpose and a chance for social interaction. Everyone knows the pages have been stolen. She can't produce them now and pretend to have found them lying around somewhere."

"I'll think about it," I said. "But I'm not getting involved. What do you think about our two professors from Blacklock College participating on Sunday?"

"I think I'd rather have a visit from the bubonic plague."

Chapter Fourteen

Wednesday evening I was preparing for the arrival of my book club. It was Ronald's day off, so before leaving for the night, Charlene helped me arrange chairs and the refreshment table in the third-floor meeting room. I didn't tell her about my visit to Maya Hughes. I didn't intend to ever let her know Maya believed Jeremy was more serious about Charlene than he'd been about other women he'd dated. Serious to the point of giving her a family heirloom.

What would be the point in telling her? She was better off without the jerk, and I didn't want her to start wondering what might have been.

"Sam Watson," she said, as I laid out glasses for tea and lemonade and plates for the cookies, "has been noticeable by his absence today."

"And that, I'd say, is a good thing. It means he's looking elsewhere for Jeremy's killer and not at our library community. Has he spoken to you again?" I ripped open the bags of cookies.

"No. And that definitely is a good thing. Why are you serving supermarket-bought cookies?"

"I fear our guests are going to be severely disappointed tonight. Josie usually brings leftovers from the bakery, although I suspect she doesn't have many leftovers, certainly not in July, but she makes up a batch specifically for us when that's the case. Even when she can't make book club, she sends something over with Steph or Grace. She's so busy this week with the extra baking for Sunday, she's working tonight and needs all her nonexistent leftovers."

Charlene studied the arrangement and selected a lemon cream cookie. "If I spent my life making pecan squares and coconut cupcakes, I'd weigh three hundred pounds. I can't imagine how Josie keeps herself so thin."

"All that energy, I suspect. You know Josie—she never stops moving. She didn't go into work last Sunday, saying she needed a day off. She used it to paint the living room."

Charlene laughed and finished her cookie. "I'm off. Have a good evening."

"Thanks. You too. Say hi to your mom."

I finished arranging the room before going downstairs to greet book club members as they arrived. We had a core contingent of regulars who came to almost every meeting, as well as library patrons who popped in if they had the time or were interested in that month's book. It being July, and the lingering daylight giving people the opportunity to go for an evening walk on the beach, dawdle over drinks on their decks or porches, or play with kids and grandkids on the lawn, I wasn't expecting a big turnout tonight. I was surprised to see a row of cars coming down the long driveway between the red pines.

My good friends Stephanie Stanton and Grace Sullivan came together. Steph explained that her boyfriend, Bruce Greenblatt, had been called in for an extra shift tonight. CeeCee Watson, wife of the detective, came, as did Mrs. Peterson and her eldest daughter, Charity.

Judging by the expression of sullen defiance on Charity's face, she thought she had better things to do of a summer's evening than come to her mother's book club.

I hoped Mrs. Peterson hadn't used book club as a punishment. No better way to turn a child off a lifetime of reading than making it something they had to suffer through. Mrs. Fitzgerald, chair of the library board, caught a ride, as she usually did, with Louise Jane.

"Before you go inside," I said, "have a look at what you all helped pay for." I gestured to the side of the lighthouse tower.

"I see nothing but a lot of dirt," Grace said.

"I know. Isn't it marvelous? What you don't see is the building crumbling to ruin."

"When are they going to be finished?" Steph asked.

"About another two weeks yet. George told Bertie they'd run into no unexpected difficulties, so everything is on schedule. And within the budgeted cost too."

"Yahoo!" Mrs. Fitzgerald gave the building a whack with her cane. It did not crumble into dust, and we all cheered.

As they filed into the library, Theodore Kowalski slid up beside me. "No news, I'm sorry to report," he whispered.

"News on what?"

"Mrs. Crawbingham's journal."

"Oh, that." I'd forgotten he said he'd check with the world of illicit historical artifacts.

"Doesn't mean it's not out there. The new owner might be waiting for the coast to be clear before offering it for sale."

"Anyone interested in obtaining it should know by now it's contents were not only stolen but associated with a murder. And thus likely to be of considerable interest to the police."

"You never know," Theodore said, "what some people want to collect. I've met people who've seen basements full of valuable artifacts that never see the light of day. Sometimes even the owner never looks at them again. Possession is enough."

"Possession of pages from a fishing wife's diary?"

"You're looking for them, Lucy. The police are looking for them. The Bodie Island Historical Society is looking for them. Half of Nags Head is looking for them. Yes, some would think that alone gives them value. Not to mention the romantic allure of a page written in code and a map leading to supposed pirate treasure."

"You mean we might never see them again? That's a discouraging thought. I guess I've been assuming that when the police find Jeremy's killer, they'll find the stolen items."

"Even if the killer's the same person who took the pages, once items slip into the underworld, they can disappear so thoroughly the person who stole them originally doesn't know where they ended up. Not to worry, that's only speculation. We still have hope for a safe return, Lucy. May I escort you upstairs?"

"I see Connor pulling in. I'll wait for him."

Theodore trotted off, and I walked up the path to meet Connor. He greeted me with a long kiss. When we separated, he said, "I don't suppose you can skip the meeting."

"No, I cannot. Even if I wanted to, which I don't. I'm looking forward to the discussion. Aren't you?"

"I am, but I thought a drink at Jake's, maybe a walk on the beach after would be nice."

"Perhaps we can do that after the meeting," I said.

"I'd like that."

To my considerable surprise, the next vehicle to arrive was Curtis Gardner's Corvette. Diane Uppiton had bought it for him so soon after the death of Jonathan Uppiton the Nags Head grapevine had been scandalized. "There's a shock," I said to Connor. "Curtis and Diane have never come to book club before. I wasn't aware they could read."

Connor chuckled. "Always a first time."

"Good evening," I said as the couple approached. "Are you here for the book club?"

Diane wrapped me in a hug. Another first. I held my breath against the scent of excessively applied perfume. She then latched on to Connor and held him even longer than she had me. I watched his ears turn pink. Curtis scowled.

"*Journey to the Center of the Earth*," Diane squealed when she finally let my boyfriend go. "I *love* that book! When I heard that your little club would be talking about it, I said to Curtis, 'We have to go!' Didn't I say that, Curtis?"

"Yes, you did," he said. "Should be . . . uh, fun."

We went into the library and climbed the stairs to the third floor. "Goodness," Diane said, "if I'd known how far up it is, I'd have worn better shoes." Her red patent leather Jimmy Choos had four-inch heels. "Now I know why you always wear such sensible shoes, Lucy."

My wardrobe choices had been insulted, but it was one in a long line of Diane's snide jabs and backhanded compliments, and so I let it go, as I always did.

By the time we got to the meeting room, the refreshments table had been decimated. Charles had taken his regular seat on Mrs. Fitzgerald's lap. He glanced up when we came in. The fur along his back rose, and he hissed at the new arrivals.

"I'll never understand why you keep that dangerous creature around, Lucy," Diane said.

If I was ever inclined to evict Charles from the library, I'd remember how much he annoyed Diane and let him stay.

Charles had proved himself to be an excellent judge of human character, and he'd taken Diane's measure the instant he met her.

"Nice kitty." Curtis reached out a hand, intending to give Charles a tentative pat.

"Do be careful, Curtis," Mrs. Fitzgerald said. "He might bite."

Curtis's hand jerked back, and he gave our library board chair a sickly grin. He poured himself a glass of tea, scooped up the last handful of cookies, and found a seat.

"Before we begin," I said, "I want to remind everyone about the Settlers' Day Fair on Sunday. It goes from one until six, and there will be activities for all age groups."

"We wouldn't miss it, would we, Charity?" Mrs. Peterson said.

Charity studied her fingernails.

"There will be prizes for best historical costume," I said.

Mrs. Peterson squealed. "I know just the thing. You can wear that dress you wore for the school play two years ago."

Charity gasped in horror. "Mother! I was twelve then. Not even a teenager."

"Prizes!" Diane said. "How exciting. I still have the dress I wore to the library's fund-raising party a few years ago. That was when Jonathan was in charge of the library, Lucy. Before your time, of course." She patted her ample hips and giggled. "Although it might be a bit loose now. Curtis, you can wear Jonathan's costume."

"I'm not—"

Diane ignored him. "Is there a prize for best couple, Lucy? Curtis and I will be sure to win."

"I don't know," I said. "The historical society is the organizer, not the library."

"I told you, Diane," Curtis said, "I'm wearing my Confederate army uniform."

"But I don't have an outfit to match it," she whined.

"The historical society wanted me to be one of the speakers," Louise Jane said, "but I suggested it would be better to invite someone new. Everyone in Nags Head's heard me many times."

"*Journey to the Center of the Earth* was written in 1864," I said. "Do you think it's aged well?"

"It's stupid," Charity said. "Like there's going to be plants and stuff growing where there's no sunshine."

"It did stretch suspension of disbelief to the breaking point and then some," Connor said.

"I loved how they practiced scaling a mountain and descending into the center of a dormant volcano by climbing a church steeple a couple of times," Steph said. "It was so cute."

"What about the old book they found at the beginning, and the code in it?" Theodore said. "That made for an exciting opening."

"The same thing happened here," Diane said.

"What happened here?" Mrs. Peterson said.

"I don't think we want to talk about—" I said.

"George's crew found a book buried under the lighthouse, and it had some silly code in it," Diane said. "The same book that disappeared when Jeremy Hughes was murdered." She glanced at the floor. "Right below our feet."

"I heard the diary itself wasn't taken," Grace said. "Only the enclosed pages."

The police had never publicly said what had been stolen, just "historical artifacts." The rumor mill had done the rest.

"It was in code?" Charity said. "Then it can't have been very old."

"Not computer code," Theodore explained. "Cipher. Secret writing."

Her eyes opened wide. "Cool!"

"I heard about a diary being found and then stolen," Steph said, "but nothing about it being in code."

"It bothers Connor that the science in *Journey to the Center of the Earth* is so unrealistic. What did the rest of you think?" I struggled to get the conversation back on track. "Did that distract from your enjoyment of the story?"

"Can I see it?" Charity asked.

"The pages were stolen," her mother reminded her. "And a man died."

"Didn't you take a picture or anything? What's wrong with you people?"

I started to lie. "We didn't—"

"We have a copy, yes," Louise Jane said.

"Shush!" I said. "That's a secret."

"Oh, a secret! Do tell." We had Charity's attention now. I'd have preferred it if she was still studying her fingernails.

"Give it up, Lucy," Louise Jane said. "We're getting absolutely nowhere trying to decipher it."

"How'd you get that cut on your lip?" Mrs. Fitzgerald asked. "And is that a bruise on your cheek you've tried to cover with makeup?"

"If you must know," Louise Jane said. "I tripped over my own big feet. Let me assure you, I did not break into the library and fight a man to the death."

"I wasn't implying—"

"We need help. We're all friends here. Right?" Louise Jane dug in her bag and pulled out a piece of paper.

"Bertie said—" I protested.

"Bertie's not here, is she? Let me see that." Grace snatched the paper out of Louise Jane's hand. She was sitting between CeeCee and Diane, and the two women leaned in closer to have a look. Curtis and Theodore got up from their seats and gathered around.

"Make more copies, Lucy," Louise Jane said.

"I most certainly will not. We don't want that document floating around town."

"Too late, I'd say." Mrs. Fitzgerald held out her hand. "Give me that, young lady. I am the head of the board of this library, remember."

Grace obediently handed it over.

"Is this evidence in the murder Sam's working on?" CeeCee asked. "Does he know about this?"

"He knows," I said. "He wants us to keep a lid on it." I looked at the circle of eager faces. "Obviously that's not going to happen."

"I bet if we all have a go, we can solve it together," Curtis said.

Mrs. Fitzgerald studied the paper. Everyone studied Mrs. Fitzgerald.

"It appears to be a substitution code," she said at last.

"We don't have the key," Louise Jane said.

"Then we must find it," Mrs. Fitzgerald said.

"Easier said than done," I said.

"I know something about codes," Charity said.

"You do not," Mrs. Peterson said.

"Gee, Mom. You don't know everything I know."

Mrs. Peterson gasped.

"How difficult can it be?" Curtis said, "if we work together. Now, what's the most common letter? That's usually meant to be an *e*. We can start from there."

"Charity, clear off the table." Mrs. Fitzgerald lifted Charles off her lap and put him on the floor. "Many hands make light work. Let's see what we can accomplish as a group."

I gave up trying to lead the book club discussion. Everyone except Connor and me wiggled their chairs closer to the table. Scraps of paper and pens came out of pockets and purses, and much muttering commenced.

"Any more of those cookies, Lucy?" Curtis called.

"No. In *Journey to the Center of the Earth*," I said to Connor, "the scientist professor decides his nephew will have more incentive to solve the code if he locks all the doors and doesn't allow any food into the house. Do you think that will work here?"

Connor chuckled.

"Your mother's family's from Denmark," Louise Jane said to Mrs. Fitzgerald. "Do you see anything that might be Danish in there?"

"Hard to tell," Mrs. Fitzgerald said. "I don't see much of anything."

"I'm taking Spanish and French in school," Charity said. "I'll try them."

"Wasn't there some sort of map that went along with this?" Diane said. "It looked a bit like this section of the Outer Banks and had eight numbers on it that didn't seem to correspond to anything."

"We believe that was nothing but a guide to places of interest to the diarist," I said. I hadn't given anyone except Sam Watson—not even Louise Jane—a copy of the supposed map. That, at least, I wanted to keep secret.

"The number seven was in the middle of the ocean," Curtis said. "I don't see—"

"That's the problem," Louise Jane said. "We don't see anything. Anything that makes any sense."

"Lucy, get me some paper, will you? I have an idea," Curtis ordered.

"I can't find a pen," Stephanie said. "Has anyone got a pen?"

"What the heck." I went to the main room and found sheets of computer paper and a handful of pens. Back upstairs I handed them out. Even Connor took one.

For the rest of the night, the members of the Bodie Island Lighthouse Library Classic Novel Reading Club struggled to decipher the code.

Most of the members anyway. Charles got bored at the lack of attention he was receiving and left the room, his tail twitching in disapproval. Diane lost interest in the code almost immediately, took out her phone, and started tapping away. Mrs. Peterson pulled her copy of *Journey to the Center of the Earth* out of the depths of her tote bag and said, "Let me refresh my memory as to how they discovered the meaning of the code in here. They read it backwards, as I recall. Has anyone tried that?" Connor went downstairs after whispering to me that he owed his mother a call and this was as good a time as any.

Despite the combined effort of the group, they had no more luck than anyone else, and by nine o'clock I was ready to throw them all out. The table was strewn with sheets of paper, most of them full of crossed out and overwritten words.

"Is there any possibility the key's in the diary itself?" Grace said.

"We've looked," I said. "Nothing."

"Nothing you've seen," Curtis said. "Why don't we all have a look at it?"

"The diary is locked up, and I don't have a key for that drawer. Sorry. I think it's about time to leave." No one paid me the slightest bit of attention.

Connor got to his feet and bellowed, "Lucy is locking the doors. Now."

Heads popped up. Louise Jane and Mrs. Fitzgerald reached for the copy of the code page at the same time. They glared at each other across it, and finally Louise Jane released it. "I can get another," she said.

"You do that," Mrs. Fitzgerald said.

"That was a waste of good drinking time," Curtis said. "Probably nothing to it, anyway."

"No one goes to that much trouble to hide nothing," Louise Jane said.

"You're assuming they meant it to be trouble," I said. "Maybe it was a game, or a love letter in a language known only to the participants."

"Oh," Charity sighed, "that would be so romantic. Their parents didn't approve, so they had to communicate in a secret language."

Mrs. Peterson huffed.

"There are plenty of tales of lost treasure along this coast," Louise Jane said.

"None of them," Steph said, "are at all believable."

"Pirates' treasure," Diane said. "You mean like gold and jewels? Wouldn't that be marvelous?"

"Plenty of ships went down in the Graveyard of the Atlantic over the years," Louise Jane said, "taking their valuable goods with them."

"In that case, these valuable goods would be at the bottom of the ocean, wouldn't they?" ever-practical Steph replied.

"It's entirely possible the treasure washed up on shore or was salvaged after the wreck," the never-practical Louise Jane said.

"The diary is dated beginning in 1858," I said. "Pirates were long gone by then. If whoever wrote the code page knew where any treasure was hidden, they would have dug it up themselves."

"It might be other treasure then," Diane said.

"That date could be more significant than you realize, Lucy," Mrs. Fitzgerald said. "It's always been rumored around these parts that some families hid their valuables at the start of the war, when the Union army attacked the forts on Hatteras Island and then took Roanoke a few months later. Curtis, you're the Civil War buff. Isn't that true?"

"So folks say. Parts of this area went back and forth between the armies in the early months of the war before the area finally fell to the Yankees in the summer of 1862."

"Were your ancestors here at that time?" Grace asked.

Curtis sat a bit straighter in his chair. "My many-times-great-grandfather was an important man in the Confederate army. My family's very proud of his record of service. And," he said, winking at her, "some that's not on the record, but should be."

Mrs. Fitzgerald smothered a laugh, and Curtis glared at her.

"*Journey to the Center of the Earth* was written two years later," Charity said. "Do you think that's just a coincidence?"

"Yes," I said.

"Where there are armies," Curtis said, "there are always camp followers and deserters, looking for opportunities to loot whatever they can get their hands on."

"What rubbish." Steph was a defense lawyer, in partnership with my Uncle Amos. Steph loved nothing more than a good argument. "What sort of treasure would a nineteenth-century fishing or farm family have had? A chamber pot? Great-grandma's milk churn?"

"It's true the Outer Banks was a mighty poor place back in those days," Mrs. Fitzgerald said, "but moneyed families spent their summers here, even then."

"That's right," Curtis said.

"All this speculation means absolutely nothing," Theodore said. "We don't know what the page says, and we probably never will."

"Whatever," Curtis said. "Let's go, babe."

Diane put away her phone. "Maybe it's a jewel, like in *Titanic*," she said to Curtis. "The Heart of the Ocean, it was called. That would look nice on me, don't you think?"

"Then again," Louise Jane said, "maybe we don't want to find it. We have to consider that it might be cursed. Did the curse get Jeremy Hughes?"

"I'll mention that to Sam." CeeCee Watson's back was to Louise Jane, and she threw me a wink. "He's always interested in your theories."

"And so he should be," Louise Jane replied as the group clattered down the spiral iron staircase.

So offended was Charles at having been ignored, he didn't even bother coming out to say good night.

Chapter Fifteen

Precisely at twelve noon on Thursday, I marched into town hall, heading for the mayor's office.

"Is he in?" I asked his assistant.

"He is, and nothing came up. His calendar's free for the rest of the afternoon."

We smiled at each other, co-conspirators.

She picked up the phone on her desk. "Connor, someone's here to see you. I tried to get rid of her, but she's a determined one and won't take no for an answer."

I leaned over the desk and spoke into the receiver. "I can be stubborn that way."

"Lucy?"

"The one and only."

"Come on in."

"I happen to know," I said after I'd returned his kiss, "that you're free all afternoon. Come with me."

"Where are we going?"

"Not telling," I said. "Think of it as a kidnapping." I took his hand and led him out of the office.

"Have a nice afternoon," his assistant called.

"Are you in on this?" he asked her.

She only smiled and turned her attention back to her computer.

I had today off, and the weather forecast said this would be the final day of the intense heat. First thing this morning, I'd checked with Connor's assistant to see if he was free this afternoon, and she told me his last meeting ended at eleven thirty. I told her what I was planning, and she promised to alert me if something came up. I had a fully loaded picnic basket and a blanket in the trunk of my car, and we were going to the beach.

Connor picked a Boston Red Sox ball cap off the front seat and was about to toss it in the back, but I said, "You'll want to wear that."

"I will, will I?"

"Yes, you will. You're going to be hot in that suit, I'm afraid, but I don't happen to have a man's bathing suit lying around my apartment."

"You're forcing me to leave the office on a Thursday afternoon and go to the beach?" he said with a laugh. "Diabolical."

I gave him a smile and was pleased to get a giant one in return.

When we got to Coquina Beach, I opened the trunk and showed him the picnic basket. He carried it over the dunes, and I followed with the blanket and an umbrella. We found a quiet spot and set ourselves up. Connor sat down and pulled off his shoes and socks. He'd left the suit jacket and tie in the car. While he made himself comfortable, I poured icy-cold lemonade into plastic glasses and laid out our lunch. I'd stopped at the market and bought a selection of cold meat and cheese, along with some fresh fruit, and then at Josie's for sandwich buns and something for dessert.

We clinked glasses and took our first sips. I kicked off my sandals and tucked the skirt of my sundress under my legs.

Connor began to assemble his sandwich. "You can kidnap me any day, Lucy Richardson."

We ate our lunch and watched the activity on the crowded beach. The waves along this stretch of the coast can get high, making swimming dangerous, but today the ocean was calm, and people splashed and played in the surf. Further down the beach, multicolored kites swooped low over the water, searching for a breeze.

"Are you still planning to come to the fair on Sunday?" I asked.

"I am. It sounds like fun. It's supposed to be a lot cooler, and that should help get people out for a day in the sun. Tomorrow I'm scheduled to spend the day at my practice."

Connor was a dentist. He intended to complete this term as mayor and then return full-time to his profession. Meanwhile, he opened the office one day a week, for long-standing patients and some pro bono work.

"Were you disappointed at book club last night?" he asked. "Not getting into much of a discussion about the book?"

"More like I'm sick and tired of that blasted code page. Every time I swear I'm never going to look at it again, I find myself looking at it again. Maybe it is cursed, like Louise Jane said. And the curse is that the reader is condemned to search forever for the solution. A librarian's version of *The Flying Dutchman*."

"It might be unsolvable," he said. "Particularly if it's not in English."

"Even if it is in English, we can't seem to do anything without the key. Professor McClanahan called me this morning and said he's making no progress. He's got a whole bunch of degrees in linguistics, so if anyone can solve it, it should be him. They must have code-breaking computer software somewhere. Maybe military intelligence or the CIA could help us with that."

"You could always ask Sam. Although I don't think the CIA would be prepared to offer you much help with a woman's diary that's a century and a half out of date."

"We can't even argue that it would provide a clue in the murder case. Deciphering the code isn't going to be any sort of help with that. Unless, I suppose, the killer manages to figure it out and . . . does whatever the code leads him or her to do."

"Assuming it leads to something and wasn't just a couple of lovers planning an illicit rendezvous."

"Or a Civil War spy's report."

"That's probably the most believable scenario of them all,' Connor said. "If it's that, it would have considerable interest to historians, if no one else."

"What's this about Curtis being a Civil War buff? I didn't know that."

"Neither did I," Connor said, "but there's a story there. He was bragging about his ancestor, and Mrs. Fitzgerald was having none of it."

"Imagine that," I said with a laugh. "A Southerner bragging about his ancestor."

"I must confess, I might have done it a time or two myself. Pass me one of those squares, will you? They look delicious."

"Josie calls it dream cake. It's a family recipe. I remember it from my childhood summers."

He bit into the buttery pastry, and a look of pure delight crossed his handsome face.

I had a slice of the cake too, and we munched in blissful silence. We sat on the beach for a long time, sipping the last of the lemonade, nibbling grapes, watching kites alternatively dancing in the air and struggling to remain aloft, and people enjoying the hot sun and the cool water, and talked about nothing much at all.

"As much as I hate to say it," Connor said eventually, "I need to get back. I have some reports to get finished for Monday meetings, and I won't have time over the weekend. Not if I want to get to the Settlers' Day thing."

I stretched and reluctantly began packing up the remains of our picnic.

"What's your role on Sunday?" he asked as he folded the umbrella.

"I don't have one. And I'm thrilled about that. I'd like to just enjoy it, although I'll probably get roped into helping set up chairs or supervising kids in the construction zone."

"Weather's about to turn." He pointed out to sea, to a line of fluffy white clouds as threatening as marshmallows, gathering on the far horizon. "Storm coming."

"If it breaks this heat before Sunday," I said, "that'll be very welcome. We don't want people collapsing on the lawn from sunstroke or heat exhaustion."

I took Connor back to town hall and then drove home full of a warm, happy glow.

* * *

My warm and happy glow didn't last until the end of the day.

"A séance," Louise Jane said.

"A *what*?"

"A séance. I will attempt to contact the spirits and ask them what happened the night Jeremy Hughes died and the pages from Mrs. Crawbingham's diary disappeared."

Thunder rumbled faintly in the distance. The storm Connor had predicted was almost here. "You mean you want to do that now?"

"Yes."

"Here?"

"Yes."

"Bertie wouldn't like that."

"Bertie isn't here, is she? And you can do what you want in your own apartment on your own time, can't you? As long as it's not illegal."

"I don't know," I said.

"Fortunately, I do." Louise Jane gave up waiting for me to invite her in and simply marched past me. "Come along, everyone. Upstairs."

Theodore Kowalski and Grace Sullivan followed her, both looking sheepish. As well they might.

"She told me this was all arranged, and you were okay with it," Theodore said.

"I should have realized this was some sort of trap," Grace said.

"Louise Jane can be very persuasive," Theodore said.

"No kidding," Grace said.

"No kidding," I said.

"Even if this works," I called to Louise Jane's retreating back, "try getting that evidence admitted in court."

"It will give you the clues you need to continue investigating," she replied without turning around.

"Me? What does this have to do with me? I'm not investigating anything. I'm not involved." I slammed the door shut on another peal of thunder and hurried after her.

It was ten o'clock at night, and I was not exactly ready for company, as I'd put on my pajamas and was reading in bed before switching out the light. Charles, who is always ready for company, bounded up the stairs ahead of my visitors. He'd been delighted when the doorbell rang and Louise Jane had demanded I come down.

I should have stayed in bed. Louise Jane hurried after Charles, and the rest of us scrambled to follow. When she reached the fourth floor, she flicked the light switch, plunging the stairway into darkness.

"Hey, I can't see!" Theodore cried.

"Take my arm," Grace said.

"Can you see anything?

"No, but if I fall over the railing we'll plunge to our deaths together," she muttered.

I hadn't bothered to lock the door to my apartment when I left, and Louise Jane simply opened the door and walked in. A sliver of light slipped out to touch the stairs, and Theodore and Grace scrambled to reach the landing before it disappeared.

"As we all know, the spirits of at least one, perhaps more, Civil War era solders live in the lighthouse," Louise Jane explained when we were gathered in a circle. Just as well she told us to sit on the floor: I don't own four chairs.

"They do not," I said. "I live in the lighthouse. No one else." Charles leapt into the center of the circle. "And Charles, of course."

"Mustn't forget Charles." Grace gave the big cat a hearty scratch behind his ears.

Louise Jane rummaged in her enormous bag and brought out a candlestick, a white pillar candle, and a lighter. She set them in the center of our circle and lit the candle. "Lucy, turn out the light."

"Don't wanna."

"The sooner we get this done," she said, "the sooner we'll leave."

"Oh, for heaven's sake." I sighed and pushed myself to my feet. I switched off the overhead light, and the room was plunged into near darkness, the only light coming from the flickering yellow flame of a single candle, which didn't reach the far corners of the room. Not that, the walls being rounded, my apartment had any corners. Before my visitors arrived, I'd pulled the drapes closed. They were thick enough to keep the light from the great 1000-watt bulb at the top of the lighthouse tower, designed to be seen thirty miles out to sea, out of my room. The stone walls at this level are four feet thick, but we could hear the rumble of thunder as the storm drew closer.

I resumed my place in the circle, between Grace and Theodore.

"Shoo," Louise Jane said to Charles. Charles did not shoo, so she gave him a poke in the ribs. In return, he gave her a nasty glare.

"Lucy, you'll have to move the cat," Louise Jane said.

"He's not in the way."

"Of course he's in the way! He'll knock over the candle or make a noise at the exact moment I need complete silence."

"Maybe our ghost is allergic to cats," Grace said.

"That might explain why Lucy has never seen him," Theodore said.

"That he's not real is a better explanation of why I've never seen him," I said.

"Lucy! Move the cat!" Louise Jane was rapidly losing what bit of patience she still had.

As she'd said, the sooner we got this over with, the sooner they'd be gone. Louise Jane was always trying to convince me that the library in general, and my room in particular, was haunted. She had plenty of stories—Civil War soldiers; laborers killed during the building of the lighthouse; a lightkeeper's small son, who fell from the upper levels; Francis, the young bride trapped in a loveless marriage to a cruel old man; a 1990s-era librarian. I didn't think even Louise Jane believed that last one.

Whether she believed in the others, I was never sure. Louise Jane prided herself on her reputation as a keeper of Outer Banks stories and legends. When I first arrived here, she wanted me gone. Out of the Lighthouse Aerie, out of the Lighthouse Library, and out of Nags Head. But after a year, with no sign of me rushing back to Boston, I thought she was beginning to accept my presence.

Was she truly trying to communicate with ghosts tonight? Did she want to brag to an interested audience that she had? Or did she want to scare me into fleeing into the night and never coming back?

I scooped Charles up and carried him, protesting every step of the way, to the door. I opened the door the moment another peal of thunder sounded, and a flash of lightening lit up the stairwell. I put the cat on the floor of the landing, blocked his attempts at reentry, and slammed the door. I then returned to my place in the circle, trying to shut my ears to his plaintive cries.

"No one say a word." Louise Jane held her arms out to either side of her, palms up. I assumed we were all supposed to hold hands, so I took Grace's and Theodore's. I closed my eyes. It might have been spooky—the dark night broken only by the flickering flame of a single candle; the feel of my friends' hands resting in mine; the four of us quiet and serious, making no sound except for our breathing; the approach of the storm, coming ever closer.

It might have been spooky—if not for the continuing cries of Charles wanting to come back in and join the party.

Despite all Louise Jane's attempts to make me believe the library was haunted, I'd never felt anything the least unworldly here. Perhaps more to the point, neither had Charles. And they say, don't they, that animals have a strong awareness of the supernatural? If there is a supernatural.

I'd experienced *something*, I didn't quite know what, over Halloween. It hadn't been part of Louise Jane's stories—she hadn't even been aware of what I'd experienced. What I thought I'd experienced at any rate.

But that was then, on the night when they say the veil between the worlds is at its thinnest, and everyone was talking about ghostly happenings and reading stories of the supernatural. I'd been able to convince myself I'd imagined it all.

I let out a little cry of surprise and gripped the hands I was holding harder as Louise Jane broke into my thoughts as she began to speak. Her voice was slow and deep, the words almost musical in their pace and rhythm. "We are here seeking answers. A man died here, between these walls, less than a week ago, but the origins of the mystery lie in our past. They lie in your past. Perhaps in your present."

All was quiet except for the sound of our breathing. Charles had given up trying to talk his way back in and had gone downstairs in search of sustenance. Minutes passed, or it might have been seconds, before Louise Jane spoke again. "Is anyone there? Sergeant O'Leary? You were here in the great War Between the States."

"Who's Sergeant O'Leary?" Grace asked.

"Shush," Louise Jane snapped. "We need complete silence here." We all breathed. I had no idea people could breathe so loudly. Theodore's hand was clammy in mine. I resisted the urge to let go and wipe my hand on my pajama legs. At long last Louise Jane spoke again. "What secrets are contained within that journal buried beneath these walls? *Why* was that journal buried beneath these walls?"

Silence again. It seemed to me as though Sergeant O'Leary wasn't going to show himself tonight.

Not that Sergeant O'Leary exists, of course.

"How long are we going to sit here?" Theodore asked.

"As long as we have to," Louise Jane answered. "The spirits can be very shy. They are unaccustomed to speaking to living people."

"Yeah," Grace muttered. "If I hadn't spoken for a hundred and fifty years, I'd have trouble getting a word out too."

I bit my tongue in an attempt to suppress a giggle. Louise Jane was rapidly losing control of the situation. She hadn't chosen her séance attendees well; she should have brought less cynical people.

A high-pitched, unworldly howl broke the hush. A crash rang out, to be immediately followed by a tower-shaking roar of thunder. My giggle turned into a scream. The circle broke as I pulled my hands in and pressed them to my chest. My heart pounded. Theodore shouted, "Oh my gosh! Someone's here!" Grace gasped and leapt to her feet. Louise Jane's voice quivered as she said, "Don't break the circle."

The howl came again, followed by another crash.

"That's coming from downstairs. Charles!" I scrambled across the room, threw open the door, and ran out of the apartment. I felt, as much as heard, the others struggle to their feet and follow me.

The light from Louise Jane's candle didn't reach the staircase. Far below a night lamp burned in the alcove on the main level, but I didn't need any more light. I know this building so well by now, I can navigate it in the dark. I ran down the stairs, twisting and turning with the spiral, my bare feet light on the solid iron beneath them. Behind me, someone slipped, and I heard a thud accompanied by a yelp of pain.

"Theodore!" Grace called. "Are you okay?"

"I'm fine," he said. "Don't worry about me. Help Lucy."

"I can't see a blasted thing," Louise Jane said.

Another crack of thunder sounded at the exact moment a flash of lightening lit up the main room. The storm had arrived, and it was directly over our heads.

I jumped off the second-to-last step. The whiteboard I'd put up by the magazine rack to advertise Settlers' Day lay on the floor; Charles crouched beside it. His back was arched and every hair stood on end.

I let out a long breath and my heart began to slow. Charles, probably because he was mad at me, had knocked over the whiteboard. Upstairs, in our heightened state of alert, waiting for something frightening to happen, with the storm raging around us, we'd seriously overacted to a bump in the night.

The room was flooded with light as Grace hit the switch. "What happened?" she said.

"They were here." Louise Jane's voice was full of awe. "Not upstairs, but down here. We have to continue with the séance, right now. Here, on the main floor. Put that light out."

"I'm okay," Theodore cried. "Don't worry about me."

I realized Charles wasn't even looking at me, and he didn't have his habitual self-satisfied smirk when he'd managed to convince me to do what he'd wanted all along.

He was staring at an object on the floor, half underneath a bookshelf.

I knelt down and pulled it out.

It was a tiny flashlight.

Chapter Sixteen

The flashlight was small, about an inch and a half long, with a small metal circle attached to it. The sort of thing you'd fasten to your key chain. I had one just like it for illuminating the lock in case the light over the front door hadn't been turned on, but mine was bright pink, and this one was black with a gold band around it.

I threw open the front door. The great first-order Fresnel lens high above us had gone into its 22.5-second dormancy, and all was dark except for two beams of white light illuminating the base of the tall red pines lining the lane and two glowing red lights heading rapidly in the direction of the highway.

A car.

At that moment rain began to fall. It didn't build slowly, starting with a drop here and a drop there, but came in a torrent as though someone had turned on a giant tap in the sky. Lightening lit up the grounds around the lighthouse, and my ears pounded from the roar of thunder.

I'd left my cell phone upstairs, on my night table. I ran for the desk phone, hoping the line would still be up in the face of the storm.

"What are you doing?" Louise Jane said. "We have to get back into the circle. They're here. They want to talk to me."

"The only thing here tonight was a flesh-and-blood intruder. I'm calling the police. Don't touch anything."

The whiteboard crashed to the floor, and I whirled around with a yelp. Grace leapt back, holding her hands in the air. "Sorry, it slipped. Just trying to help."

I decided to call Sam Watson himself rather than go through 911. I'd earlier tucked his card into the top desk drawer. He'd written his personal cell phone number on the back.

He answered at the first ring. "Watson."

"It's Lucy, at the library. I—I'm sorry to bother you so late." I glanced at the clock on the wall. To my surprise it was eleven thirty. Louise Jane and the rest had been here for an hour and a half. It had felt like minutes.

"What is it, Lucy?"

"Someone tried to break in. They did break in, but Charles scared them off."

"You mean that cat?"

"He can be quite frightening, if he wants to be."

"Are you all right, Lucy?"

"Me? I'm fine. Charles is fine too. I didn't see who it was, but it has to do with the death of Jeremy Hughes and the theft of the journal pages. It has to—don't you think?"

"Are you alone?"

"Some of my friends are here. There are four of us. Not including Charles."

"That's good. Tell everyone to stay put. I'm on my way. Don't touch anything."

I hung up the phone. "We're not to touch anything."

"As this seems to have been a lost cause, and now you've got Sam Watson coming here, spreading cynicism everywhere he goes, I'm going home," Louise Jane said. "We'll try again tomorrow."

"We will not," I said. "I'm never going through that again."

Louise Jane's expression indicated that she had other ideas, but she wisely said nothing. I was not in the mood to argue. "Sam wants everyone to stay here until he arrives."

Theodore had dropped into the wingback chair next to the magazine rack. He rolled up his pant leg and poked at his ankle. His ankle, I couldn't help but notice, was as thin as a twig. "Nothing seems to be broken," he said.

"That's good," I said.

"Fortunately, this time I have a good alibi," Louise Jane said. "No one can accuse me of trying to break into the library."

"I don't know," Grace said. "We had our eyes closed, like you told us to. You might have slipped away."

"And it was dark," I added.

"It wasn't that dark," Louise Jane said. "I didn't break the circle of hands. I could hardly have gone downstairs and run back up to—"

"We're kidding," Grace said. "Relax. I'll testify you were with us the whole time."

Louise Jane sniffed. "Most amusing." She did not care to be made fun of.

"Any chance of a cup of coffee while we're waiting, Lucy?" Theodore asked.

"I suppose that would be okay. I don't think our intruder got any further than this room."

"I'll get it," Grace said. "I know where everything is. You wait here for the police."

We didn't have to wait long before I spotted headlights coming up the driveway. Two pairs of headlights, breaking through the pounding rain. Watson was in his own car, but he was followed by a cruiser. The desk phone rang and I answered it.

"Stay inside, Lucy," Watson said, "while we check out the grounds."

"Okay."

Theodore, favoring his left foot, and Louise Jane, Grace, and I gathered at the window to watch as Sam Watson and Butch Greenblatt shone their flashlights around the parking lot, the path, and then the steps. Overhead, jagged bolts of white lightning filled the sky, turning night into day; thunder roared, and the rain fell in steady sheets.

Eventually, the police officers came in, bringing a lot of water with them. "Did you find anything?" I asked.

Butch shook off raindrops like a dog who'd been for a swim. Watson stood in a spreading puddle of his own making and said, "No. Until this very moment, it hasn't rained since Monday, so we've not got much of a chance of finding any tire tracks. We checked the fence around the construction site, but nothing seems out of place there. You think you saw a car driving away?"

"Definitely," I said.

Watson glanced at the crowd of people behind me. I was aware I was still in my pajamas.

"Having a sleepover?" he asked.

"Something like that," I said.

He raised one eyebrow. "Teddy? Want to explain what you're doing at this sleepover?"

"Wasting my time, it would seem."

"If you must know, Detective," Louise Jane said, "although it has nothing to do with what transpired here tonight, we were putting our heads together one more time to try to figure out what the coded page is attempting to tell us."

"Not that again," he said. "It's not attempting to tell you, or anyone else, anything. Otherwise it wouldn't be in code, now would it? Want to tell me what happened?"

Theodore, Louise Jane, Grace, and I spoke at once. Watson lifted his hand. "One at a time, please. Lucy?"

"We were upstairs . . . uh, talking. Charles was being annoying, so I put him outside the apartment and shut the door on him. He must have come down here. We heard a crash, which was probably that falling over"—I pointed to the whiteboard—"and Charles started howling."

"Scared the life out of me," Grace said.

"Scared the life out of our intruder also, I suspect," I said. "We came running down to see what was going on, and I saw that." I pointed to the small flashlight on the floor. "Then I ran to the window and saw a car driving away."

Butch pulled an evidence bag out of his pocket and used it to pick up the flashlight. "Do you recognize this?" he said.

"No," I said. The others shook their heads.

"I've seen plenty of ones like that at the convenience store and discount stores," Theodore said. "They're very common."

"Are you sure it wasn't there earlier?" Watson asked. "Maybe someone dropped it during the day."

"Pretty sure," I said. "Whoever's last on the circulation desk at the end of the day does a quick sweep after closing. We find all sorts of interesting things people have left behind. That wasn't me today, as I wasn't working, but I had a quick look around before going upstairs. I would have seen that if it had been here. I did not. Therefore it wasn't. Here, I mean."

"How did this person get in?" Watson asked. "The door doesn't seem to have been tampered with this time."

I grimaced. "I forgot to lock it."

He raised one accusing eyebrow. "You forgot to lock the door? After everything that's happened here, you still forgot to lock up?"

"I wasn't expecting my visitors to stay long. Sorry." I'd run after Louise Jane, intending to make her turn around and leave. Instead, we'd all trooped upstairs, and despite our new lock and sturdy new door, an intruder had marched in.

Watson shook his head. Rainwater flew.

Charles jumped onto the nearest bookshelf and settled down to wash his whiskers with an air of satisfaction. Once again, Charles had saved the day.

Watson studied the four of us in turn. "You were all together the entire time?"

Grace, Theodore, and I nodded. Louise Jane puffed up her chest in indignation, "If you are attempting to accuse me, once again, of—"

"I'm not accusing anyone," Watson said. "I'm asking."

"We were together the entire time," I said. "No one could have left the fourth floor without the others noticing."

"What do you mean by once again, Louise Jane?" Theodore asked.

"Nothing," she said.

"Any idea what this person might have been after?" Watson asked.

I'd been thinking about that while we waited. "If it wasn't a common or garden thief, after whatever they think we might have left lying around—"

"Which, for now we will assume it was not."

"Right. Then they have to be after Mrs. Crawbingham's diary. Whoever took the code page and the map must believe they need the rest of her diary in order to solve the code."

"Where's the diary now, Lucy?"

"Bertie put it in the rare books room, and that room's always locked unless someone's working in there."

"Let's have a look and see if it's there," Watson said. "You might have surprised the intruder on their way out, you know, not coming in. Lucy, you show me. The rest of you, wait here. Need I point out that I expect you to keep knowledge of this conversation to yourselves?"

Grace, Theodore, and Louise Jane nodded enthusiastically.

"You can count on my discretion, Detective," Louise Jane said, "in this as in everything. I know how to keep a secret, and my knowledge of Outer Banks history and—"

"One minute," I said. "I have to get the keys." I ran upstairs. While there I took the opportunity to throw a sweater over my pajamas and slip shoes onto my bare feet. I keep a complete set of keys in the apartment, in case of a fire or emergency evacuation in the night. I grabbed them out of the kitchen drawer and ran back downstairs.

Watson and I went up the back staircase. We found the door to the rare books room securely locked and everything inside neat and orderly. Nothing appeared to have been disturbed. I unlocked the main cabinet. Mrs. Crawbingham's diary lay there, as enigmatic as ever. I studied it for a brief moment, wondering if this little bit of old paper and aging leather really was worth killing over.

"All is as it should be?" Watson asked.

"Apparently so," I said. "If the person who was here tonight was after the diary—and we don't know that for sure—they likely would assume it was still in Bertie's desk drawer, as it was on Monday."

"Bertie's office next," Watson said.

That door wasn't locked, but when I opened it, we could see that it was undisturbed. Bertie hadn't yet replaced the broken lock on her desk, and all it now contained were boxes of paper clips and staples and her secret stash of chocolate bars and peanuts. The cabinet in which she kept budget papers and staff records was locked. I did not have a key for that.

Satisfied our intruder had not gotten this far, we rejoined the others.

"Have you tried reading it backward?" Butch was saying. "That's how they solved it in *Journey to the Center of the Earth*, wasn't it?" Louise Jane had taken her copy of the code page out and was showing it to him.

"We've tried that," she said. "I'm working on the premise that it's not in English. Your ancestors were German, weren't they? Do you see anything Germanic about it?"

"Even my grandfather didn't speak German," Butch said, "much less me or my brother."

"If I never hear another word about that blasted code," Watson muttered to me, "it will be too soon."

"Can I have a copy of that?" Butch asked Louise Jane.

"I'll get Lucy to make you one," she said.

"I will not," I said. "It was given to you on the grounds that you don't show it to anyone, Louise Jane."

"I wouldn't call Butch just anyone. He can be trusted, can't you, Butch?"

Butch tried to look trustworthy.

"Of course," Louise Jane said, "it would help if we had a copy of the map."

"The map . . ." I said.

"What about it? What have you remembered?"

"I don't know. Something about the map popped into my head. It's gone now."

"Well, get it back," Louise Jane ordered.

Watson cleared his throat. "If we can return to what brought us here tonight . . ."

Butch had the sense to look embarrassed. Louise Jane, who was never embarrassed by anything, nodded and said, "Please continue, Detective."

"Did you find anything in the back?" Grace asked.

"No," I said. "Looks like they didn't get that far, thanks to Charles."

Charles preened.

"You should give him an extra serving of kibble tonight," Theodore said.

"Meow," Charles said.

"I don't know why I bother," Watson muttered.

"Sorry," Grace said. "Don't mind us. I for one am not doing very well at coming down from such a fright."

"What are you thinking, Detective?" Theodore asked.

"Unless I have reason to think otherwise, I'll assume this is related to the death of Jeremy Hughes and the theft of the diary pages. Our intruder might have come here tonight intending to break into the library, or he might have been watching and found the door fortuitously left unlocked." Watson glared at me. "Regardless, he came inside. He or she. It would appear he was startled by Charles and dropped the flashlight. He panicked when he heard the lot of you coming, and ran off. We can hope he, or she, didn't wear gloves, and we can get some prints off the flashlight. None of you touched it?"

We shook our heads.

"Have you thought of anything else I should know?"

Louise Jane, Theodore, Grace, and I chorused, "No."

"Good night then," Watson said. "You will lock the door, won't you, Lucy?"

"Yes," I said meekly. "Uh, one thing, please."

"What?"

"Can you please not mention this to Connor? Any of you. I don't want him worrying about what's going on here at night."

"I see no need," Watson said. "I'll make a report, of course, but as no harm has been done, it's unlikely His Honor will hear about it."

"Thanks," I said. "Butch?"

"I never discuss police business in personal conversations, Lucy. You can count on me." He gave me a wink and followed the detective out.

I stood in the doorway, watching them walk up the path, heads close together as they talked. Rain continued to fall, but the storm was moving on, leaving puddles the size of small lakes in the parking lot.

"Turn out those lights, and we can get back at it," Louise Jane said. "I can only hope Sergeant O'Leary and his fellows haven't been scared off."

"My ankle hurts," Theodore said.

"I'm beat," Grace said. "I'm going home."

"It's just you and me then, Lucy," Louise Jane said.

"No." I said.

"It's worth a try. Even with just the two of us, we might be able to make a powerful enough circle to convince the spirits to return."

"If you don't leave, right now, this very minute, I'll call Butch to come back and arrest you for trespassing," I said.

"Perhaps we can try another time then," she said. "I'll agree there's been too much activity for the spirits tonight." Louise Jane almost ran out the door.

Grace wiggled her eyebrows at me, and then she held her arm out to Theodore. "Here, lean on me."

"Not quite the excitement I expected, but exciting nonetheless," Theodore said, accepting Grace's arm.

"How did you two get roped into this anyway?" I asked.

"Louise Jane phoned me," Theodore said. "She told me she had an idea for finding the stolen items and needed my help. I assumed she meant help searching historical records."

"I was expecting to play bridge," Grace said.

"Bridge?"

"She called and said she needed a fourth for tonight. I thought she meant a fourth in bridge. When she said to meet her here, at the library, I assumed a bridge club was having an evening. Sorry. Next time, I'll ask for details. I did think ten o'clock was late for bridge, but I don't have school tomorrow, so . . ." Her voice trailed off.

"I'm glad you were here, both of you," I said. "Who knows what might have happened if it had been just the two of us."

"Who knows what might have happened had Charles not been on the ball," Grace said.

Charles washed his whiskers.

I locked the door behind my friends, tested to make sure it was secure, and then I went upstairs. Charles held his tail high and ran nimbly up the railing ahead of me.

Before collapsing into my bed, I opened a tin of salmon and dumped it into his bowl.

Chapter Seventeen

"No one by the name of Crawbingham ever lived on the Outer Banks," Phil Cahill said.

"They might have visited, of course," Lynne Feingold added, "but they didn't live here."

"That's worth knowing," Charlene said, "but it doesn't tell us much. Maybe she vacationed here or came to visit friends. My research found records of a family over near New Orleans by the name of Crawbingham. They had a mighty big plantation in the years leading up to the war, but the family seems to have died out in the decades following."

"Might be them," Phil said. "The women and children of wealthy Louisiana families often spent the worst of the hot, disease-ridden summer months away from home."

"Even if that was the case," I said, "and we don't know it was, it makes no sense to me that a wealthy Southern antebellum woman would keep a weather diary. Surely she'd have preferred a record of parties and dances and dinners and what everyone was wearing."

A smile touched the edges of Charlene's mouth. "Maybe she wasn't interested in those things, Lucy. Maybe her secret lover, the one her family disapproved of, was a fisherman, and so the movement of the weather was the most important thing to her."

I pretended to be shocked. "Charlene Clayton! What sort of historian are you? Making up stories of doomed lovers."

She grinned at me. "I'm forced to admit, as a historian and academic librarian, I'd have preferred a record of dances and dresses and what food was served at such things. But I can imagine in the absence of facts."

"I don't think we'll ever know," Lynne Feingold said with a deep sigh, "what it all means. Poor Jeremy. He died for nothing."

Phil snorted. "Jeremy died trying to steal a historical document for his own ends. Good riddance to him, I say."

"You can't mean that!" Lynne said. "We don't know what he was doing here that night. Perhaps he suspected someone intended to steal the dairy, and he came in an attempt to prevent them."

"Then he should have called the police. Or at least Bertie here. No, he was up to no good. Face facts, Lynne, the man was trying to find a way to pretend he was a big man around town."

"May I remind you that Jeremy provided the funds to put on Settlers' Day?" Lynne said.

"I don't need to be reminded." Phil leaned back in his chair. "Again."

Bertie coughed lightly. "Can we please continue? We're getting off-topic here. Again. Mabel, transportation for the guest speakers has been arranged?"

"Under control," she said. "I never have to be asked twice."

The meeting continued. The arrangements for the Settlers' Day Fair appeared to be in place. The Historical Society committee had everything under control, and best of all, I didn't have any responsibilities. The event was being held on Sunday, when the library was closed, so no one needed to be at work inside.

"The weather report looks promising," Bertie said as she put the last tick mark next to her list of items to be discussed.

"Thank heavens that dreadful heat has broken," Lynne said.

"Quite the storm last night," Phil said. "A few trees came down, some houses were flooded, and some cars hit by flying debris, but not much real damage. It could have been a lot worse."

Bertie and I exchanged glances, but we didn't say anything. I'd told no one but her, Ronald, and Charlene about the break-in last night, and didn't intend to.

I'd spent a restless night, listening to the storm retreating, running lines of indecipherable code through my head, and wondering who could be so desperate for those pieces of paper they'd kill to get them.

If they had killed to get them. It was possible that the disappearance of the code page and map had been incidental to the murder of Jeremy Hughes. Something the killer grabbed on the way out the door or stuffed in their pockets to look at later.

What of the diary? Why would the killer—if last night's intruder had been the killer—come back for it? Did they think the clue to the code would be found within? We'd thought of that, and Charlene had gone through the diary page by page, searching for something. Anything. But all she found were dates and recordings of the weather and the movement of the tides.

Mrs. Crawbingham had been a particularly focused individual if all she cared about was the weather. I considered that for a while. Was it possible she was a far more detailed diarist, and she kept her personal thoughts, ambitions, and dreams secretly in the pages of another book?

Was there another book?

If there was, it had almost certainly been lost to time.

And what of the map itself? How important was it in all of this? I'd thought of something when I was downstairs with Watson and Butch, but whatever it was had disappeared before I could put my finger on it. Something about the map . . .

I'd finally fallen into a disturbed, restless sleep. As Charles snoozed beside me, I dreamt I was frantically trying to write something dreadfully important in the sand as waves washed my words away.

"It's going to be a marvelous day." Mabel Eastland got to her feet, pulling me out of my thoughts. The rest of the historical society scrambled to follow. "I hope you're coming in period dress, Bertie."

My boss's eyes twinkled. "I might be."

"What about you, Lucy?" Mrs. Eastland asked.

"Me? I haven't given it a thought. I don't have anything to wear."

"You don't have to dress as an antebellum lady, all crinolines and petticoats. We're celebrating all the settlers to our land, from the first Native Americans to the most recent escapees from the concrete jungle."

"So I can wear my own clothes? I came here from Boston a year ago."

"The point of a costume," Lynne pointed out, "is not to look like you do every day. It's not a costume if no one knows you're wearing one."

"I'll think about it," I said, intending to do no such thing.

"I have some ideas," Charlene said. "Let's talk about it, Lucy."

"Are you coming in costume?" I asked her.

"Oh yes. I have just the thing. Something I've been saving for the right occasion."

Bertie's phone rang, and she reached for it. "Hold on a minute, Lucy. I want to talk to you."

"I'll show you out," Charlene said to our visitors. "I'm bringing my mother on Sunday, and she's very much looking forward to it."

"Good morning, Eddie," Bertie said into the phone. She listened for a minute as her eyes opened wider and wider.

"We certainly did," she said. "How did you come to hear about it? It's not been picked up by the media."

I couldn't hear what was being said on the other end of the phone, but whatever it was had taken Bertie by surprise.

"Yes, I think I should, but I can't exactly phone to make an appointment. Can you do that for me?" She made a "hold on" gesture to me and drummed her fingers on her desktop. "Good. If we leave now, we can be there before noon. Are you still planning to come on Sunday? See you then." She put down the phone.

"What?" I asked.

"I asked you to stay back so we could complete your performance review. That will have to wait." Bertie pulled her handbag out of her desk drawer—the one with the broken lock—and stood up. "That was Eddie."

"What happened?"

"He gave one of his fellow professors a ride into the college this morning."

That didn't sound all that earth-shattering to me. "So?"

"Said professor's car had to go to the repair shop to have a new window put in. Seems the back passenger window suffered some damage in the storm last night when a branch flew into it."

I still didn't see that it mattered. "What of it? Phil said trees and branches were down all over."

"All over the Outer Banks, yes. Nothing like that happened in Elizabeth City, Eddie tells me. Only a light rain fell last night."

"Oh, I get it. I assume you're talking about Professor McArthur. She, or her car, might have been in the Outer Banks last night. You think—"

"Not McArthur, but Hoskins. I think it's worth a trip to Elizabeth City. You can come with me. Someone broke into our library last night, and I'd consider finding out who that was to be library business. Wouldn't you?"

* * *

Bertie called Charlene's office, quickly explained our errand, and asked her to take the desk for most of the day.

In preparation for Sunday's Settlers' Day festivities, the children's programming today was all about Outer Banks history. As we left the building, a steady stream of primary school children and their parents was arriving. Some of the children were in costume—I saw plenty of pirates and location-inappropriate cowboys and cowgirls. Ronald wore his own pirate costume, complete with black eye patch and stuffed parrot fastened to his shoulder, to greet his patrons.

As we walked to my car, we passed the Washington twins, tearing up the walkway. They were dressed in neat white caps and brown aprons over dresses in a checked yellow-and-brown pattern that trailed in the dirt. The dresses had high collars, long sleeves, and rows of small buttons up the front. Their mother followed, wearing jeans and a T-shirt. She gave us a smile and said, with one eye on a little girl in a repurposed Halloween princess costume, shouting at the twins to hurry up, "Do you think I'm overdoing historical accuracy?"

"It's important," Bertie said, "to remember that we're not all descended from royalty and wealthy land owners. Our ancestors built this land with a lot of hard work, and sometimes not much to show for it. You're right to teach your girls to be proud of that."

She grinned at us. "Thanks. They're dressed today as their father's great-grandmothers would have been when the family were members of the Freedmen's Colony. Neil's mother made the outfits."

"What about your ancestors?" I asked. "When did they arrive?"

She spread out her arms. "I'm it. I was born and raised in Chicago and first came here in 2002 for a summer job with the National Park Service. I loved it so much, I moved here as soon as I finished college. I met Neil shortly after that and never wanted to leave."

"The story of all settlers," I said. "We come from other places and do our best to make it in our new home."

"Charlotte wanted to come as a Native American princess, and Emily as Orville Wright, but I convinced them those outfits might be better saved for another occasion."

Bertie and I laughed and continued on our way.

* * *

"What's your plan?" I asked my boss once we were on the highway heading out of Nags Head.

"You are assuming I have a plan," she said. "I do not. Perhaps I'm simply, and naively, hoping Norman Hoskins will break down in the face of my righteous indignation and confess all."

I laughed.

"I'm afraid you're right," she said. "My sense of Norm and Lizzie is that she's the one who calls the shots, and he simply goes along with it. Breaking and entering is a felony, and if I can convince Norm he doesn't want to go to jail because of some plot of Lizzie's, he might tell us what they're up to."

"We aren't even sure he, or his car, was at the library last night," I pointed out. "He might have been in the Outer Banks on other business."

"That's what we're hoping to find out," she said. "Absence of evidence is not—"

"Evidence of absence."

"Precisely."

"How do you know he's going to be available to talk to us?" I asked Bertie. "He might have classes or seminars or student appointments. Are we going to hang around all day? If he knows we're waiting, he might sneak out the back door."

"I'm better at subterfuge than that, Lucy," Bertie said with a chuckle. "Eddie used the college's online appointment system to reserve a half an hour of Hoskins's student consultation hours at twelve thirty. I could have any time slot I wanted, Eddie said. Norm's appointment book is almost completely empty, as it is every day. His students don't normally bother wasting their time talking to him. Or so Eddie tells me."

As someone who worked for years in the libraries at Harvard, the physical appearance of Blacklock College doesn't impress me much. Most of the buildings were built in the 1960s and 1970s: blocks of solid gray concrete with small, narrow windows and not a touch of history or charm. But a university is more than weather-worn stone buildings and clinging ivy. Students lounged on the grass of the common, reading, gossiping, or flirting in the shade of white oaks and sugar maples, or tossing around footballs in the hot sun. On a Friday in summer, not many people were around, but there were enough to give it the feel of the best of college life. It was quarter past twelve as Bertie and I crossed the grassy common, heading for the languages building in which the North Carolina history department had a small office. We took the elevator to the third floor and emerged into a narrow hallway. The paint on the walls was chipped, and the industrial carpet needed to have the dust pounded out of it. All the doors running off the hallway were shut, and the dim bulbs in the ceiling barely broke the gloom. The door we were after—the one marked Professor Norman Hoskins—was situated next to a utility closet. Bertie knocked lightly and pushed the door open at the grunted command "Enter."

Norman Hoskins's office was much like the man himself: nondescript, boring, beige. The potted plant on the windowsill appeared to have abandoned all hope. The books on the shelves lining the walls were covered in a thin layer of dust. Three coffee mugs, half empty under a layer of curdling cream, sat on his desk amid piles of papers and magazines.

He looked up from his computer and blinked.

"Good afternoon," Bertie said. "May I?" She gestured toward a chair and, without waiting to be invited to take a seat, did so. It was the only visitor's chair in the office. I leaned against a wall. Norm glanced between Bertie and me. His eyes flicked toward his computer, confirming something on the screen. "I'm sorry, Ms. James, but I have a student arriving shortly for a consultation."

"No student," Bertie said. "Just us."

He glanced at the computer in confusion.

"Professor McClanahan was kind enough to mark off some time in your . . . busy schedule," Bertie said.

"That was an unusual thing for him to do. What do you want?" His eyes darted between Bertie, me, the computer screen, and the door. He knew, I thought, why we were here. I crossed my arms over my chest in an attempt to appear formidable. I thought of myself as Bertie's enforcer.

"Let's get straight to the point, shall we?" Bertie said. "You failed in your attempt to get Mrs. Crawbingham's diary last night. If you'd simply asked to be allowed to study it, we would have given you permission to do so at a later date. Therefore, I have to ask why you thought it necessary to break in and attempt to steal it."

If anything, the air-conditioning in this office was turned up way too high, but beads of sweat began popping up on the professor's forehead. He flicked through the stack of papers on his desk and avoided our eyes. "I've no idea what you're talking about. If you'll excuse me, I'm a very busy man."

Bertie leaned back in her chair and settled herself comfortably. The colorful folds of her long cotton skirt swirled around her legs. "Lucy, here, can identify you. She saw you quite plainly. Didn't you, Lucy?"

"I did? I mean, I did. Yes. Last night. You broke into the library and activated our silent alarm." Charles was as good as any alarm, although he certainly wasn't silent. "Which alerted me to the fact that we had an intruder. I was on the steps, standing on the first bend, watching as you ran away."

"I can explain." He wiped sweat off his forehead. "I wasn't there to steal anything. You left the door open, anyway. I considered that an invitation to enter."

"The door was not locked, I'll admit," I said, "but it was not open, and you were not invited in."

"It's a public library. I assumed—"

"You assumed you were welcome to walk right in in the middle of the night? I find that difficult to accept," Bertie said. "Which still leaves the question of why you were there and what you were after."

"I only wanted to . . . uh . . . borrow the diary. I would have left a receipt."

Bertie didn't look as though she believed him. "Borrowing without asking is also called stealing, Professor. Didn't your mother teach you that?"

He stopped fiddling with student essays. "I'm sure you can understand, Ms. James. My position here at the university is tenuous. To say the least. Not just me but the entire department. After we failed to secure the Ruddle Collection, we've been left high and dry, waiting for the axe to fall."

Last year, Professor McClanahan had told Bertie and me that the North Carolina history department was in danger of being folded into the college's regular history department, if not eliminated entirely. Blacklock College was primarily a school for literature and languages, ancient and modern, and highly regarded in that field. In a time of budget cuts, the college board wanted to let institutions that specialized in North Carolina history do that, and leave Blacklock to concentrate on it's core mandate.

Needless to say, Professors McArthur and Hoskins were vehemently opposed to any such suggestion. Eddie had also told us their reputations in the academic community were such that they'd have trouble finding positions at another prominent institution of higher learning.

"You have to understand my position." His tone turned wheedling as he glanced between Bertie and me. "Publish or perish—that's the rule in academic life. I haven't got so much as an idea for a book. I need to find something groundbreaking, something truly original. The Civil War era was a time of great change in the Outer Banks, but every aspect of that has been covered many times before. I thought . . . I hoped . . . one previously undiscovered fishwife's diary would lead me to something. Something . . ." His voice trailed off ". . . worthwhile. All I need is an idea." His shoulders shook, but he recovered himself, and he lifted his head. "I couldn't wait. You refused to allow the diary to be available for examination, pending the police investigation into the murder that happened at your library the other night. That wasn't right; the diary doesn't belong to you, but to the people of North Carolina. Besides, no harm done, now was there? Except for my car, I'm sorry to say. I had an excessively wet and uncomfortable drive home. How about I make an appointment to view the diary at a mutually convenient time? Say tomorrow afternoon at two? You'll make an exception for me, I'm sure." Norm Hoskins smiled at Bertie. He might have thought it was a smile, but it was more the edges of his mouth turning up in a strained grimace.

Bertie didn't return the smile. She studied his face for a long time before she suddenly said, "Did you return to the library on Monday night after everyone else had left? Did Jeremy Hughes interrupt your attempt to *study* Mrs. Crawbingham's diary that night? Did you kill him when he got in your way?"

Norm leapt to his feet. "What! No! You can't pin that on me. I was at a faculty function that evening. I went there immediately after getting back from Nags Head. Fifty people, highly respectable members of this university and the community, can testify to that. Ask anyone. They'll tell you."

I believed him. Professor Hoskins wasn't much of a liar. I was about to ask again about last night and what he'd hoped to achieve, when I realized he'd spoken in the singular. Not the plural. "Was Professor McArthur also at this faculty function?" I asked.

He glanced at the papers on his desk and shuffled a few of them around. "I . . . uh . . . don't remember."

Before I could press the point, the office door flew open. Professor Elizabeth McArthur stood there, her mouth set in a tight line and her eyes ablaze. "You really are a fool, Norman. Why are you even talking to these people? They aren't the police—just a couple of busybodies. Sit down and shut up."

He dropped into his chair and pinched his lips tightly together.

"Good afternoon," Bertie said amiably.

"Get out," Lizzie replied.

Bertie folded her hands neatly in her lap. "If you weren't at the faculty function on Monday, Elizabeth, where were you?"

"Not doing anything that's any of your business. Please leave. Now." She pulled her phone out of a pocket of her ill-fitting trousers. "Or I'll call security and have you escorted out."

Bertie stood up. "Very well. Have a nice day. Thank you for your time, Professor Hoskins."

We left the office, and the door slammed shut behind us. Bertie put her finger to her lips and leaned closer to the door. I did the same. It was a thin bit of wood, hastily installed when a larger room had been broken up into smaller ones, and we could clearly hear Lizzie scream, "Are you out of your tiny mind? You tried to steal that diary? Did you think no one would notice when it showed up here?"

"I thought—"

"I don't ask you to think," she yelled. "How many times have I told you, Norman, leave the thinking to me."

At that moment, a door further along the hallway flew open, and chattering students streamed out of the classroom. Bertie and I made our escape.

* * *

"That was interesting," Bertie said once we were in my car and rapidly heading away from the college.

"Interesting personal inter-dynamics there for sure," I replied.

Bertie took out her phone and called Sam Watson while I drove. She put the call on speakerphone so I could listen. Briefly, she told Sam that Norman Hoskins had confessed to us that he'd broken into the library last night in search of Mrs. Crawbingham's diary.

"Why on earth would he do that?" Watson asked. "He could hardly use the thing if it had been illicitly obtained."

"I suspect he didn't think that far ahead," I said.

"He might have planned to give it to McArthur and hoped she'd know what do to with it," Bertie said.

"Why?" Watson asked. "Without the map and the code page, it's nothing but a weather record."

"Competition can be brutal in academe," I said. "Trust me. I worked at Harvard. Brings a whole new meaning to the word *ambitious*. Not to mention *vindictive*."

"Glad I work for the police then," Watson said. "Do you want to press charges for the break-in at the library?"

"No," Bertie said, "No harm was done, and if I haven't scared him off trying again, McArthur certainly has."

"Did anyone check their alibis for the night Jeremy Hughes died?" I asked. "Maybe last night wasn't the first time one of them tried to get their hands on the diary."

"Let me see. Hold on a sec." We heard computer keys tapping, and then Watson said, "An officer from Elizabeth City paid a call on them. Both professors said they were at a party given by the chancellor to welcome new faculty. When the officer checked with the chancellor's assistant, she told him the party ran from seven until ten." The gathering at the library to view the contests of the iron box had broken up—when Bertie kicked everyone out—before six. Blacklock College was an hour and a half's drive from the lighthouse, meaning they would have been able to make it to the reception in time to be fashionably late. "Attendance had been mandatory, and Hoskins and McArthur were expected to attend. The officer asked if they had, and the chancellor's assistant said the night was busy and the room crowded, so she couldn't remember every individual present. She did go on to imply that Hoskins' and McArthur's positions are tenuous at the college, so they would have been at the party if they knew what was good for them."

"Not an alibi then," Bertie said. "Did anyone follow up?"

More keys clicked. "Doesn't look like it. Someone dropped the ball, and I can only apologize for that. I'll have someone go around to the college and try to pinpoint them, but almost a week has passed. Memories fade quickly."

"I'd suggest you concentrate on McArthur," Bertie said. "Norm told us about the faculty party, and I don't think he would have if he wasn't there."

"Don't be so quick to take things at face value, Bertie. Some people can be sneakier than you think."

"Which is why I'm glad I'm a librarian." Bertie pushed the red button to end the call.

"Norman told us he didn't remember if McArthur had been at the faculty party or not," I said. "Considering how closely they work together, I'm taking that to mean she wasn't there. He doesn't strike me as the friendly, gregarious type who gets along with everyone at a cocktail party. If she'd been in the room, he would have stuck close to her the entire time."

"Agreed," Bertie said. "But just because she didn't attend a boring staff party doesn't mean she was out killing someone."

Chapter Eighteen

Saturday is always the busiest day of the week at the Lighthouse Library. Ronald has a full schedule of children's programming; high school and college students need Charlene's help with their history papers; and people who work during the week come in on Saturday to take out books. Bertie usually takes Saturday off, but she'd dropped in today to make sure everything was on track in preparation for Settlers' Day tomorrow.

Work on the building had shut down for the weekend, but our miniature version was open and busy all day. Theodore and my Aunt Ellen took the morning's volunteer shift to keep an eye on the rambunctious and enthusiastic prospective construction workers.

At five minutes before noon, feet pounded the stairs as the fifth-grade reading club let out. Parents emerged from between the stacks, gathered up their own collections of books, and fell into line at the circulation desk.

By the time I'd checked all the books out, the afternoon volunteer shift—Mrs. Peterson and Grace—had arrived to take over.

"Have fun?" I asked Aunt Ellen.

She took off her sun hat and gave me a big grin. "I sure did. There's something about being around laughing, playing children that makes a woman young again."

"Give Josie time," I said. "She's only been married for five months."

"That long?" Ellen's light laugh rang out. "You must be a mind reader, Lucy. I don't recall saying anything about hoping for grandchildren."

I smiled at her. "You didn't have to. The look on your face is enough." For me, the pressure to present my mother with grandchildren is off. My three older brothers are all married with kids. Not so for Josie, the eldest child in her family. Aunt Ellen would never say anything, but Josie told me she knew her mother had her hopes.

"It's lunchtime," Ellen said. "If you want to take your break, I'll watch the desk for you."

"Thanks," I said. "Ronald and Charlene are around, and I'll be upstairs if you need anything."

I have the worlds' greatest commute, and I trotted upstairs to my apartment. I reheated the leftovers from a takeout chicken curry I'd first enjoyed last week and sat down at the kitchen table to eat.

I'd been intending to research the Freedmen's Colony Janelle Washington had talked about, and now seemed as good a time as any. I opened my iPad and read.

The colony had been established on Roanoke Island in 1863, at the height of the Civil War, to be a safe haven for slaves seeking refuge or those freed when the Union took control of Confederate areas. At first the colony thrived as the settlers built homes, worked their land and fished, established trades, and set up their own churches and schools. Some even joined the army or worked as spies, scouts, or guards for the Union. They were paid wages for their work and encouraged in their independence. Literacy spread and families stayed together.

The population grew and the colony soon became so crowded infectious diseases began to take hold. Farming failed on the poor soil of the island; men were involuntarily conscripted for war work.

The colony struggled on.

When the war ended, President Johnson ordered all property seized by Union forces to be returned to its previous owners. That included the people at the Roanoke Island Freedmen's Colony. The families living there were told they had no rights to the land they'd been promised, on which they'd built homes, farms, workshops, and a community.

The settlers dispersed and the colony was abandoned in 1867. A few years later, only a handful of the freedmen remained on the island. Janelle's husband Neil came from one such family.

It was a sad story, but so was much of history. Nevertheless, I found it fascinating, and I wanted to learn more. I'd ask Janelle if her husband would be interested in telling me stories passed down through his family. When I had time, I'd see what Charlene could produce from the archives.

Speaking of time . . . I was running out of it. I had to get back to work.

Connor phoned as I was washing up my single bowl.

"Feel like a little excursion tonight, Lucy?" he asked.

"I'm always up for an excursion. What do you have in mind?"

"I got some news a few minutes ago. It seems as though good news never arrives on a Friday afternoon."

"What's happened?"

"Monaghan Corporation has filed a motion in court to put a stop to the environmental review on that plot of land where they're hoping to build their golf resort."

"Can they do that?"

"They can and they have. They can ask the courts to stop it, yes. Doesn't mean the court has to agree, of course, but legal action costs money. There are people on the town council who won't want to fight it. I won't say some of my esteemed colleagues are in the pockets of developers but—"

"But they are," I said. "What does this have to do with our excursion?"

"I want to go to the site and have another look at it. I haven't been there for a few months. If we're going to fight this, I need to have a pretty good idea in my mind what I'm fighting for. I called Monaghan's offices and got permission to go this evening. I thought you might like to come. What time do you get off work?"

"We close at six. I can be ready at one minute after six."

"I'll pick you up then," he said. "I don't suppose you have any news about the code page and map? You didn't decipher it and forget to tell me?"

"Sadly, no. I've pretty much given up on it. Some secrets are meant to remain secret, I suppose."

"I haven't heard anything more from Sam or the police chief about the progress of the investigation into Jeremy Hughes's murder. I hope that's something that won't remain a secret much longer."

"I've heard nothing either," I said. It was obvious Sam and Butch had kept my confidence and hadn't told Connor about the break-in on Thursday night. Otherwise, Connor would be sure to have had something to say about security around here.

* * *

Connor was nothing if not punctual. At one minute past six, I was standing on the lighthouse steps as his car pulled up. I checked to ensure the door behind me was locked—for about the tenth time—and ran to join him.

Two of our patrons were standing by their cars chatting while their children chased each other across the lawn. They smiled at me as I ran past.

"Hot date tonight, Lucy?" one called.

I felt myself blushing.

"I remember when I ran to greet Greg," one of the women said. "I felt as though I had wings beneath my feet."

"These days," the other said, "I run past my husband when he comes in the door. Let him handle the kids for a while."

As if to prove her point, one of the little boys started crying. "Mommy, she hit me!"

"Did not! You hit me first."

"Did not!" Screaming children ran toward us.

"And so the romance dies," the first mother said with a tired sigh.

"Hopefully," the second said as her weeping son collapsed against her, "to be replaced by something even better. Enjoy every moment, Lucy. I'd better get these guys home. It's long past dinnertime. Stop crying, Stewart. You're not hurt. Will we see you tomorrow, Lucy?"

"At the Settler's Day Fair?" I gave the little girl, grinning from ear to ear at the prospect of getting her brother into trouble, a rub on the top of her head. "Definitely. I'm looking forward to it."

I waved good night and jumped into the BMW.

"Good day?" Connor asked as he drove away.

"Every day at the Lighthouse Library is a good day," I said, "except when it isn't."

Traffic was heavy coming toward Nags Head as people returned from a day exploring Cape Hatteras National

Seashore and the remote communities of Rodanthe and Buxton. We didn't have far to go before Connor slowed the car and made the turn onto a bumpy construction road. Other than the road itself, I could see no signs of work being done. We bumped along for not more than thirty seconds before we reached a chain strung across the road and a prefabricated shack. A "No Trespassing" sign was slung onto the chain. Connor parked and we got out of the car. A man came out of the shack, dressed in the beige uniform of a local security firm.

"Hey," he said.

"Good evening," Connor said. "I'm Mayor McNeil, and I'm here to have a look around."

The guard nodded. "I was told you'd be here. Go ahead." He waved to the sand dunes. "Knock yourself out."

"Won't be long." Connor took my hand, and we rounded the barrier. The road turned into a small track weaving between the beach grasses and the dunes. At places the path disappeared beneath the ever-shifting sand. As the noise from the highway died away, my ears became accustomed to the quiet, and I could hear the soft shuffling of the sand and the murmur of the sea rushing to shore on the other side of the dunes. Seagulls flew in lazy circles overhead, and the wind—accompanied by a good number of sand particles—tore at my hair. I breathed in deeply. The air was fresh and pure and salty. We climbed up sand dunes and down again. Not much grew in this harsh environment, and everything that did was tough, hardy, and small. I was able to identify sea rocket, sea oats, pennywort, and prickly pear cactus. Trees didn't stand a chance here.

"Strange place for a golf course," I said. "Will grass even grow in all this sand?"

Connor didn't reply. We climbed another dune, and the ocean stretched out before us. Sandpipers and oyster-catchers dashed through the surf; avocets searched the shallows; a lone pelican glided majestically above the water; and higher up, gulls circled as they cried out to one another.

It was unbelievably beautiful.

Connor pointed south, further down the beach to where a single house perched on the dunes. It was a typical historic Outer Banks house, all dark, unpainted wood and blue shutters, built on stilts, four stories tall with outdoor staircases, multilevel balconies, and covered verandas. A path led to the sea. It was hard to see from here, but a fenced-in area at the back of the house was probably a pool and patio.

"That's the Monaghan house," Connor said. "First built in the 1930s by Nathanial Monaghan."

"You mean Rick's father? The one who died recently? He must have been mighty young back then."

"The Monaghans are a long-lived family. Zebadiah died at ninety-seven, rare in those days, and Nathanial was one hundred and two."

"How old is Rick? I've never met him, but his wife Cheryl seems to be around fifty."

"He's the same age as her. Nathanial was a recluse. He didn't marry until late in life and had only one child, Rick. I believe Nathanial was in his late fifties when Rick was born. They were long-lived men, but not very procreative. Nathanial was Zebadiah's only child, also born late in his father's life."

"If that's Nathanial's house, this must be the land you told me he walked every day."

"It is. They say he insisted on going on his morning stroll in the face of an incoming hurricane. Rick's plan is to convert the old house into part of the hotel and conference center, and extend the building north, toward where we're standing now, and inland. Separate buildings—guest cottages and the club house—will be built along that ridge there." He pointed. "The golf course will be across the dunes behind us."

"The beach environment will be destroyed."

"Yes, it will. Although he's going to argue he's doing everything possible to preserve as much of it as is feasible."

"And when it turns out it's not *feasible* to save much, everyone will say, 'Gee, that's too bad'?"

"Probably. Don't look now, Lucy, but we're being watched."

Of course I looked. Two figures stood on one of the upper balconies of the old house. They held binoculars to their eyes and were looking directly at us.

"Should I wave?" I said.

"That would be unnecessarily provocative," he said with a chuckle. He waved.

The binoculars were lowered. I thought I recognized Cheryl Monaghan. The man with her was tall and round bellied. "Is that Rick?"

"Yes. Let's go. I've seen enough. How about dinner?"

"A good idea. I need to get the taste of this development out of my mouth." I stuck out my tongue and picked particles of earth off it. "As well as the taste of this sand."

Chapter Nineteen

I decided not to wear a costume for Settlers' Day. If anyone asked, I'd explain that I was a true settler, being new to the Other Banks, so I was coming as myself.

I wouldn't tell the truth—which is that I hate dressing up, mainly because I have no imagination. Other people seem to be able to whip together an authentic-looking, humorous, or whimsical costume at the drop of the hat with a handful of things pulled out of the back of their closet. I'd considered renting a long dress from a costume shop, but I forgot about that until I was turning in on Saturday night after dinner with Connor.

I can't even rent a costume efficiently.

It shouldn't matter what I wore. Plenty of other people could be counted on to show up suitably attired, if not always historically appropriate.

Connor and I had enjoyed a nice dinner at Jake's. We hadn't talked about our walk among the dunes, nor did we discuss the code page or Mrs. Crawbingham's diary. I said nothing about Thursday night's break in at the lighthouse or Bertie and my trip to Blacklock College and what we learned there. Instead, I told him I'd been doing some research into the Freedmen's Colony.

"Did you not know about that?" he said. "The Fort Raleigh National Historic Site over in Roanoke has information about it."

"I knew about it, yes. I vaguely remember reading about it when we toured the site many, many years ago. Come to think of it, that might have been the summer I was fourteen. I had other things on my mind that year." I rested my chin on my hand and twisted my face into something resembling deep thought. "I wonder what that might have been."

The edges of his mouth turned up, and his sea-blue eyes twinkled. "Oh yes. That summer."

I first met Connor McNeil when I visited my Outer Banks cousins the summer I was fourteen and he was fifteen. We had the sweetest, most innocent of summer romances, which ended when I went back to Boston for another school year, and we fell out of touch. When we next met again last summer, we found the feelings we'd had way back then, waiting to be rekindled.

"Do you know Neil and Janelle Washington?" I asked.

He shook his head. "Don't think so."

"Neil's family was part of the Freedmen's Colony. I guess meeting someone with such a direct, personal interest has sparked my curiosity. I'm hoping to learn more about it."

"One thing the Outer Banks has," Connor said, "is no shortage of history."

"Even as someone coming from Boston," I said, "I can agree with you on that."

We'd then lifted our wine glasses in a toast to history.

I enjoyed a long lie-in Sunday morning, only getting out of bed when Charles's pleas to be fed got too insistent to ignore any longer. I drank copious cups of freshly brewed coffee and munched on muesli and yogurt while checking the online news from Boston and the Outer Banks gossip. The historical society had started a Twitter meme of #OBXSettlersFun, and plenty of people were chiming in to say they were looking forward to it.

Breakfast finished, I showered, washed my hair, and dressed in white capris with a blue stripe down the leg, a blue-and-white-striped T-shirt, and sturdy sports sandals. A costume of sorts—the twenty-first-century newcomer.

"Is that what you're wearing?" Ronald said when I came downstairs, ready to dive into helping with the setup.

I eyed his pirate costume: big hat with sweeping feather, parrot on the shoulder, eye patch, pants tucked into high leather boots. "The role of Captain Jack Sparrow has already been cast," I said.

"Nice of you to say that I do a good imitation of Johnny Depp," he replied. The stuffed parrot wobbled, and Ronald adjusted it.

"What's Nan coming as?" I asked, referring to Ronald's wife.

"Anne Bonny."

"Who's that?"

"A notorious pirate in her own right. She was born in Ireland and came to the Carolinas in the early 1700s. For their time, pirates could be remarkably gender neutral. Several women had reputations as efficient pirates and good fighters."

"I'm constantly amazed at how much North Carolina history I still have to learn," I said.

The library door opened, Charlene swept in, and Ronald and I burst out laughing.

"Like it?" she said with a big grin.

"Perfect," I said.

"I came early in case you need some help setting up. I have to go back for Mom at one, but in case I get held up, I didn't want to have to worry about getting changed later."

Charlene was dressed in oil slickers, with a big yellow hat and heavy boots, looking exactly like a fisherman returning to land after a day spent on the water. "I'm my great-great-grandfather on my dad's side. They came from England and got jobs on the fishing boats. All I can say is thank heavens that hot spell is over. What are you going to wear, Lucy?"

I held out my arms. "This is my costume. I put a lot of thought into it and decided to come as a settler from Boston who moved to the Outer Banks to work as a librarian in the twenty-first century."

Charlene laughed. I had the feeling I was going to get very tired of explaining myself before the day was over.

"Now," she asked, "what have we got to do?"

"Nothing, really, until the historical society people get here. They're bringing everything."

"Looks like them now." Ronald pointed out the window. "A truck's pulling up."

We went outside in time to see a rental panel van, followed closely by a small car, slow to a stop. Phil Cahill jumped out of the car, and two men got out of the truck. They opened the back doors and began pulling out stackable chairs and loading them onto trolleys. Ronald, Charlene, and I hurried to help.

The rest of the historical society soon followed, along with vendors and performers. Cars and trucks backed up and unloaded, and people ran about jostling for the best position to advertise their wares. Jewelry makers, hat sellers, potters, a couple of painters of local scenes, several food booths, an ice cream truck, a face painter. The people from Island Bookstore erected a big tent, where they set up a table covered with volumes on local history, both fiction and nonfiction, and to do with the environment of the Outer Banks. Many of the titles were aimed at children.

My cousin Josie arrived, and she and her assistant, Blair, set up their booth. Before she'd even opened for business, volunteer workers were lining up for fresh bakery-made cookies and tarts or warm-from-the-oven Danishes and croissants.

By quarter to one, the lighthouse lawn had been turned into a fairground with tents and tables under colorful umbrellas and a small stage facing neatly laid-out rows of chairs. Almost all the vendors had come in some sort of costume. A cheerful yellow sun shone in a brilliant blue sky, and a light cooling breeze blew off the ocean, sending the decorative flags fluttering.

"Couldn't ask for a better day for it," Bertie said to me.

Bertie hadn't come in costume, or perhaps, like mine, hers was so subtle I didn't realize it was a costume. I didn't ask.

"We're not working today," she said. "And this is not a library function, but it is on the library grounds, so we will need to keep an eye out. Did you lock the front door, Lucy?"

"Yes." I'd checked about ten times already.

"Good. No one's to go in the building for any reason whatsoever. Present company excepted."

"Got it," I said. "A couple of porta potties have been set up around the back."

Mabel Eastland, Lynne Feingold, and Cheryl Monaghan picked their way across the lawn toward us.

Mabel wore a simple dress of brown cotton that swept the ground, under a white apron, and a white bonnet, and Lynne was in something similar, but her dress was dark gray rather than brown. Cheryl, on the other hand, might have been presiding over afternoon tea at a Louisiana plantation, in a yellow satin and lace gown stretched over wide hoops and yards of crinolines. Her hat was weighted down with feathers, fake fruit and stuffed birds, and still more lace. A steady stream of sweat dripped from under the brim and ran down her bright red face. I figured she was probably already regretting trying to dress like a lady of the manor. Those clothes were suitable for sitting on the covered front porch in the heat of the day, sipping mint juleps, and being fanned by servants. Not for running around an open patch of lawn under a bright sun.

"This is so exciting," Mabel said. "Looks like people are starting to arrive early." A steady stream of cars was making its way down the long driveway.

The Washington twins ran past us, and their mother hurried after them. The girls were dressed in the costumes they'd worn to the library, and Janelle had on the clothes of a farm wife or servant woman of the nineteenth century. She stopped by our little group to say hello.

When we'd exchanged greetings, Bertie asked who would be the first speaker.

"A professor from Duke, talking about the constantly changing landscape of barrier islands," Mabel said.

"How dreadfully exciting." Cheryl suppressed a fake yawn.

"I'd think you'd find what she has to say both interesting and important," Janelle said, "considering your family's plans to build a multimillion dollar hotel on a foundation of sand."

"Thank you *so much* for your concern, dear," Cheryl said. "When I want your advice on my husband's business matters, I'll ask for it."

"Never hurts to listen to what the experts have to say." Janelle kept her voice calm and even.

"We have consulted with plenty of experts, dear—don't you worry about us."

"Oh, I never worry about you, Cheryl," Janelle said.

"Does everyone like my costume?" Cheryl said, wisely changing the subject. "I've come as Eula, Mrs. Zebadiah Monaghan, Rick's grandmother. They say Eula was the greatest beauty of her generation, and Zebadiah was one of the most important men in the Outer Banks in his day. He owned a lot of land around these parts."

"I think we're all aware of who Zebadiah was, dear," Mrs. Eastland said. "We are members of the historical society, after all."

Cheryl gave her a poisonous look before turning to me with a strained smile. "*Newcomers* such as Lucy might not be aware of the importance of my husband's family's history to this area."

"So helpful of you to ensure everyone knows," Mrs. Eastland said.

"Is that Fred McIntosh, I see?" Cheryl said. "Why, I do believe it is. I need to speak with him. Do give me a shout, Mabel, if you need any help." Cheryl bustled off, lugging her heavy skirts.

"I could use lots of help," Mabel said. "But for some reason Cheryl never seems to be around when the time arrives."

Bertie and Lynne chuckled.

"I wasn't aware Cheryl was a member of the historical society," I said.

"Only peripherally," Lynne said. "And only when it suits her to remind us how important her husband's family is."

"Don't let her needling get to you," Mabel said to Janelle. "She speaks to everyone that way."

"Everyone she regards as her inferior on the social scale," Lynne said. "I'm quite sure she's not talking to Fred McIntosh like that. I heard she and Rick are desperate to get Fred to invest in their project. He, however, has the brains God gave him, and he doesn't want any part of it."

"Don't y'all worry about me," Janelle said. "I got my brains from my mama, and I know better than to let Cheryl bother me." She turned to me. "I came over to ask if the children's construction site is going to be usable today."

"Feel free, but be aware Ronald won't be on hand all day to supervise."

"Thanks. The twins have already lost interest in stories of their family history and want to play at building things." She hurried after her children. I started to walk away but turned around when I heard Lynne mutter, "What on earth is *she* doing here?"

Maya Hughes had also come as an antebellum lady of means, but in her case I thought the costume might be more suitable to running a house of ill repute rather than a respectable plantation. The long dress was tight in all the right places, the neckline plunging, the shoulders bare. She lifted her skirts in both hands and picked her way across the lawn, teetering in her twenty-first-century stiletto heels.

"Isn't this a lovely turnout," she said. "Mabel, darling, it's been far too long." She exchanged air kisses with Mrs. Eastland. I managed to dodge a perfume-scented hug by thrusting out my hand. She returned the shake limply and said, "Nice to see you again, Detective. Are you making any progress on the brutal murder of my husband?"

I avoided looking at Bertie and the others, and said to Maya, "Nothing official. I'm here to enjoy Settlers' Day."

Maya turned her smile on Lynne. "I don't believe we've met."

Lynne crossed her arms over her chest and scowled.

Deciding the other woman wasn't worth worrying about, Maya turned back to Mrs. Eastland. "I hope you're going to pay tribute to Jeremy today. The historical society, and this day, was so dreadfully important to him." She sniffed delicately, pulled a lace-trimmed, lavender-scented handkerchief out of her glove, and wiped at dry eyes.

"I plan to mention Jeremy's dedication to the historical society when I say a few words to open the afternoon," Mrs. Eastland said.

"Why don't I do that?" Maya said. "I knew him best, of course. I went to the trouble of preparing a few words." She smiled at Mrs. Eastland. Mrs. Eastland looked at me. I looked at Bertie.

"Why not?" Bertie said.

"Good, it's settled then," Maya said.

"I hardly think you're the appropriate person to talk about Jeremy," Lynne blurted out. "After all, he was about to leave you for another woman."

Mrs. Eastland's eyes opened wide. "I don't think—" she began, but Maya cut her off with a wave of her hand.

"I assume you're referring to yourself." Maya laughed, the sound low and cruel. She openly studied Lynne, top to toe. "As if. You poor little dear, you don't need to tell me. He was leaving his miserable shrew of a wife to take up a life of middle-aged bliss with you. You can count yourself lucky he died before he laughed in your face." Her eyes narrowed. "Or did you kill him because you knew he was about to dump you as he did all the others before you?"

"You're lying." Lynne spat out the words. "He loved me. Me! He stayed with you all these years because he was a man of honor who wanted to respect his marriage vows, but your constant demands were becoming too much for even him to bear."

Maya laid a gloved hand on Lynne's arm. "If it helps you sleep at night, dear, go ahead and believe it. It must be so hard to be your age and realize your best-before date is long past."

Lynne shook her off. "Maybe it was you who killed him because you knew he was about to leave you. Leave you, and take all his money with him."

"His money?" Maya threw back her head and laughed. "He told you he had money of his own? How absolutely delicious. Everything Jeremy had was courtesy of either his mother or me."

Lynne's eyes filled with tears. Her mouth opened and closed as she searched for a cutting response, but nothing came. She ran away.

"That wasn't kind," Mabel Eastland said, watching her go.

"I've never pretended to be kind," Maya replied. "But I can always be counted on to speak the truth."

"When it suits you," Mrs. Eastland said.

Maya batted her eyelashes in response and then looked out over the crowd. A steady stream of people were arriving, and cars cruised the lot, searching for a parking spot.

"If you'll excuse me," Bertie said. "I've things to do."
She walked away, shaking her head. I considered following her but hesitated. I had absolutely no desire to hear
any more of Maya Hughes's catty pettiness, but the subject of a possible motive for her husband's murder had
come up. I was on the verge of asking Maya if this was
her first visit to the lighthouse, when she spoke again.

"I'll be ready as soon as you want me to speak,
Mabel. But don't wait too long. People will start getting
restless. Oh my goodness. There's Mayor McNeil. Isn't he
quite the handsomest man in Nags Head? I heard he has
a girlfriend, but I'm sure that's only temporary." She
laughed. "If not, I can make it so."

"Speaking of best-by date," Mrs. Eastland said, "isn't
Connor McNeil a bit young for you, Maya?"

"Oh, darling, they're never too young for me." Maya
scurried off.

I recovered my wits. "Good heavens. She's a . . .
not-nice person, isn't she?" I watched as Connor caught
sight of Maya descending on him, a hawk intent on her
prey, and ducked behind my Uncle Amos.

"She and Jeremy were made for each other, all right,"
Mrs. Eastland said. "Do you have a cane handy, Lucy?"

I blinked. "A cane? Are you okay?"

"I'm fine, but I might need to hook it around Maya's
neck to drag her off the stage."

She walked away, and I glanced around, looking for
something I could be helping with. Two library volunteers were at the children's play construction area, keeping one eye on the kids while they chatted. A handful
of people had found seats in front of the impromptu
stage, waiting patiently for the program to begin, and
the booths and tents were busy. A clown wandered
through the crowd, twisting balloons into fascinating,

complicated shapes for eager children. Holly Rankin had come dressed in street clothes, walking with a man about her age. I saw Butch munching on a hot dog while Stephanie flicked through the books on display at the Island Bookshop table. They both were in their regular clothes, as were about half the people here. The rest had come in some sort of costume, like the elaborately attired woman talking to Aunt Ellen. As if sensing me watching her, the woman turned and waved at me.

I realized my mouth must be hanging open. I snapped it shut, gave my head a shake to make sure I wasn't imagining things, and made my way toward them.

The woman was a vision out of another time, in pale blue silk. The dress was enormous, yards and yards of fabric draped over hoops and crinolines, the edges trimmed by yellow satin. Her dark hair was twisted up and fastened in place under a huge hat of matching blue with a wide yellow satin band tied into a bow under her chin. She grinned at me and twirled the lace-trimmed blue parasol she held in one of her wrist-length, fingerless yellow gloves.

"You look absolutely amazing," I said to Louise Jane. "Where on earth did you get that?"

"A little something my mother's had in the back of her closet for years," she said.

"Louise Jane's mother was an actress," Aunt Ellen told me. "She had a few good parts in Hollywood movies in her youth, as I recall."

"That career ended when her costumes, as well as other props, kept disappearing from the wardrobe room," Louise Jane said. "Or so my grandmother says. Oh well, Hollywood's loss is Nags Heads's gain." She swirled around, her huge skirts flaring out. "Like it?"

"I love it. But I'd hate to wear it—doesn't it weigh a ton?"

"All fake. The underneath is made of lightweight modern materials, and there are a few discretely placed breathing holes here and there." She lifted her arm to show me a slash running down the side seam. "And if it should rain, I'm ready." She opened the parasol, tucked it over one shoulder, and cocked her head, giving me a broad wink and a friendly grin.

I smiled back, realizing this was probably the first time Louise Jane and I had exchanged smiles that didn't have layers of tension and hidden meaning beneath them.

"Too bad you didn't take the time to go to any trouble yourself, Lucy, honey," she said, because she was, after all, Louise Jane and had probably had the same thought I had. "Ronald and Nan look splendid in their pirate costumes, and Charlene is a real Outer Banks fisherwoman."

"Speaking of costumes," Aunt Ellen said, "look who's just arrived." Louise Jane and I turned to see what she was pointing at.

Curtis Gardner had gone all out as a Civil War soldier. His gray uniform was immaculate, complete with knee-high black boots, double-breasted frock coat, high collar, and gold sleeve brocade. A gold sash was tied around his waist above the sword belt holding a replica sword. Not a soldier fresh from battle, but a general on parade, Curtis walked through the crowd, nodding left and right and accepting compliments. Diane Uppiton scurried along behind, her heels sinking into the soft grass. She wore her usual attire of pastel-colored skirt suit with pearls and heels, totally unsuited to a summer outdoor festival on the Outer Banks.

"Poor Curtis," Aunt Ellen said. "He's determined to make sure everyone knows his ancestor was an officer in the Confederacy."

"Wasn't he?" I asked.

Louise Jane laughed. "If Curtis would just let the story die, no one would care that his great-grandfather was a private who apparently ended up deserting. We all have skeletons in our family closets. Which makes for far more satisfying stories than being the pillar of respectability as your family was, Ellen."

Aunt Ellen winked at me. "I believe someone made mention of skeletons."

"That story will have to wait for another day," I said. "I'm going to get one of those hot dogs. Aunt Ellen, can I get you something?"

"No, thank you, dear. I see Mabel heading for the stage. I'll find myself a seat, as I want to hear the first speaker."

"A hot dog sounds good to me." Louise Jane fell into step beside me.

Mrs. Fitzgerald veered toward us when she caught sight of Louise Jane. "You look absolutely splendid, my dear,"

Louise Jane beamed. "So do you."

Our board chair was dressed in a poodle skirt and saddle shoes. "Did your family move to the Outer Banks in the 1950s?" I asked.

"We arrived on these shores long before that, Lucy. But this is my Halloween costume, and I didn't feel like making up another. One costume a year is enough for me. Unlike Louise Jane here, who can always rise to suit the theme of the day."

"I do my best," Louise Jane said, flushing with pleasure at the compliment.

More admirers approached to ask Louise Jane about her costume or take pictures. I left her to chat and pose and joined the queue at the hot dog cart. Connor caught up to me in the line. He slipped his hand into mine and said, "I'm hiding from an overly friendly citizen."

"The Widow Hughes."

One eyebrow lifted. "Is that who that was? Jeremy Hughes's wife?"

"Plantation girls gone wild? Yup, that was her."

"She has a unique interpretation of widow's weeds."

I laughed, wrapped my arms around him, and leaned my head into his chest.

"Keep the line movin' there, Mr. Mayor," a man shouted. "We haven't got all day here to wait while you do your courtin'."

I pulled away, my cheeks burning, as everyone in earshot laughed.

"Leave the man alone, Milt. Lucy doesn't want to wait some twenty years for him to make his move like you did with Ethel Stainsbury."

"I was worth the wait," Milt replied, and the lineup laughed again.

Connor and I got our hot dogs and piled the buns high with condiments. I took the first welcome bite and chewed happily. I caught sight of Elizabeth MacArthur and Norman Hoskins checking the selection at the bookstore tent, and chewed less happily. *Couldn't those two stay away?* They seemed to have an unhealthy fascination with the Lighthouse Library and were always popping up. They'd not come in costumes. No doubt they thought history too serious to be played at.

I tried to remember if I'd locked the front door of the library.

Yes, I was sure I had. But I'd better go back and check, just in case.

"The stage program's about to start," Connor said, wiping mustard off his chin. "I want to hear the first speaker. He's done some original research into shoreline erosion. Are you coming?"

"You go ahead. I'm not officially working today, but I feel some responsibility to keep an eye on things. I can listen to the opening remarks from here."

He kissed me lightly on the cheek and walked away. I watched him cross the lawn, exchanging greetings with almost everyone he passed. I felt a smile cross my face, and then I realized two elderly ladies were watching me, sparkles in their eyes and grins on their faces. My cheeks caught fire once again, and I buried my face in my hot dog.

"Young love," one of the women said to the other. "There's nothing on this earth like it."

"You think so, Esther?" her friend replied. "Been so long, I've forgotten."

"I haven't," Esther said.

* * *

The Settlers' Day Fair was a huge success. Everyone seemed to be enjoying themselves enormously. I know I did. I checked, for about the twentieth time, that the door to the library was locked, and then spent some time at the construction playground, keeping an eye on the children, but mostly I just chatted to friends and library patrons.

The day's first two lectures—the one on the dunes environment and the talk on gardening in the early days—were well attended, but much of the audience left before the third lecture: Elizabeth McArthur on the industrialization of North Carolina. She was, to put it mildly, an uninspiring speaker, and gradually people began getting up from their chairs and slipping away. Some of them had the grace to look shame-faced about it. Soon Professor McArthur was speaking to a crowd of no more than half a dozen people. Those people, I thought, must either be very interested in the topic or too polite to walk away.

"Glad I'm not one of her students." Charlene carried a tray with two pulled pork sandwiches and drinks.

"How's your mother doing?" I asked.

"Great. She's really enjoying herself. She's meeting up with so many people she hasn't seen in a while. Although I fear at the moment Lizzie is sending her to an early nap." Charlene nodded to the back of the row of chairs, to where Mrs. Clayton sat in her wheelchair. "We'll probably be leaving once we've finished eating. See you tomorrow, Lucy."

Norman Hoskins had taken a seat in the front row. He nodded enthusiastically at everything Lizzie said.

Which reminded me . . .

I took a minute to walk around the lighthouse in search of a moment's privacy. A few people had done the same and were strolling on the boardwalk that leads through the marsh to a dock on the sound. I pulled out my phone and called Sam Watson. He answered.

"Good afternoon, Detective," I said. "Lucy here."

"What have you got, Lucy?" he asked.

"Uh. Nothing. Sorry. I'm at the lighthouse for Settler's Day."

"CeeCee and her mother have gone to that."

"I saw them," I said. "They seem to be having a good time." I didn't mention that CeeCee had showed me her husband's birthday present. A book on The Lost Colony.

"Glad to hear it. Is that why you called?"

"No. I was wondering about Elizabeth McArthur's alibi for Monday night. You were going to check on that?"

A long silence came down the phone. "Why do you think I would share that information with you, Lucy?"

Fortune favors the brave, or so they say. I plunged in, trying to be brave. "Because I've been of help to you in the past. And I'd like to be of help again. McArthur and Hoskins are here now. She's boring the audience. What's left of her audience anyway."

"Elizabeth MacArthur did not attend the faculty reception. No one we spoke to remembers seeing her there. A few people spoke to Hoskins; they remember him."

"Meaning she doesn't have an alibi," I said.

"Meaning no one saw her at the party. Still doesn't mean she was in the Outer Banks. I have a call into her as it happens. You say she's there now?"

I peered over the top of the crowd. McArthur was still on stage, standing behind the podium, her arms stiff at her sides, her back erect, droning on. "Yes."

"Thanks. I think I'll drop by. Don't tell her I'm coming, Lucy, and don't ask her about her alibi."

"I won't."

He hung up. I put my phone away, feeling quite proud of myself. I had been of help to the police.

So there.

Next I went to the bookstore tent. The selection, I noticed, was thinning out. If I wanted to get something I'd better do it soon. I bought a couple of books on Outer Banks fishing history for my mother's Christmas present, even though I knew she'd probably not bother reading them. She'd gladly left her family's fishing past behind her when she married into a patrician Boston family, but all the talk today about people who'd settled here had reminded me of how important the contributions of everyone had been to building this marvelous community. Maybe my mom needed to be reminded of that.

I took my purchases and turned, almost colliding with Phil Cahill.

"Sorry," I said.

He grinned at me. "No harm done." Phil had come as a nineteenth-century farmer—overalls, big hat, checked shirt.

"Are you pleased with the day?" I asked. "I'd say it's a huge success."

"So it seems. I've been busy at my booth. I'm taking a break to grab something to eat before it's all gone."

"I'm impressed with the trouble some people have gone to over their costumes. Everything from farmers or fishermen to pirates, to soldiers, to gentlemen and ladies of leisure."

"The intention was that everyone came as *their* ancestor." Phil said. "I doubt very much Curtis Gardner is descended from a general in the army of the Confederacy or that Louise Jane's ancestors swanned about in dresses like that one. Not to mention that ridiculous getup Maya Hughes is in."

He actually looked angry at the thought, so I tried to make light of it. "Louise Jane is genuinely wearing her ancestor's clothes. Her mother was an actress, and that was one of her movie costumes."

"Not exactly what I meant."

"People are in the spirit of the day—isn't that what counts?"

As if to prove my point, a man slipped past us, heading for the book table in red breeches; white stockings; blue vest over a wide-sleeved, high-collared white shirt; and a metal hat that reflected the light from the sun. "You're from the Lost Colony, I assume," I said, referring to the group of Elizabethan settlers on Roanoke, the first Europeans to permanently settle in North America, who'd disappeared without a trace.

"Got it in one, Lucy," he said. "Great day, Phil. Good job."

Phil harrumphed.

"If you'll excuse me," I said, "I want to hear the results of the costume contest." McArthur had finished, to weak, scattered applause, and left the stage. It was quarter to five, but the grounds were still busy and business brisk at all the booths. Most of the items listed on the blackboard at Josie's table had been crossed out.

"At least I don't have to put up with whatever Jeremy was planning to wear," Phil said.

"Pardon me?"

"Jeremy was a snob. He had airs considerably above his station. He would have wanted to come as George Washington or maybe J. P. Morgan."

"Was J. P. Morgan from the Outer Banks?"

"No. Which is my point, Lucy. Jeremy would have made the day all about him. We're better off without him." Phil walked away.

Phil Cahill seemed not to have heard of the expression *Don't speak ill of the dead.* How worried had he been that Jeremy would ruin the Settlers' Day Fair?

Worried enough to kill him?

It seemed rather a drastic step to go to in order to make sure the man didn't wear an inappropriate costume. Still, I filed the comment away in the back of my mind. Sam Watson had said he was coming to speak to

Elizabeth McArthur. When he got here, I'd let him know what Phil had said.

Bertie, Connor, and Mrs. Eastland had climbed onto the stage. It was time for the awarding of the prizes for best costume. Almost everyone who was still here gathered around. To no one's surprise, Louise Jane won for best women's costume and Curtis Gardner for best men's. The best child's costume was a double award, given to a brother and sister who came dressed as an eighteenth-century farming couple, complete with miniature hoe (him), baby doll (her), and a well-behaved cocker spaniel dressed like a cow. The award winners and the award givers posed for photographs, and then they left the stage, accompanied by enthusiastic applause.

The last lecture of the day was to be on the Lost Colony and the Roanoke Island Freedmen's Colony. My bit of reading yesterday had simply whetted my appetite to learn more, so I found myself a seat in a center row. Janelle Washington took the chair beside me, tucking her skirts around her.

"The twins okay?" I asked.

"My mother-in-law's watching them," she said, "so I can pay attention to this talk. I was so hoping Neil would be able to come with us today, but his back was acting up something terrible this morning, and he had to bow out."

"I'm sorry to hear that. It must be tough for you—for both of you."

She turned to me with a radiant smile. "It's hard sometimes, but a lot of folks have it a lot harder. His parents are a great help with the twins. Neil texted me just now to say he's feeling better and will have supper ready when we get home. Not that we'll need anything for supper with the hot dogs and baked goods and ice cream the girls have been devouring all day, but I didn't have the heart to tell him that."

I chuckled and glanced around me, interested to see how many people wanted to hear the lecture. Most of the seats were taken. Professors McArthur and Hoskins stood at the back, behind the last row of chairs. Neither of them had happy smiles on their faces. I suspected they were attending the talk in order to find fault with it.

A rustle of anticipation ran through the crowd, and I twisted in my seat. The speaker, a short, round man in a tweed suit with a red bow tie, was standing at the edge of the stage, flipping through his notes.

"I'm surprised she's come to this," Janelle said.

I followed her gaze to see Cheryl Monaghan settling herself into a seat in the front row. Two seats, in fact, needed to accommodate all her skirts. The woman in the row behind her shifted over because the hat was blocking her view. "Why does that surprise you?" I asked. "It should be interesting."

"All Cheryl and her husband care about is ripping up the precious environment to make a couple of bucks. Nothing about the people or the history. Particularly not *our* history."

The speaker took his place in front of the microphone and cleared his throat, and Janelle and I settled back to listen.

The topic was fascinating, but the speaker was so dry they could rent him out to put fractious infants to sleep. He droned on and on and on, in a low steady monotone, never once looking up from his notes. I noticed more than a few people shifting uncomfortably in their seats and heard the rustle of fabric as the lucky people in the back rows got up and slipped quietly away.

Janelle leaned over and whispered to me, "I'm going to suggest they vet their speakers better next year. First that woman from Blacklock, and now this guy. I don't know where they get them."

"Not that there aren't interesting and knowledgeable people living around here," I whispered back.

"They should have used Louise Jane," Janelle replied.

"Shush!" a man chastised us.

Janelle and I exchanged glances and struggled not to laugh.

As the lecture continued, my thoughts began to wander. Mabel Eastland's opening words had been short and to the point. She simply thanked everyone for coming and acknowledged the board of the historical society, the volunteers, and Connor as the mayor. She thanked Bertie for providing the library grounds and then mentioned Jeremy Hughes's contribution to the day. Whereupon Maya climbed onto the stage and began a recitation of Jeremy's numerous virtues, managing at the same time to make sure we all knew what a solid support she'd always been to him and how much she'd shared his interests. She looked to be settling in for the duration when Mabel stepped forward, yanked the mic away, thanked her, and introduced the next speaker.

I realized that all the people I considered to be the prime suspects in the murder of Jeremy Hughes were here: Phil from the historical society board, who had no love lost for Jeremy; Maya, the not-grieving widow; Lynne, the soon-to-be-ex-girlfriend; Curtis and Diane, who'd been at the initial inspection of the found documents; Professors McArthur and Hoskins, desperate for the career boost they'd get if the diary turned out to be important—as long as they had possession of it.

The printouts of the code page and the map were still on my kitchen table, and I still glanced at them every time I passed, but I'd largely given up hope of being able to decipher the code. So many people had tried, but all to no avail. Maybe it was nothing but a pile of nonsense scribblings or in a language so obscure none of us recognized it.

At long, long last the speaker droned to a halt. A scattering of polite applause broke out, and I joined in.

What a shame," Janelle said.

"You mean the talk?"

"The history of the Freedmen's Colony is so important, not to mention fascinating, and he managed to make it about as interesting as the verbal equivalent of watching paint dry."

"I've an idea," I said. "At the Lighthouse Library we take our history seriously. Why don't you talk to Charlene about putting together an exhibit about the Colony? Maybe you could give a talk on it yourself."

"Oh, I couldn't possibly. I don't know enough."

"You know more than most of us. Give it some thought. Something aimed at the children maybe."

A smile touched the corners of her mouth. "I just might do that. Give it some thought, I mean. Neil is the storyteller in our family, not me."

I got to my feet. It was quarter to six, and the day was supposed to be wrapping up, but not many people seemed inclined to leave, and many of the booths were still doing a brisk business. The scent of roasting meat from the hot dog cart and the food truck drifted on the air, and the shouts of excited children came from the marsh and the construction play area.

Connor and my Uncle Amos were standing apart from the crowd, talking. I could tell by the set to their faces that they were discussing something serious. Ronald was pretending to make his parrot talk to a group of children while Nan smiled at him fondly. Charlene and her mother had stayed to the end after all and were watching the clown twist balloons into fantastic animals. Josie and her staff were in the process of breaking down her booth. Every item on the blackboard had been scratched out. Mrs. Eastland and Lynne Feingold chatted to Bertie and Mrs. Fitzgerald, and Maya Hughes and Cheryl Monaghan had taken seats together. I hadn't realized they knew each other. Phil Cahill was still at his table, showing a family his books. McArthur and Hoskins stood in line at the food truck.

I didn't see Sam Watson anywhere.

I'd spoken to Detective Watson an hour ago, but he hadn't arrived. Maybe something had come up. He had other cases on his desk, although I'd have assumed a murder investigation took priority.

Diane and Curtis were standing by themselves, and I realized I hadn't spoken to them yet today. I didn't like either of them much, and I didn't trust their intentions for my beloved library, but it never hurt to be polite. I said goodbye to Janelle and went to join Curtis and Diane, still clutching the book that was to be my mother's present.

"You look great, Curtis," I said. "Totally authentic. Congratulations on your award."

He smiled at me. Another first. "Thanks, Lucy. Civil War history is an important part of my life. My great-great-grandfather served in the army of the Confederacy. Did you know that?"

"No, I didn't. Of course, I'm a Yankee myself." My father's family could trace their lineage back to Revolutionary Boston.

"We'll forgive you," Diane said. I didn't think she was joking.

"Heritage is important to us Southerners," Curtis said.

"So it should be," I said.

"My grandfather was a highly decorated officer, who went undercover behind Yankee lines. Very dangerous job. I—"

"All of our history is important," I interrupted. "Janelle Washington and I have an idea for a library presentation on the Freedmen's Colony. Her husband's ancestors were part of it."

Diane stifled a yawn.

"Are you getting anywhere with the code page, Lucy?" Curtis shifted his belt, and his sword jangled.

"Afraid not. We've all pretty much given up trying. Sam Watson was going to ask some people who work in cryptography to have a look at it, but he warned me that they have more immediate problems to handle first, and it might be a long time before they get around to it. Probably a waste of time. It means nothing."

"It means something, Lucy. It has to. I know it."

I was surprised by the vehemence in his voice.

"Can we leave now, Curtis?" Diane said. "I'm sick and tired of hearing about that silly map." She turned to me. "It's all he talks about anymore. The map, the map, the map. Trying to figure out what those nonsense scribbles mean. As if Civil War treasure and military reports are sitting around waiting to be found. Any decent treasure would have been dug up long ago. Oh look—the jewelry booth lady is starting to pack up. I've decided to get that necklace after all." She tottered away, her sharp heels digging into the grass.

I wanted to get going also. I should start saying my goodbyes and help with the chairs and anything else that needed doing. But that little something that had been niggling at the back of my mind for days was tapping on my consciousness, begging to be allowed in. Something about the map . . .

"That was a great day, Lucy. Be sure and thank everyone for us, will you?" Mrs. Fitzgerald called as she and a group of her library volunteer friends headed for their cars, giving me a wave as they passed.

"You should make this an annual event," one of them said.

The booths were being torn down now, and parents were rounding up tired children. Ronald and Connor helped stack chairs, and Charlene wheeled her mother, a huge smile on her face and clutching a balloon in the shape of an elephant to her chest, down the path. A flock of Canada geese flew overhead.

"Sam's getting help with the code, is he?" Curtis said. "That's good. Is he here today? I didn't see him."

"He didn't come. Probably still working on the murder."

"Oh yeah. That. I'll ask him to let me know if he learns anything. Just 'cause I'm interested, you know. Civil War history's a hobby of mine."

"Diane said you've been trying to decipher the code page. You're not getting anywhere either?"

"No. It's tough." Curtis shrugged, appearing to lose interest, but the intense expression in his eyes meant he couldn't quite pull off the casual look.

"You're obviously interested in the war itself, but I get the feeling this is something more personal for you, isn't it, Curtis?" That was just a guess on my part. I remembered how at book club he'd talked proudly of his ancestors' participation in the Civil War, how Mrs. Fitzgerald had laughed in his face, and his furious expression.

"Folks around here say my great-great-grandfather was a deserter. That's not true!" Curtis's voice rose. "He had letters, commissions from the army, ordering him to go behind enemy lines. It was dangerous work. The most dangerous. The most valuable. If he'd been found with those orders, they'd have killed him. So he had to bury them. He intended to go back for them later, when the war was won and it was safe."

"But that didn't happen."

"No. He suffered an injury, a blow to the head. He couldn't remember. He died in disgrace not long after the war ended."

Whether that was true or not, and I thought it highly unlikely, it didn't matter. All that mattered was that Curtis believed it was true.

He turned quickly away from me. "What's Diane found to spend her money on now? Time to round her up and get going."

"The map's not helping?" I hoped I was better at pretending causal disinterest than Curtis was.

"Nope. Nothing there I can find." He took one step away from me and then froze momentarily before spinning on his heels and facing me once again. "'Course I only got a quick glimpse of it when we all did."

And the nagging feeling burst out of that quiet spot in the back of my head into my brain.

"No, Curtis. You didn't." I drew up a mental picture. People gathered in Bertie's office, eager to see the diary and its contents. Jeremy, wanting to begin examining it right then and there; Bertie telling him he'd have to wait for Charlene to supervise. Everyone clustered around the desk. Everyone but me, because I let the others get close, thinking I could see it later. And Curtis, who stood against the wall. "I remember now. On Monday at five, when everyone else was jostling at Bertie's desk for the best view of the diary and its contents, you didn't join them, Curtis. You kept yourself too far away to read anything. But at book club the other night, you knew the number seven was drawn in the ocean."

His eyes narrowed, and he gave me a look I didn't care for. "I don't like what you're implying, Lucy. Diane told me what was on the map."

"Diane did no such thing. I don't like to be rude, not too rude anyway, but Diane has no interest in the diary, the map, or the code page. She wouldn't have remembered anything about it, not unless the code had been written on the inside of a diamond ring."

Curtis shifted his sword belt. "You'd be right about that, Lucy, except that someone mentioned the word *treasure*. That got Diane's attention fast enough."

"Perhaps it did. But not enough to memorize the numbers on the map. At that time we were interested in the possible historical significance of the diary. The only reason you can possibly know what's written on the map, Curtis, is because you've looked closely at it. You didn't do that on Monday. No one has a copy." Except me, but I saw no reason to mention that. "Which has to mean you have the original. But it's proving to be of no use to you, as you can't figure out what it means. At first I thought Diane meant you'd been trying to work out the code from the few notes you took when we were looking at it at book club, but that's not it either, is it? You have the original copy of the code page as well as the map, but you can't decipher it. That's why you came to book club, hoping we'd provide the key you need. I should have realized at the time that Diane wouldn't be the least bit interested in talking about *Journey to the Center of the Earth*. Diane doesn't care about books at all. I went to her house after Jonathan died, and she was planning to throw out his entire library to make a bigger room."

Curtis's eyes narrowed. He gripped the hilt of his fake sword and took a step toward me. I took a step back, realizing—too late—that I'd said too much. I should have kept my mouth shut and called the police. I could see Connor and Bertie on the far side of the lawn, chatting to Aunt Ellen and Uncle Amos. Too far away to hear me shout.

I shifted Mom's book to my left hand and fumbled in my pocket for my phone with my right. My fingers closed around it, and I pulled it out.

"Put that away," Curtis said, his voice low and menacing.

I kept my eyes on him as I stepped backward. "Okay. No harm done. We're just talking, right?"

The phone in my hand rang. I was so startled I almost dropped it. Instinctively, without conscious thought, I answered it. "Hello?"

"I've been held up," Sam Watson said. "Are McArthur and Hoskins still—"

"It was Curtis! Curtis has the map. Curtis killed Jeremy!"

In one smooth movement Curtis pulled his sword out of his belt. I hadn't paid much attention to the weapon at his side, assuming it was a wooden or plastic thing like kids waved around at Halloween. But it was a real sword all right, the steel bright and shiny, recently polished, the blade sharp.

I yelped and dropped the book and the phone.

The metal slashed through the air. I screamed and ducked and felt the air move beside my head. I turned and ran. Heavy footsteps pounded the ground behind me.

"Help!" I yelled.

"That Curtis," a woman said as I ran past. "He's always playing soldier."

"Wasn't his great-grandpappy a deserter in the War Between the States?" her companion said.

"That's what they say," a man said.

"Help!" I yelled again.

People stopped what they were doing to watch. Some clapped. They were all smiling.

"I'm not pretending!" I shouted as I rounded a small boy.

"Just a game, son," Curtis said from behind me.

"Go, General, go!" the boy shouted.

As Curtis and I talked, the crowd had largely thinned out, but a few people remained scattered across the lawn, packing up their booths, finishing the last of the snacks from the food truck, chatting to friends.

A group of old men applauded as Curtis and I ran past. "You go, General Gardner. Teach that Yankee not to mess with us Tar Heels."

"It's not a very good historical reenactment," someone said, "if Lucy isn't wearing a costume."

I'd run blindly, without thinking, fleeing the look on Curtis's face and the way he held the sword in his hand. He wasn't going to kill me in front of a couple of dozen people, was he? If he hit me with the sword, and blood began to flow, surely people would realize we weren't playing Yankee versus Rebel?

Of course, by then I might be dead.

I kept running. I was heading away from Butch and Connor and anyone else who might realize I was in trouble, in the direction of the construction zone. The children's toys were plastic, not much use to defend oneself against a real sword. The wire surrounding the earth-moving equipment and the big hole at the base of the lighthouse tower loomed up in front of me. I reached the fence and whirled around, putting my back to the wire. I had nowhere else to go.

Curtis stopped a few feet in front of me. He stared at me, breathing deeply, gripping the hilt of the sword tightly.

"People are watching," I said. "You can't kill me in front of an audience."

"Can't I?" he said. "A little historic rivalry getting out of control. I'll tell them I'm sorry." He lifted the weapon. I shut my eyes.

Chapter Twenty

I opened them at the sound of running footsteps and a high-pitched screech.

A flurry of blue and yellow hit Curtis from behind, knocking him off balance. He twisted around, recovered his footing, lifted his sword and swung, but it was swiftly parried by another sword. No, not a sword. An . . . umbrella?

Blue and yellow silk and satin twirled and spun. Gray wool and gold braid dodged and wove. Curtis was being relentlessly driven back toward the fence, his sword doing nothing but keeping the flurry of blows from the parasol from making a direct hit. I skipped nimbly out of the way as he crashed into the wire. Stunned, he shook his head. The parasol saw its opening and slashed down onto Curtis's right hand. He let out a sharp squeal of pain and dropped the sword.

The umbrella hit him hard on the side of the head, and he fell into a gray heap on the ground.

"Oh my gosh," I said.

Butch and Connor reached us the moment Curtis fell. Connor kicked the sword out of the way while Butch pressed Curtis into the ground with one knee and pulled his arms up behind him. He snapped cuffs on the groaning man.

My legs gave way, and I dropped to the ground.

Louise Jane stood in front of me. Her long skirt was tucked into her belt, her face was flushed, she'd lost her hat, and her hair cascaded out of its pins. She was breathing heavily and a huge smile crossed her face. "You okay, Lucy?"

"I . . . I think so."

"Good." She shifted her parasol to her left hand and held out the right. I took it in mine, and she hauled me to my feet.

Seeing that Butch had control of Curtis, Connor ran for me. He gathered me in his arms and stared into my eyes. "Lucy? Are you okay?"

"I am." I wrapped my arms around Connor's solid bulk and nestled into his embrace. "Thanks to Louise Jane." I looked at her. "Thanks. Where did you learn to do that?"

"Ellen might have failed to mention that one of my mother's most renowned roles was as a pirate queen. The climax of the movie was a long, intense sword-fighting scene, and she practiced long and hard to get it right. She taught me everything she learned." She glanced at Curtis, shaking his head as Butch pulled him to his feet. "I've always hoped I'd get the chance one day to use what I learned. I can't wait to tell her it worked."

"Thank you," Connor said to her.

She nodded in reply.

A circle of people were watching us. Someone broke into applause and others joined in. Beaming, Louise Jane curtsied deeply.

"Cool," Emily Washington said.

"Will you ask her if she'll teach me to do that?" Charlotte asked her mother.

Curtis did not take a bow.

Chapter
Twenty-One

Curtis's once-perfect uniform was covered in dirt, the gold brocade torn, the sash askew, and dust caked his tall black boots. He yelled and screamed and struggled and tried to get away, but he was no match for Butch, particularly not with handcuffs on. He insisted he and I had been play-acting, and for some unimaginable reason begged me to agree.

"He attacked me," I said. "He was trying to kill me. He would have killed me if not for Louise Jane."

Holly Rankin arrived at a run to give Butch a hand.

"Guard that sword," he said to her. "Don't let anyone touch it until a detective gets here."

She stood over the weapon, glaring at the crowd as though daring anyone to try and pick it up. Charlotte crept forward, trying to be unobtrusive. Her mother yanked her back. "I wasn't going to touch it," the girl said. "I just want a look."

"That's mine!" Curtis lunged at Holly. "I demand you give it back to me. Right now."

Butch pulled Curtis's arm. "Let's go, Curtis."

"I demand you unhand me!" Curtis yelled.

"Not likely," Butch said.

Sirens sounded in the distance, getting closer. Blue and red lights broke through the trees. Brakes squealed as cruisers pulled into the parking lot.

Connor kept his arm around me, holding me close. I felt strangely calm. Shock, no doubt, would come later. Louise Jane accepted accolades on her fencing ability. Bertie simply looked baffled, whereas Ronald, in his pirate outfit, fit right in alongside Confederate General Curtis and Antebellum Lady Louise Jane.

Sam Watson ran up the path. He took one look at the crowd and shook his head, and then he turned to the man with Butch. "Curtis? You got anything to say?"

"Arrest them! Louise Jane's lost her mind. She attacked me and Lucy helped her."

"That's not what I saw," a man said. Onlookers murmured agreement.

"I don't know what I saw," someone else said, "but that's a genuine sword you got there, and it's dangerous."

Watson directed uniformed officers to move through the crowd, getting names and phone numbers of people to contact for statements later. He then came over to where Connor and I stood with Louise Jane, Bertie, and Ronald. "What did you try to tell me on the phone about Jeremy Hughes?" he asked me in a low voice.

"Curtis has the original of the map. When I realized that, I knew he must have killed Jeremy to get it."

"Why?" Bertie said.

"Diane said something about the map and code possibly leading to lost military reports from the Civil War era. I believe Curtis hoped these reports would exonerate his much-maligned ancestor."

A woman handed me my phone and the book for my mother. "You dropped these."

I smiled my thanks.

"Lucy and Louise Jane," Watson said. "You'll have to come down to the station to make statements."

"I'll drive them," Connor said.

We began to walk toward the cars. The onlookers stood respectfully back and let us pass.

Butch followed with a still-protesting Curtis.

The crowd shifted momentarily and I caught a glimpse of pink Chanel cowering in the back as, for once in her life, Diane Uppiton tried to be unobtrusive. "Diane!" I called. "Stop right there. You have to have known something about this."

As one, the multitude turned to face her. Diane attempted to smile. "Me? I don't know a thing. What have you gotten yourself into now, Curtis?"

"Diane!" Curtis screamed. "Tell them! Tell them it was your idea."

"It was nothing of the sort. Don't you try to pin your foolishness on me, Curtis Gardner." She glanced at the onlookers, seeking support. "Don't believe anything he says. I was about to end our relationship. He's out to get revenge on me."

"I didn't get the impression ten minutes ago that anything was wrong with your relationship," I said.

"I was being polite in public," she replied, "as befits a proper lady. Never make a scene, my mother always taught me."

Beside me, Louise Jane snorted.

"I'm sorry, but I have another appointment," Diane said. "Can't be late. So sorry. If you need my help, Detective, you know where to find me, I'm sure." Diane threw Watson what she probably intended to be a flirtatious grin.

"You'll have to miss your appointment, Mrs. Uppiton," Watson said.

"It rained heavily early in the evening on Monday," I said, "but not until after the five o'clock meeting had broken up and everyone left. I went into town, and when I got back, Jeremy's car was in the parking lot. Other than mine, his was the only car there." I kept my eyes on Diane. The slash of deep red lipstick stood out in a face gone very pale. "Jeremy Hughes himself was inside the lighthouse, and he obviously had not come alone. The police found one set of distinctive tire tracks in the mud. They were able to locate the person those tracks belong to and that person has been cleared of any wrongdoing."

"Not before time," Louise Jane harrumphed.

Ronald threw her a questioning look. "What have you been up to Louise Jane?"

"Saving the day, it would seem," she replied smugly.

"Connor McNeil's car also left prints in the mud, as did the emergency vehicles," I said. "But whoever had been with Jeremy inside the lighthouse got away without leaving tire tracks behind them. The police searched the entire parking lot. That means Jeremy's killer didn't drive him or herself. I suppose they could have walked back, but it's a long, long way to town, isn't it, Diane?"

She threw Watson a panicked look. "I don't know what you're implying, Lucy. Poor dear, you're not yourself. You've obviously had a shock."

"I've been wondering about that," Watson said. "How Jeremy's killer managed to get away without leaving tracks behind him."

"You were quick enough," Louise Jane said with a sniff, "to accuse someone else of being the killer because you followed their tracks."

"Will you shush, Louise Jane," Bertie whispered. "This is not the time to complicate things."

"Only making my point," Louise Jane said.

"When I interviewed you about the night Jeremy Hughes died," Watson said, "you stated that you had dinner with your mother, left her house at nine thirty, and drove yourself directly home. You claimed you didn't go out again. Do you have anything to add to that statement, Mrs. Uppiton?"

Diane's eyes were wide. She searched the faces of the crowd, looking for support. No one moved. Even the children had fallen silent. "I . . . I . . ."

"Accessory to murder," Connor said, "is a serious charge."

"I didn't know he'd killed anyone!" she yelled. "He told me he'd gone to the library with Jeremy to try to have another look at the diary, but no one was there. Jeremy suggested they break in, and Curtis wanted no part of it."

"That's right," Curtis said. "I left him knocking on the door of the library. How was I to know he'd go and get himself killed?"

"It was raining," Diane said. "I picked Curtis up at the end of the road. He was soaked right through. I didn't think anything of it."

"When you heard the next day that Jeremy had been killed, you didn't think I might want to know you'd been there?" Watson said.

"I—I didn't realize. I thought someone else must have killed him after Curtis left. Curtis told me I wasn't to tell anyone he'd been there with Jeremy. I didn't want to get involved. He told me it was an accident!"

Curtis pulled himself out of Butch's grip and hurled himself at Diane. She screamed and leapt behind a shocked Grace. Grace yelped.

Sam Watson grabbed Curtis's arm and almost yanked him off his feet.

Curtis spat at Diane. "You're lying. It was all your idea. I only did what you told me to do."

"You said the map led to Civil War treasure," Diane said. "You told me if we found it first, we could have it all." Once again, Diane took in the circle of onlookers. "You have to believe me. I didn't know he was going to kill someone. I was only trying to help." She glared at Curtis. "And then, with all your fancy talk about treasure maps and jewels, you couldn't even read the blasted thing. I never should have believed you."

Watson took her arm. "Diane Uppiton," he said, "I am arresting you."

* * *

Louise Jane and I made our statements, and then we were allowed to leave the police station with Connor. Watson walked us to the door. "I don't think," the detective said dryly, "I'm going to have a lot of trouble making my case. Diane is confirming that Curtis phoned her that night saying he needed a lift, and she picked him up at the end of the lighthouse road. Curtis is saying he killed Jeremy in self-defense because they fought over the items, but Diane put him up to trying to steal them. He seems to think that's some sort of defense."

"What will happen to Diane?" I asked.

"She'll be charged, at a minimum, with being an accessory after the fact and lying to the police. Curtis is saying the theft was her idea, but that doesn't really matter. Not if we can't prove she was present at the break-in and the subsequent murder."

"He must have thought he could decode the page, and the map would lead him to buried treasure," Connor said. "What a fool."

"Not treasure," I said. "I suspect he told Diane that so she'd think of gold and jewels, but he was hoping to find some lost military report that would exonerate his ancestor."

"He was somewhat overconfident of his own cleverness," Louise Jane said. "Considering the best minds in the Outer Banks have been trying for days to decipher the code with no success."

"Do you include yourself in that group, Louise Jane?" Connor asked.

"Naturally," she replied. She gathered the tatters of her gown around her. It was torn in several places, but, as she told me, it was easily fixed, as it was a movie costume made to come apart easily.

* * *

As I said from the very beginning, all we needed was the key.

Watson phoned Bertie first thing the next morning, and Bertie immediately called Charlene and me. I left my apartment without even showering or having breakfast.

Last night, the police had searched Curtis and Diane's house, and found the original map and code page. Watson was inviting us to down to the police station to see them.

The sun was rising over the ocean as three excited librarians gathered in the interview room at the police station.

"Before we see them," I said, "I've got one last question. We've figured out why Curtis wanted the code page and map, but I don't see why he killed Jeremy. Fueled by a couple of drinks, they went to the library together, broke in, and took the pages. But then they fought and Jeremy died. Curtis said it was self-defense. Why would Curtis have to defend himself against Jeremy?"

"From what I can make out," Watson said, "all Jeremy wanted was to examine the papers first and somehow get one over on the historical society. Curtis had other plans. He wanted to take the pages and use them to find the supposed lost military documents himself. Jeremy laughed at Curtis's story of his ancestors' army papers. Curtis didn't like that. And one thing led to another."

"Poor Jeremy," Charlene said.

Watson opened the top drawer of the table, took out two sheets of paper wrapped in plastic, and laid them on the table in front of us.

"This is evidence we'll need for Curtis's trial," Watson said. "So you can't touch the papers themselves, but I knew you'd like to have a peek."

We stared at the pages, so familiar from the photos I'd taken and printed out and pondered over long into the night.

"I was hoping," Charlene said with a sigh, "there'd be something so faded it didn't show up in the photo. But I don't see anything like that."

"No," Bertie said.

"What about the back? Maybe something's written there," I said. "Can you turn them over, Sam?"

He did. First he turned the code page. It was blank. Then he flipped the map over, and we saw it immediately. The writing was very faint, aged with time, but legible. Watson handed me a magnifying glass and I put it to my eye and leaned in while Bertie and Charlene held their breath.

8559
9360

"Eight five five nine," I said. "And nine three six zero."

Watson groaned. "Not another puzzle."

"It's got to be significant," Charlene said. "Every piece brings us closer to solving it."

"But what do you suppose it means?" Bertie said. "Map coordinates? Longitude and latitude?"

"If so, that's nowhere around here," Watson said. "More like near the North Pole, if my college geography holds up."

"They might be dates," I said. "August fifth eighteen fifty nine?"

"September third eighteen sixty," Bertie said.

We took a collective breath.

"Those dates appear in Mrs. Crawbingham's diary," Charlene said. "I don't recall anything exceptional about them, though."

"Thanks, Detective," I said.

"We might be back," Bertie said.

"Have a nice day," Charlene said.

We rushed for the door.

"You're not going anywhere without me." Watson ran after us. Butch Greenblatt was at his desk. Holly Rankin stood over him, pointing at something on his computer. Butch jumped to his feet with a cry. "You've solved it!" He hurried after us. Rankin fell into step behind him.

Startled officers and civilian clerks watched the six of us falling all over one another to get to the doors.

"I'm calling Connor," I said. "He'll want to know."

Charlene and I had come with Bertie. We leapt into her car, and she tore out of the police station.

Charlene twisted around and looked out the back window. "Sam's right behind us. Oh, and Butch has grabbed a cruiser. Better slow down, Bertie."

Bertie eased off the gas. "It would be just like Sam Watson to have me arrested for speeding so he could get to the diary first."

"We can play at that game also," Charlene said. "If he tries to pass us, I'll report him for driving dangerously."

I checked behind us. "Connor's coming down the town hall steps. He's running for his car."

We drove in a stately procession of four vehicles to the Lighthouse Library, sticking exactly to the speed limit.

It was early and the library wasn't open yet. Bertie unlocked the door, and we stumbled in.

I'd let Charles out of my apartment when I left, not even stopping to give him his breakfast. His blue eyes opened wide at the sight of the crowd with me.

"I'll get the key," Bertie shouted. She headed for her office, and the rest of us, including Charles, pounded up the back stairs to the rare books room, where we waited impatiently for the door to be unlocked. Charles waited impatiently for me to remember that a cat needs sustenance.

"Are you sure you've solved it?" Connor asked.

"No," I said. "But we have a solid clue."

"I'm looking forward to seeing this map," Holly Rankin said, "that everyone's been talking about."

I patted my pockets. We'd had to leave the originals behind, but I had the printouts with me.

Bertie unlocked the door, and we fell into the room.

"No pushing or shoving, everyone," Bertie said. "As Charlene is the expert on historical documents, we'll let her handle the book."

Bertie unlocked the cabinet. Charlene slipped white gloves on and slowly, carefully got Mrs. Crawbingham's diary and laid it out.

Charles leapt onto the table. Charlene shrieked. I scooped him up and tapped his little nose. "Not for you." I put him outside and shut the door against his protests.

Charlene turned the pages slowly and carefully. My heart pounded with excitement.

August 5, 1859: Wind is high.

We let out a collective sigh of disappointment. I felt my entire body deflate.

"I was hoping for something more meaningful," Bertie said.

"It was a windy day?" Holly said. "What does that mean?"

"It means," Butch said, "that it was a windy day."

"Try the other date," Bertie said, and Charlene turned the pages.

Sept 3, 1860. Rain is heavy at 2:08.

"It's raining?" Watson said. "I have to confess I was expecting something more dramatic than that."

"I hoped . . ." Bertie said.

"I guess we'll never know," Connor said. "Some secrets are meant to be hidden after all."

"The wind is high," Charlene said.

I rolled the words around in my mouth. And then I had it. No!" I said. "Not *the* wind. But wind. Wind is high: *w* is *h*."

"Yes!" Charlene shouted. "That's got to be it."

"Be what?" Butch said.

I grabbed a piece of paper out of the printer next to the desk. I wrote so quickly my hands shook.

$w = h$

$x = i$

$y = j$

"It is a substitution code!" Charlene shouted. "And

we have it. Give me a piece of paper, Lucy." I handed her one.

We both started writing as fast as we could.

"Oh my gosh," Connor said as proper English words and sentences began to form on the page. "It actually works."

Some of the words were incomplete, missing vowels or double consonants, words ran together, or were broken in random places. But essentially, this is what we wrote:

My beloved Aunt Petal's youngest son died when he was swept away in a flash flood. A year later she was widowed when a sudden storm brought down a tree on the plantation where we lived and killed her husband. She became obsessed after that day with recording the weather. Even after war broke out and we escaped and headed north, she continued her strange habit.

We started at a tap on the door. It opened, and Ronald's curly gray head popped around the corner. Charles took advantage of the opportunity to sneak between his legs. "What on earth is going on? What are all you people doing here? It's past opening time. Are we opening today, Bertie?"

"We've found the key," Bertie said.

"The key to the code? Really? That's great."

"Really. Go ahead and open. Will you mind the desk, please? I'll let you know what we've found as soon as I can."

Once again I grabbed Charles and shoved him at Ronald. "And can you feed this ravenous beast, please?"

Ronald took the cat. "Sure." His head withdrew. "Never a dull day at the Bodie Island Lighthouse Library," he muttered as he descended the stairs.

I continued translating.

She insists that her beautiful journal was given to her

by her mistress as a gift. I do not know if that is true, but
such is possible as her owners were kind people who taught
her to read and write. And so she taught me.

A slave family," Butch said.

"Sounds like it," Bertie said.

"Crawbingham," Charlene said. "I found a record of
a plantation family in Louisiana with that name. Sometimes slaves took the surnames of their owners."

Suddenly, the words stopped making sense, and
Charlene and I were writing lines of gibberish.

"What does that mean?" Watson asked, as he stud-
ded a row of jumbled letters.

"The substitution has changed," Charlene said.
"Let's try the other date."

Sept 3, 1860. Rain is heavy at 2:08.

"*R* equals *h*," I said. "That seems to work."

"Let's just hope he didn't change the code again,"
Charlene said. "We have no other clues."

We set to the translation once more.

Aunt Petal went to her reward last night. I hope she
finds peace and is reunited with those she loved. I know she
would not mind her journal being put to good use. And so I
will use it to help my children find their inheritance. If such
becomes necessary.

I have hidden the land grant in a field near where they
are building the new lighthouse. I sense danger approaching.
The old man is on his deathbed, and his son is getting desper-
ate. The fire in my boat shed was not an accident. I was
lucky to get out unharmed.

"Oh my gosh," Charlene said. "Someone's trying to kill
him."

"A one-hundred-and-fifty-year-old attempted murder case," Watson said. "Bring it on!"

I may have hidden it too well. My sons will need to be

able to find it if I am not here to show them. Aunt Petal's journal will be their guide along with a map my daughter drew for me as part of her schoolwork.

I will place a box containing Aunt Petal's journal at map point 2.

We scrambled for the map.

Connor pressed his finger to the number two. "This has got to be the lighthouse. The map's not entirely accurate, but this place looks about right, and most importantly it's where we found the diary."

They are starting work on the new lighthouse. I will go there tomorrow, on Sunday when the workers will not be around, and bury the box to keep it safe until I need it. Or until it is safe to reveal its location to my sons.

From point 2, walk 30 years to the east.

"Thirty years?" Butch said.

"He must mean thirty yards," I said. "We're translating as fast as we can, and a lot of letters are missing or words run together."

"Which would be part of the reason we couldn't decipher the code earlier," Connor said.

And there I have buried the hopes of the future of my family.

We looked at each other. Then the stampede for the door began.

We galloped down the stairs and through the library. It was shortly after nine, so not many people were around. What patrons there were came out from the stacks and fell into step behind us. One woman was sitting in the wingback chair with Charles on her lap. She leapt to her feet and clutched the cat to her chest. Ronald stared at us, open-mouthed. Then he also ran after us.

"I have a severe sense of déjà vu," I said to Connor.

"Never a dull day, as I believe someone recently said," he replied.

As we emerged from the library, Louise Jane's rusty van pulled to a stop in the parking lot, and she leapt out. She fell in beside me. "So you broke the code, did you? Looks like I arrived in the nick of time."

"How did you find out?" I asked.

She tapped the side of her nose. "I have my sources, Lucy."

I assumed someone had called to tell her about the mad dash out of the police station and the town offices parking lot. Louise Jane's network of contacts and informers rivaled that of the FBI.

George's crew was hard at work this morning. Jackhammers rattled, men called to one another, dust flew. George and his son were standing off to one side, consulting an iPad.

"Zack!" I yelled. "We need you. Get men and all the shovels you can find."

"What the heck's going on?" George demanded.

"We've cracked the code," Bertie said.

"You mean it really is buried treasure?" George asked.

His men dropped their tools; library patrons whispered among themselves. The word *treasure* spread. Charles meowed.

"Treasure of a sort," Charlene said, "but not gold or jewels."

"It's buried thirty yards east of where you found the first box," Connor said.

The workers stared at George. They stared at one another. Then they ran for picks and shovels. Zack calculated the distance and led the way, holding his iPad in front of him as we fanned out behind. Police officers, library patrons, librarians, the mayor of Nags Head, construction workers, assorted interested persons, and one big cat trotted after Zack.

"Makes me think of the story of the Pied Piper," Connor said. "I hope none of us will never be seen again."

I squeezed his hand.

The land around the lighthouse is flat and low lying, and the ground is soft. No trees, bushes, or rock formations create landmarks. Thirty yards brought us just short of the boardwalk winding through the marsh to the calm waters of Roanoke Sound. A handful of birdwatchers and hikers were out this morning. They gave the strange group questioning looks but carried on about their business. The backhoe trundled after us, and it was maneuvered into position.

"Are you sure it's safe to use that?" Bertie asked George. "We don't want to damage anything."

"It'll loosen the surface," he said, "and then we can dig by hand."

"We might have to cover a fair bit of ground," Connor said. "Whoever buried whatever this is wouldn't have had the benefit of GPS technology like Zack here does. He could have been off by a few degrees."

"You do realize," I whispered to Bertie, "that we've left the library unattended."

"Do you want to go back and watch the desk?" she asked me.

I recoiled. "No!"

"Nor, I think, does anyone else."

A flock of ducks lifted off from the marsh. Charles tilted his head to watch them go. No doubt he was seeing treasure of another sort. "Don't put Charles down," I called to the woman holding him.

"Has anyone considered," Charlene said, "that the letter writer came back and dug up whatever he'd buried without bothering to get the box with the diary first?"

"I don't want to even think that," Louise Jane said.

"We'll find out soon enough," Ronald said.

The backhoe broke the surface of the earth, and the men moved in. Connor threw his jacket onto the ground, rolled up his sleeves, and grabbed a shovel. Sam Watson did the same. Butch didn't bother to loosen his sleeves.

"It shouldn't be far down," Bertie said. "The box with the diary was buried quite deep because it was put in a hole that had already been dug."

"Can't you dig any faster?" Holly Rankin said to Butch. "Give me that."

"Get your own shovel," he said.

She did so.

They only worked for a few minutes before Connor yelled, "I've hit something." He threw down his shovel and dropped to his knees.

Everyone gathered around and leaned in. The hole he'd dug wasn't more than two feet deep. At the bottom, metal gleamed in the light of the sun.

"Lucy?" Connor said. "Why don't you do the honors?"

I glanced at Bertie. She gave me a nod. I crouched down. Connor and I brushed dirt away to reveal a tin box. I reached in and lifted it up. It was slightly smaller than the one we'd found at the base of the lighthouse but made of the same material and around the same age.

Once again, I carried a box up the steps to the library, followed by an eager pack of onlookers.

"Take it into my office, Lucy," Bertie said. She turned to face the crowd, planted her feet apart, and crossed her arms over her chest. "Sorry to bother you, everyone—please return to your business."

"Time is money," George bellowed. "If my men aren't back outside ASAP, I'll dock your pay. And that includes you, Zackary."

"Which presumes you actually pay me," Zack mumbled. But he left quickly enough, followed by the rest of the work crew.

"That goes for you two as well," Watson said to Butch and Holly.

"I was hoping to see what all the fuss is about," Holly said.

"I'm sure you'll hear about it soon enough," Watson said.

"Mrs. Cartwright," Ronald said, "I can help you find that book you were asking about."

Eventually only Sam Watson, Connor, Charlene, and I went with Bertie into her office.

And Louise Jane, of course. Somehow Louise Jane is always able to place herself exactly where she wants to be. At that, she's even better than Charles, who'd tried to slip in unnoticed. I'd been too fast for him, and he was left in the hallway, whining plaintively.

I put the box on Bertie's desk. She gave me a nod and I opened it.

No treasure lay within. No gold or jewels or Spanish doubloons. Just two pieces of yellow paper.

Charlene handed me white cotton gloves. I put them on and took out the pages and laid them on the desk. The top one was in the same handwriting as the coded letter that had led us such a merry dance but—thank heavens—it was not in code.

I began to read.

It is not my intention to write here the story of our family and how we came to be in Roanoke. Another day, perhaps. The war is over and the Freedmen's Colony where we made our home has been broken. We have been betrayed. Many have left. I have decided to stay. I have been granted a piece of land by Mr. Ethan Monaghan and intend to claim it when the time comes. I have hidden the land grant in fear that his son Zebadiah will try to kill me rather than see me get a share of his inheritance. I know he will try to overturn his father's wishes. He has many rich and powerful friends. Mr. Monaghan lies on his deathbed, and he cannot help me now. Once Mr. Monaghan is dead, I will produce my document for the court.

Signed Thaddeus Washington

We were silent for a long time. The faint sounds of people moving about and chatting in the library came through the walls. Charles had given up hope and gone in search of more friendly company.

"Wow," Bertie said.

"That's incredible," Connor said.

"Thaddeus Washington was an ancestor of Neil Washington, who lives in Nags Head," I said. "Neil's wife, Janelle, told me that. She also told me the family had been part of the Freedmen's Colony. She'll want to see this."

"What does the other letter say?" Watson asked.

I opened it. It was dated April 22, 1871.

"Work on the lighthouse started on June 13 of that year," Louise Jane said.

Before I began to read, I glanced at the signature at the bottom of the page: *Ethan Monaghan.*

I gave the paper to Connor. "You're the mayor, and I think you're about to have a very hot political potato on your hands."

Connor read. "It seems that Thaddeus Washington saved the life of Ethan Monaghan's daughter when she fell off a boat into the sea. In gratitude Mr. Monaghan has left a section of land to Thaddeus and his heirs."

"What land? Does it say?" Watson asked.

"I recognize the coordinates. I should, I've been reading enough about them lately. It's that patch of land along the shore to the north of the Monaghan house. Not a particularly large tract, but enough for Thaddeus to build a home for his family and some outbuildings from which he could run his business. It doesn't say what that business was."

"He was a boat builder, Janelle told me." I said.

"You're saying this document proves that the heirs of Thaddeus Washington own some of the land Rick Monaghan wants to build his golf resort on?" Watson said. "That is a political hot potato, Connor. Is this paper valid, do you think?"

"I've no idea," Connor said. "That will be for the courts to sort out. The paper is signed and dated, so it should have some validity."

Louise Jane turned to me. "I hope you're prepared to admit that I was right all along."

"Right about what?"

"The spirits did communicate with us. Like I told you they would."

"We found an old letter. Not phantasmal scribblings on the walls or disembodied hands leading us on."

"Regardless of the method, the result was the same. Messages sent from worlds beyond our own."

"Nonsense," I said.

"The spirits work in mysterious ways. Have you considered that if Curtis hadn't stolen the code page, we might never have turned it over and thus found the key?"

"I think we would have figured that out eventually, LJ," Charlene said. "We didn't need any help. We only needed the real document."

"Which is neither here nor there," Bertie said, "as we have it now. Take this into custody, Sam. I do not want this piece of paper in my library one minute longer. Not if it's likely to be fought over."

"Not before I take a picture," I said.

"Be sure you get both sides, Lucy," Louise Jane said. "Just in case."

Chapter
Twenty-Two

A t that moment Sam Watson's phone beeped with an incoming text. He glanced at it and then gave us a grin.

"Curtis's lawyer has arrived. It seems Mr. Gardner wants to talk to me. Diane Uppiton has also lawyered up. I suspect I have an interesting day ahead of me. I'll take this box with me and put it someplace safe."

"I'll call Janelle Washington," I said, "and let her know it might be of some interest to them."

"I'll talk to Rick Monaghan," Connor said. "You'll probably be able to hear him yelling from here."

"You can tell people we found some interesting personal letters from the immediate postwar era," Bertie said, "but please provide no details. It's up to the families concerned if they want to take this further."

"Understood," I said. "The Washingtons don't have much money. I can't see that they'll be able to mount a court challenge against Monaghan and his company."

"Bankers are a proud people and respectful of our history," Louise Jane said. "All of our history, including the bad parts. I think the community will come down awful strong on the side of Thaddeus's heirs."

"That remains to be seen," Bertie said. "Let's get back to work everyone."

I walked Connor to the door, conscious of the library patrons watching us.

He gave me his private grin. "Life with you, Lucy Richardson, is never boring."

"Sometimes," I said, "I wish it could be just a little bit less exciting."

His blue eyes twinkled. "Never."

* * *

Sam Watson returned to the library at closing time. He'd called Connor and invited him to come too.

We gathered in the main room. Bertie pulled up the wingback chair; Charlene sat behind the circulation desk. Ronald leaned against the wall, and I stood next to Connor. Watson faced us. Charles sat on a shelf next to Watson's shoulder, as eager as the rest of us to hear what he had to say.

"I feel like I'm between the pages of a Lord Peter Wimsey novel," I said. "All the characters have gathered in the library, eagerly waiting for the detective to make the big reveal."

"All the characters except for the accused," Watson said, "which is why I'm here. I figured you'd want to know the most recent developments. Curtis is claiming self-defense. He admits that he was here, at the library, with Jeremy that night. They'd met at a bar in town, as we knew, and had a couple of drinks. Far more than the one he'd told me about in his initial statement."

"Imagine that," Ronald said.

"As they drank, Jeremy got increasingly angry at being, in his words, 'kicked out of the library to wait for'—again in his words—'some flit of a girl' to let him examine the documents. He decided he wasn't going to stand for that, and he'd go back to the library and demand to be let in."

"Curtis agreed and they drove to the library together in Jeremy's car. Now, according to Curtis, when he realized the library was closed and no one was around, he wanted to leave."

"Totally believable," Connor said sarcastically.

"That will be up to a judge and jury to decide," Watson said. "Fortunately, not me. It just so happened that Jeremy had a sledgehammer in the trunk of his car."

"Why?" Bertie asked. "He didn't seem the handyman type to me."

"Apparently he was. His wife tells us he liked to fix things around the house. She added that she usually had to call a contractor to unfix them. We found a well-stocked tool box in his car and similar items in the garage."

"You didn't tell me that," I said. "I was wondering where the sledgehammer came from."

"I don't tell you a lot of things, Lucy," Watson said.

I pondered that for a few moments.

"Jeremy got the hammer and broke down the door. Curtis, according to Curtis, was appalled, but he followed Jeremy into the library in order to prevent him from doing more damage."

"That worked well," Ronald said.

"Jeremy then forced open Bertie's desk. When Curtis realized that rather than just looking at the papers, Jeremy intended to steal them, he tried to stop him. They fought"—Watson glanced at Louise Jane—"meaning pushing and shoving at each other and knocking things over. No injuries were found on Jeremy's face, nor on his hands, which is why we discontinued that line of investigation."

Louise Jane smirked.

"Jeremy fell and hit his head," Watson continued. "Panicked at what he'd done, Curtis fled the library, calling Diane to come and pick him up."

"What, the documents just happened to fall into his pocket?" Bertie said.

"He claims he grabbed them from Jeremy and in his panic took them with him."

"Hogwash," Bertie said.

"I'm inclined to agree," Watson said. "He might well have panicked, and he probably did, but he took the documents with him."

"But he didn't show much interest in the pages," I said, "Not when everyone was here. It was his obvious disinterest that first clued me into suspecting his guilt. What do you suppose changed?"

"After a few drinks," Watson said, "Jeremy, who should have known better, told Curtis the map might lead to a cache of previously undiscovered Civil War documents. It was Jeremy's idea to steal the map and follow to where it led, but it was easy enough, I suspect, to get Curtis to agree to the plan. All of which is largely irrelevant. I don't know what caused the men to argue and get into a fight, but not only did Curtis not report to the police when he'd sobered up and calmed down, he tried to use the documents to his own end. He came to your book club, pretending to know nothing about their whereabouts, and joined the discussion about cracking the code. I think we have a pretty solid case."

"What did he hope to do with the pages if he did manage to crack the code?" Bertie asked.

"Curtis's family has long maintained that their ancestor wasn't a deserter, as everyone believes, but instead an army spy pretending to be a traitor to the cause. They claimed letters that could prove such had been lost."

"When we first saw the pages," I said, "Louise Jane suggested they might lead to a report a spy had had to bury. Curtis didn't seem all that interested at the time, but I bet he said something to Jeremy about his ancestor when they talked later, and Jeremy played it up."

"What a fool," Connor said.

"Knowing Curtis," Charlene said, "I'll guess he didn't bother with the diary because he thought it nothing but the ramblings of a fisherman's wife. A foolish assumption on his part. Therein lay the beginning of the trail."

"What about Diane?" I asked. "What's she saying?"

"She says she didn't tell me she'd picked him up on the library road because I didn't ask. She told me, in her words, 'a little white lie' because Curtis had asked her to. She didn't ask when word got around about the documents missing."

"That I believe," I said. "She didn't show much interest when they came to book club. She is, if I may be honest, not very smart and not very observant, and not at all interested in anything to do with anyone else. She did what he asked her to do because she didn't bother to think it through."

"Diane has been released on bail," Watson said. "Curtis has been denied."

"I'll give Eunice Fitzgerald a call," Bertie said. "She might want to suggest Diane step down from the library board."

"Now," Watson said, "who'd like to go into town for a drink? My treat to thank you all, Lucy in particular, for a job well done."

Charles was the first to reach the door.

Chapter Twenty-Three

Two weeks later, I was standing on the library steps with Connor, when Janelle Washington and the twins arrived. Connor had been in a budget meeting with Bertie, and I'd stepped outside with him to get some air and enjoy a quick private moment together in the middle of the day.

The girls made a beeline for the children's construction area. Today was the last day for it. The real work was finished. George and Zack and their crew had packed up all their equipment and driven away, leaving only a scarred patch of earth and a gigantic bill. The landscapers were due to arrive tomorrow to put the lawn back together, and Ronald and his volunteers would take down the play area.

The man with Janelle walked slowly, tilting to one side. Lines of pain were etched into his face, but his dark eyes glowed with warmth as he watched the girls greet Ronald and the other children.

"Good afternoon," I said. "Lovely day." The sun was warm on my face and a light salty breeze stirred my hair.

"It is," Janelle said. "Lucy, Connor. I don't think you've met my husband, Neil."

We shook hands. Neil's grip was solid—strong but friendly. "My girls have been talking about nothing but this play area for weeks," he said. "I think I have two new crew bosses in my family. Grimshaw Contracting had better watch out."

I smiled and we watched the children play for a few minutes.

"I wanted to come and meet you," Neil said. "To thank you for all you did for my family."

"I did nothing, really. We were all desperate to find out what was in that coded letter. What's happening now?"

"It's going to take a long, long time to sort out," he said. "Rick Monaghan has, as you can expect, surrounded himself with lawyers."

Connor put his arm around my shoulders. "Some of Monaghan's backers on the resort project are getting cold feet and pulling out. They don't want anything to do with a protracted legal battle. I'm cautiously hopeful that'll put an end to the project once and for all."

"He offered us money if we'd drop our claim," Janelle said.

"Might not be a bad idea," Connor said. "This could last a long time."

Neil shook his head firmly. "My family's been waiting for a hundred and fifty years. It isn't up to me to take the money and let it go."

Janelle smiled at her husband. "We're thinking it would be a lovely spot to have an oceanfront B&B. But early days yet."

"Do you know what happened to Thaddeus Washington?" I asked. "Why he never went back to get his land grant?"

"Thaddeus was my great-great-grandfather," Neil said. "My great-grandfather was his oldest son, John. Thaddeus disappeared when John was twelve."

"Disappeared?" Connor asked.

"Yup. Went out in his boat one calm June night in 1871, telling his wife he'd be back in a couple hours. Boat washed up a few weeks later. Thaddeus was never seen again. My great-great-grandma was left with five kids under twelve and no husband."

"You think . . ." I said.

"We think Zebadiah Monaghan killed him. Probably the very night Thaddeus buried the map to the land grant. Family story goes that his eldest son, John, was supposed to go out with his daddy that night, but he'd fallen and twisted his ankle earlier. It's likely Thaddeus was going to show John where to find the papers. But he never got a chance." Neil's face darkened.

"A sad story," I said.

"No sadder than many others," Janelle said. "We have two pieces of good news."

"You tell them, hon," Neil said. "Watching all that digging going on makes me want to join in."

We watched him limp away. His daughters squealed in delight when they saw him approaching.

"What?" I said. "Don't keep us in suspense."

"First, Cheryl Monaghan has left the real estate company where I work, so I don't have to worry about her any longer. Things were getting tense, to say the least, between us."

"Why did she quit?"

"Rick's company has had to lay off some support staff as he tightens his belt, so she's gone to help out. She wasn't a very good realtor in the first place."

"And the other news?"

"Best of all. Our story hit the papers."

I nodded. "Big time." It must have been a slow week for news. The story of a long-hidden land grant, a mysterious disappearance, and a generations-old family feud got a lot of attention in the national media.

"A TV production company called us. They're doing a major multipart documentary on the history of black families in the Civil War. The Freedmen's Colony is going to be a big part of that. They've hired Neil as a consultant. Imagine that! He loves nothing more than to tell stories passed down through his family, and he's going to be paid to do it. And now we have Thaddeus's letters to add."

"That's great. I can't wait to see the program."

She laughed. "Neil Washington, TV star! There'll be no living with that man now. We've also been approached by another movie producer who's considering making a movie about Thaddeus, Ethan, and Zebadiah. He's going to pay us what he calls an option on our story. Meaning money whether or not the movie goes ahead."

"It's quite the story," I said. "I can see it making a great movie. I assume Zebadiah will be the villain. I can't see that helping Rick's development project any. Can I have a part? I can play the local librarian, sticking her nose in everything."

"And I'll play the mayor," Connor said, "but only if I can be a bad guy. I've always fancied having a mustache I could twirl."

We turned at a scream of laughter. Neil had plopped one of the bright pink construction hats on his head and picked up a tiny shovel.

"Dig, Daddy, dig!" Charlotte cried while Emily clapped her hands in delight.

"If they keep going like that," I said to Janelle, "they might well find the passage to the center of the earth."

"Nothing," she said, "would surprise me." She went inside the library, leaving Connor and me alone on the steps once again.

We looked out over the lawn, the children's play area, the scarred earth soon to be repaired, the boardwalk to the marsh, the long line of tall red pine trees. A flock of Canada geese flew overhead, calling to stragglers to keep up, and children laughed.

"I don't think you'd make a very convincing villain," I said at last.

"Probably not. All that mustache twirling must get tiring." He took a deep breath. "Lucy, I—"

The door behind us flew open. "Connor!" Louise Jane shouted. "Bertie tells me you've approved an expenditure for a fall series of historical lectures. You know my rates are entirely reasonable." She grabbed his arm. "Not to mention my breadth of knowledge. As you're not doing anything right now, let's go to Josie's and talk about it over a coffee. I haven't had lunch yet."

She dragged Connor away. I gave a brief thought to wondering what he might have been about to say when Louise Jane interrupted him and decided there was no point in speculating. I laughed and went back to work.

Author's Note

In order to make Lucy's descent toward the center of the earth more dramatic, I have taken liberties with details of the foundations of the Bodie Island Lighthouse.

The Bodie Island Lighthouse is a real historic lighthouse, located in Cape Hatteras National Seashore on the Outer Banks of North Carolina. It is still a working lighthouse, protecting ships from the Graveyard of the Atlantic, and the public is invited to tour it and climb the two hundred fourteen steps to the top. The view from up there is well worth the trip. But the lighthouse does not contain a library, nor is it large enough to house a collection of books, offices, staff rooms, two staircases, and even an apartment.

Within these books, the interior of the lighthouse is the product of my imagination. I like to think of it as my version of the TARDIS, from the TV show *Doctor Who*, or Hermione Granger's beaded handbag: far larger inside than it appears from the outside.

I hope it is large enough for your imagination also.

Read an excerpt from

A DEATH LONG OVERDUE

the next

LIGHTHOUSE LIBRARY MYSTERY

by EVA GATES

available soon in hardcover from
Crooked Lane Books

CROOKED
LANE

NEW YORK

Chapter One

Reunions can be tricky things. Everyone involved approaches the gathering bursting with excitement and full of high expectations. Sometimes it turns out well: friends reconnect, photos of children and grandchildren are shared and exclaimed over, accomplishments praised, new friends made, and old enemies reconciled. Sometimes—not. Long-buried grievances are given fresh air, friendships doubted, old jealousies and resentments remembered, and new ones discovered.

Everyone goes home miserable and tells their loved ones they had a marvelous time.

Ten years later they do it all again.

I don't actually know this from personal experience. I missed my high school class's tenth reunion because it was the same weekend as my second brother's wedding. I would have preferred to attend the reunion. My brothers and I are not close, but family is family, my mother says when it suits her to think so. Besides, my sister in-law has no sisters or female cousins, so I had to be a bridesmaid. I'll never forgive her for that frilly shocking-pink dress I was forced to wear. I'm short enough that I looked like a cartoon character in it. The humidity had done its work on my curly dark hair, adding to the cartoon aspect, and the color didn't go well with the bad case of sunburn I'd suffered the weekend before.

Last year, I missed my college's tenth reunion because I'd just arrived here, in the Outer Banks, to take up the post of assistant director of the Bodie Island Lighthouse Library. Everyone wrote to tell me they'd had a marvelous time.

Right now, I was sincerely hoping Bertie James's fortieth reunion to mark her class's first day of undergrad studies would turn out to be the success she was expecting.

"Our exhibit might not exactly be worthy of the Bodleian," Charlene Clayton said, referring to the great English library where she'd worked for a few years, "but it's impressive enough."

"Speaking as a North Carolinian," Bertie replied, "I'm mighty impressed."

"Your friends and colleagues will love it." I added under my breath, "I hope."

We stood back and admired the display—the history of libraries in North Carolina. Charlene and I had gathered artifacts from near and far and worked hard over the past few days to put it together. We were proudly showing it off to Bertie James, our boss and the library director.

The idea for the exhibit had been Charlene's, something to show Bertie's college class when they gathered tomorrow evening for the start of their reunion weekend at the Bodie Island Lighthouse Library.

* * *

We'd put the display together in secret, working into the night after Bertie had left for the day, our activities concealed behind old sheets strung across the entrance to the library's alcove, and "Keep Out" signs prominently displayed. When the library was open, we'd stationed

Charles, one of our more formidable staff members, at the entrance to keep the curious—Bertie most of all—out.

Now it was time for the big reveal. At closing time on Thursday evening, library staff, board members, invited Friends of the Library, and lingering patrons had gathered to see it. Charlene ripped away the sheets; Charles returned to his favorite wingback chair next to the magazine rack to wash his whiskers and have a snooze; and everyone had suitably oohed and aahed.

"I doubt," Ronald Burkowski, our children's librarian, said, "the Bodleian could have done better with the materials available."

Bertie clapped her hands. "You people are amazing."

"I'll second that," Charlene said modestly.

"Meow," added Charles from his chair.

The exhibit was a collection of old photographs of libraries in North Carolina, as well as items librarian friends had sent us or we'd been able to uncover in the depths of the town hall basement. Stuff was down there that probably hadn't been seen by a human being since the building was first built.

We'd found a real card catalog and displayed it with the narrow drawers open to show the neat rows of little typewriter-printed cards; there was also a selection of photos showing enormous rooms full of row upon row of the neatly labeled wooden cabinets.

Charlene pointed to a sign I'd hung on the back wall next to the window, showing a woman's plump red lips with her index finger pressed to them, and the word "Silence" in loud black print. "I cannot begin to imagine how they kept the kids quiet when story time let out."

"I have a vison of them descending the stairs in a calm, neat little row," Ronald said, "faces scrubbed, hair combed, socks pulled up, shirts tucked in, not saying a word under the stern eye of the children's librarian. *Not.*"

One of the photographs was of two women, in floor-sweeping skirts, high-necked blouses with puffy sleeves, and hair pulled sharply back, organizing a bookshelf, and another showed a woman on horseback, with a jaunty hat and split skirt, cradling a stack of books in her free hand. We laughed over a staff picture from the 1960s of the librarians—all women of course—with their big hair and orange and brown dresses or twin sets with pearls. Photos of patrons showed more big hair, along with flowery orange or checked pants or jeans with wide lower legs they called bell bottoms. A stern-faced librarian, complete with horn-rimmed glasses, hair pulled back into a tight bun, and high-necked blouse, sat behind a huge manual typewriter, her fingers poised above the keys. We'd dragged a similar machine out of storage, dusted it off, and displayed it next to a still-sharp letter opener, a memento of some long-ago Nags Head anniversary.

"I've just noticed," Charlene said, "there isn't one man in any of these pictures. Librarian was a woman's career back then and still largely is"—she acknowledged Ronald with a smile and nod that he returned—"but even the patrons in these pictures are all women."

"Is that Bertie's office in that picture?" Mrs. Fitzgerald, the chair of the library board said. "It must be. The window's the same, and there's a slice of the marsh showing. Look at all those filing cabinets—there's scarcely room for the director's desk. Never mind that hideous broadloom, covering up the marvelous original flooring."

"The floor in my office isn't that old," Bertie said. "The broadloom was pulled up along with layers of ply-wood and linoleum and some rotting hardwood back in the 1990s, and new wood laid down then."

"I feel so old," my aunt Ellen, one of the Friends of the Library, said. "I remember this stuff like it was yester-day, and now it's ancient history."

A small stack of books had been placed on one side of the desk. I opened the cover of one to show everyone the withdrawal slip. A small cardboard pocket had been glued to the inside of the cover, and a handwritten record of people who checked the book out and a stamp for the day it was due back had been slipped inside. The book was *The Celestine Prophecy* by James Redfield, and the last due date for it was July 11, 1995. The book itself had suf-fered some damage—a spilled cup of coffee by the look of it—which would be why it had been removed from circulation. All these years later, we still got requests for that book.

"Nineteen ninety-five," Aunt Ellen muttered. "Ancient history."

"At least we've no cuneiform tablets or rolled-up parchment scrolls to show you," Charlene said with what I thought was a tinge of regret.

"The Lighthouse Library," Mrs. Fitzgerald said, "came late to computer cataloguing, as I remember. Not many places were still using record cards like that one by the mid-nineties."

"The things that matter the most," Bertie said, "haven't changed. And that's people reading good books and loving literature and wanting to improve their knowledge of science and history."

"Hear, hear," Mrs. Fitzgerald said, and everyone murmured their agreement.

"I remember that book." Mr. Snyder, one of our regular patrons, pointed to *The Celestine Prophecy*. "It was a huge bestseller. Bunch of made-up nonsense pretending to be a novel."

"Which," Charlene pointed out, "is pretty much the definition of a novel."

"You know what I mean," he said.

"I do," Bertie said. "*The Celestine Prophecy* struck a chord in a lot of people at the time."

"I don't see any pictures of the library cat," fifteen-year-old Charity Peterson said.

Bertie laughed and gave Charles an affectionate glance. "Perish the thought. An animal in a library!"

"Speaking of ancient history," Aunt Ellen said. "Look at that computer. It's huge."

From the depths of the town hall basement, we'd excavated a real, although no longer working, Commodore 64. Charlene had searched the newspaper archives and found an article on the purchase of the machine, along with a picture of the then library director proudly showing it off to wide-eyed children.

"That's a computer?" a pre-teenage boy said. "I thought it was a TV or something." At that moment his phone buzzed. He pulled it out of his pocket and checked the screen. "Mom's here." He hefted his book bag and ran out of the library.

"A computer a child carries around in their pocket," my aunt said. "Whoever would have thought?"

"When you put it like that," Mrs. Fitzgerald said, "we are old, Ellen." Turning to us, she continued, "My congratulations to Charlene and Lucy for honoring Bertie and her class with such a thoughtful gesture." Bertie's class had gone to the University of North Carolina, but after graduation several of the women settled in the eastern part of the state, and those from further afield liked the idea of a summer weekend in the Outer Banks, so they'd decided on Nags Head as the perfect spot at which to gather.

Bertie, normally calm, unflappable, the very picture of the yoga instructor she was, had been excited about the forthcoming reunion for weeks. She was in touch with some of the women regularly, she said, but others she hadn't seen for years.

Our library isn't large: there are plenty of better places for gathering twenty women to laugh about the joys and terrors of their youth; show off pictures of families and pets, homes and holidays; and brag about their careers. But the Lighthouse Library is something very special, and Bertie was proud to offer it as a venue for the kick-off party. And Ronald, Charlene, and I were determined to show it off to its best advantage and to make Bertie proud.

"You've done a splendid job," Mrs. Fitzgerald said.

"Did you really wear your hair like that?" Charity Peterson peered at a photo at the front of the display. Bertie's freshman class: the group of beaming young women, arms around each other, posing on the wide steps of an ivy-covered building. "Ugh."

Her mother poked her in the ribs.

"What?" Charity said. "That sweater? Purple, orange, and brown stripes? Ugh."

I'd been thinking much the same thing, but I didn't say so.

"Which one are you, Ms. James?" Charity asked.

"Second on the left," Bertie said. "In the purple, orange, and brown sweater."

Charity slipped a peek at Bertie and said nothing, clearly thinking that Bertie, today wearing a light flowing dress of pale blue, had changed.

Which she had. That college picture was forty years old. Taken before I was born, never mind Charity.

"The 1980s and '90s," Louise Jane McKaughnan said, "were not known for the elegance of fashion."

"I like it," Theodore Kowalski said. "Everyone looks so young and free."

"Oh yes," Bertie said, "those were the days. We *were* young and free."

"You still are, Bertie," Connor McNeil, mayor of Nags Head, said.

She gave him a big smile.

"You've done a fabulous job with this collection of old junk," Connor said. "Feel free to come around any time and clear out the basement."

I studied the photo of a row of cabinets with neatly printed little labels on them. "Hard to imagine having to do all that on paper."

"We managed," Bertie said, "just fine."

"Some of this stuff's well before your time, isn't it, Bertie?" Connor asked.

"Charlene and I gathered whatever we could find," I said. "This exhibit isn't meant to be only about Bertie's year, but about the history of libraries in general. We thought the women would get a kick out of it."

"When do your friends arrive?" Mrs. Fitzgerald asked.

"Tomorrow," Bertie said. "They'll be dribbling in throughout the day and gathering here tomorrow evening for a welcome reception."

"Which is not," I reminded Mrs. Fitzgerald as well as Connor, who, as the major of Nags Head, was the overall boss of the library, "an official library function.

Charlene, Ronald, and I are working it as a favor to Bertie, and the refreshments are being paid for by the attendees themselves."

The three—four including Charles, and one must never forget Charles—employees of the Bodie Island Lighthouse Library were a close group and extremely fond of Bertie. We'd do just about anything for her. Including acting as waitstaff and cleaning crew for her college reunion. We'd been through some tough times together, and Bertie always had our backs.

"You don't have to keep reminding me, Lucy," Connor said.

"She's afraid someone will complain about inappropriate use of library resources," Louise Jane said. "But you needn't worry, Lucy, honey. I'll be here to set them straight."

"Thank you so much LJ," Charlene said. "We can always count on you."

"I would hope so," Louise Jane sniffed.

Connor put his arm loosely around my shoulders. "The town's fully supportive of Bertie hosting her class here. We're happy to have the tourist dollars, if nothing else. Where are they all staying?"

"Most of them are at the Ocean Side," Bertie said, "but a few have friends or family to visit, or are coming with their families to make a vacation out of it. One or two of the women live locally."

We studied the exhibit for a few moments more, and then Bertie turned to us. It might have been a trick of the light, but I thought I saw tears in her eyes. "Thank you so much. Lucy. Charlene. Ronald. This weekend means the world to me."

Louise Jane shifted from one foot to the other and cleared her throat.

"And you as well, Louise Jane," Bertie said. "You've proven yourself to be a valuable member of our library community many times."

Louise Jane waved her hand in the air and sniffed again, but I could tell she was pleased.

"I can't wait to show it to Helena," Bertie said. "She's going to love it."

"Is she in one of these pictures?" Connor pointed to a picture of the 1990s-era library staff.

"I don't see her," Bertie said.

"She wasn't one for the limelight," Aunt Ellen said. "She pretty much stayed inside her office and never came out unless she had something or someone to criticize."

I cast a quick glance at my aunt Ellen, who rarely ever had a bad word to say about anyone. Helena must have rubbed her the wrong way somehow.

Helena Sanchez had been the library director before Bertie. I'd never met her because, on retirement, she moved to Florida, and as far as I knew, she'd never come back before now. It was just a coincidence that she was in the Outer Banks for a visit at the same time as Bertie's reunion, but when Bertie heard about it, she invited her predecessor to come to tonight's party, mainly to see our historical exhibit and talk about the old times in libraries.

Charles leaped off the shelf and landed nimbly at my feet. He rubbed himself against my legs and meowed as though to say, "Enough of this standing around and talking. It's dinner time."

Bertie agreed. "Thank you for coming everyone. It's time to close the library. We have a busy day tomorrow."

"As do we all," Theodore Kowalski said. "I haven't even started the current book club selection yet, and I'm very much looking forward to it. *The Moonstone.* One of my absolute favorites. Are you reading it, Connor?"

"I'm trying," Connor said. "When I can find the time. It's a big book."

"As are most of the great works of literature. Go big or go home—isn't that what young people today say?" asked Teddy who was all of thirty-three years old. He, unlike almost every other person on planet Earth, likes to pretend he's older than he is. He thinks it gives him, and his rare-book-dealing business, a more serious air.

"*The Moonstone?*" Charity asked. "Is it about travel to space? I like those old-timey books about rocket ships and weird aliens."

"The Moonstone of the title," Theodore said, "is a precious jewel with a mysterious past that's stolen during a house party in England. It's a mystery novel. *The* mystery novel, some would say."

The group began to disburse. While Theodore explained the plot of our book club selection to Charity, Mrs. Fitzgerald called good night and walked out with Mrs. Peterson who, as always, had some suggestions for expanding the children's programs at the library. Ronald and Charlene collected their briefcases and left; the remaining patrons gathered their books, and I went behind the desk to check them out. Bertie headed down the hall to her office to gather her things.

Soon only Connor, Louise Jane, and I remained in the library.

"Uh, can I help you Louise Jane?" I asked.

She looked between Connor and me.

"What?" he said.

"Would you mind," she said.

"Mind what?"

She jerked her head toward me.

"Oh," he said. "Right. I'll be outside, Lucy. When you're ready."

I eyed Louise Jane suspiciously as the door closed behind Connor. "What's up?"

She threw a quick glance at the historical exhibit before turning back to face me. "You know I said I'm happy to help here tomorrow night, at Bertie's reunion."

"Yes," I said. "And we appreciate that. Is something wrong?"

She studied my face intently. I studied hers equally intently in return. Louise Jane and I had never exactly been friends. She'd resented me since the moment I first stepped foot in the library to take up the job of Assistant Library Director. Louise Jane had thought the job should be hers, not bothering with the minor fact of her being not at all qualified. As far as she was concerned, being a fierce lover of the library as well as a descendent of long lines of proud Bankers (as natives of the Outer Banks are called) and a storyteller of local renown, should be enough. But it wasn't and I got the job. Louise Jane had made some feeble attempts to frighten me away from the library and back to Boston, but here I was a year later, comfortably settled into my position. She'd saved my life recently, and I was grateful. Extremely grateful. I'd thought we could be friends now. But I still wasn't entirely sure I could trust her.

"Historical items are all well and good, but you need to be careful when dredging them up."

I sighed. Louise Jane was not just a collector of legends and a storyteller. She was a ghost hunter. Although she'd never quite put it that way.

"I don't think we have anything to worry about," I said. "Look at the faces in those old photographs.

Everyone's smiling. If they're not smiling, it's because they're so interested in what they're being shown."

"Appearances," Louise Jane said, "can be deceiving."

I didn't have the time, nor the interest, to engage with Louise Jane tonight. Sometimes, pretending to go along with her is the only way to bring things to a conclusion. "You'll be here in case anything untoward happens, right?"

"Yes. Yes, I will be."

I switched off the computer. "Now, if we're finished here, I have a date with the handsomest man in Nags Head, North Carolina."

"And I have a date with a stack of reference books."

I shouldn't have asked, but I never learn. "What are you reading about?"

"The haunting of this library. As you know, between my grandmother, her mother, and me, there's scarcely a story about the ghostly happenings in these parts that remains a secret. But in this case, 'scarcely' is the important word. Great-Gran said something the other night about a librarian who came to an unnatural end, and the story was hushed up."

"Not that again. This building has only been a library for a couple of decades. No ghostly librarian haunts the shelves."

"Your Yankee pragmatism does you credit, Lucy. Sometimes. You worry about what you can find of card catalogues, old photos, and manual typewriters. Let me worry about the spirit world."

If Louise Jane had been wearing a cape, she would have swirled it about her shoulders and made a suitably dramatic exit. Instead, she hoisted her leather satchel over her shoulder and stalked out of the library. That is, she would have stalked had she not had to do a nimble little dance to avoid Charles, who'd slipped unnoticed between her feet.

I shook my head. Charles washed his whiskers.

Chapter Two

Friday evening I dressed in black slacks and a crisp black blouse with a stiff white collar, and twisted my hair into a knot on the top of my head. If I was pretending to be a waitress, I wanted to dress the part.

I posed for Charles, stretched out on my bed. "How do I look?"

He yawned.

I studied myself in the mirror. My mother's a beautiful woman. I've occasionally been called "cute." I'm cursed with a thick mane of out-of-control black curls and round cheeks (more cuteness) that turn red far too easily when I'm embarrassed. Unlike my cousin Josie, who gets her height from her father's side of the family, I get mine from the Wyatt women, meaning not much of it. I like to think I have nice eyes, although I'd never tell anyone that. They're large and round and a soft brown color with green flakes that, Connor tells me, dance when I laugh.

I smiled at the thought and decided I'd do.

"Bertie said you can come down and join the party," I told Charles. "But behave yourself, or I'll bring you back here."

He jumped off the bed and ran to the door.

I have the world's best commute. I live above the library in what I call my Lighthouse Aerie. My apartment is tiny, but perfect for me at this stage of my life, and I don't mind living several miles outside of town. Taking the hundred steps up and down the twisting spiral iron staircase several times a day saves on gym membership.

Charles and I went downstairs to help with the setup for the party. We had an hour between the library closing at six and guests arriving at seven. Charlene and Ronald had brought a change of clothes with them, and they were clearing space in the main room for chairs and refreshment tables. Like me, my colleagues were dressed in black pants. Ronald's shirt was black, and Charlene's blouse white. Ronald had accented his outfit with a huge, yellow polka-dot bow tie. I arrived as my cousin Josie O'Malley came through the doors, laden with bakery boxes. Connor was right behind her, bearing a case of wine.

"I've more in the car," Josie said. I took the first load from her and went into the staff break room while Ronald hurried to help Connor.

I took platters down from the shelf and began arranging the treats. Josie owns Josie's Cozy Bakery, one of the most popular spots in Nags Head. She often provides desserts for library functions, but tonight she'd done canapes as well. I used what little self-control I have to keep myself from diving into the miniature crab cakes, crostini with smoked trout, cucumber roll-ups, and phyllo triangles.

Charles sprang onto the table. Charles has absolutely no self-control. "Not for you," I said as I put him on the floor.

Josie came in with more boxes, and my mouth watered as I helped her arrange the selection of baked goods. I'd had a small salad for lunch and no time for dinner. That, I realized as I studied the treats, might have been a mistake.

"You can have one if you want," Josie said.

"How'd you know that was what I was thinking?"

She grinned at me. "That's what everyone's thinking when they see my food. Try one of those." She pointed to a small chocolate-covered square.

I picked one up and studied it. It consisted of a dark crumbly base, a thick layer of custard, and a topping of chocolate ganache. I took a tentative bite, and I almost swooned as the flavors exploded in my mouth.

"Oh my goodness," I said. "This might well be the best thing I've ever eaten. What is it?"

"It's called a Nanaimo bar. A baker friend of mine moved to Vancouver Island, and she sent me the recipe. Trust me, you might think you want another one now, but don't. They're really filling."

I popped the rest of it in my mouth and chewed happily.

"Mom says this is a party for Bertie's library school crowd," Josie said, referring to my aunt Ellen.

"Yup. The start of a reunion weekend. They'll be doing the usual tourist stuff tomorrow and Sunday."

"Where did Bertie go to college?"

"She did her undergraduate studies at the University of North Carolina. That's close enough that some of her class settled in this area, but far enough many of them didn't. So they don't see each other much. I gather it's the anniversary of the first day of class, when they all met, not their graduation. This is strictly a classmates' weekend, from what Bertie tells me. Meaning, the women didn't bring husbands and families with them, or if they did, said husbands will be left to their own devices."

"Not hard to entertain oneself in the Outer Banks in summer." Josie studied the arrangement of canapes, cookies, squares, and tarts on the trays. "How's that look?"

"Good enough to eat."

She laughed.

"Be sure you have a peek at the historical exhibit Charlene and I put together before you leave. The only non-schoolmate coming tonight will be Helena Sanchez, who was the library director here before Bertie. She also went to North Carolina, but before Bertie and her crowd, so Bertie invited her. Did you ever meet Ms. Sanchez?"

Josie's pretty face twisted. "I've met her, but only once or twice, when I was with Mom."

"Was your mom a Friends of the Library member back then?"

"She was. I vaguely remember hearing her telling Dad she was going to quit. Something about not being able to get along with the director. That was several years ago, and I had plenty of other things on my mind, so my memory of that fleeting conversation might be faulty. Shortly after that, Ms. Sanchez retired, Bertie was hired, and Mom stayed on. If you're okay here, I'm off. Jake's taken the night off work, and we're having a date night."

"Have fun," I said. Josie had married Jake Greenblatt over the winter. She still had that newlywed glow about her. I hoped she always would.

I walked her to the door, and we hugged good night. Then I turned to face into the room. Connor and Ronald had set up the bar, and Charlene was arranging plates and cocktail napkins on the table where we'd put the food. Most of our bookshelves are on rollers, and we'd pushed them back to create a larger space for people to mix and mingle. We were expecting twenty-one guests, which was easily doable even for our small library. We'd had far larger parties before. Somehow the Lighthouse Library seems to be able to stretch at the seams to accommodate everyone who wants to come in.

"I offered Ronald a hand when the guests arrive," Connor said, "but he says the three of you have it all under control."

"We do," I said. "The food's made, so all we have to do is serve, tend bar, and keep things tidy. And then clean up, of course, so we look like a library at opening time tomorrow."

He pulled me into his arms and kissed me lightly on the top of my head. Then, conscious of Ronald and Charlene trying not to watch us, he pulled away. "Good night, Lucy,"

"Good night," I said.

He touched my arm lightly and called, "Break a leg," to Ronald, who had a background in theater before becoming a librarian. On the way out, Connor held the door for Louise Jane.

Ronald and Charlene stopped what they were doing, to stare. I might have stared myself.

"Goodness," Charlene said.

"Where'd you get that?" Ronald asked.

"A little something from the back of your mother's closet?" I asked.

"I always believe in dressing the part." Louise Jane wore a proper maid's uniform circa 1920s. Calf-length black dress buttoned to the throat and down the sleeves, white apron, black stockings, thick-soled black shoes. Her hair was pulled back and tucked under a crisp white cap with lace trim. She surveyed the room. "You seem to have everything under control in here. Has the food arrived?"

"It's in the break room," I said.

"I'll help you bring it out then."

"We're waiting until the guests arrive. Then you and I will circulate with the dishes. Ronald's tending bar, and Charlene will keep an eye out for potential spills or dirty napkins needing to be whisked away, and talk to the guests about our historical display."

One eyebrow rose. "Do you think that's wise, Lucy, honey? The room will get quite crowded. We don't want any accidents."

"Which is the potential spills part of my job, LJ," Charlene said. "It's all been decided. No need to worry your pretty little head about it."

"I'm only providing the benefit of my experience at this sort of thing," Louise Jane said.

Ronald and I exchanged looks. Charlene and Louise Jane never did get on. Charlene is an academic and historical librarian. The history of shipping along the eastern coast of North America is her specialty, and she's so qualified she'd worked for a time at the Bodleian Library at Oxford University in England. Louise Jane, on the other hand, is an enthusiastic amateur. She probably knows as much, if not more, history of the Outer Banks than Charlene, but her knowledge came not from history books, but from family stories and local legends, which are not always completely reliable. If Louise Jane didn't know something, she simply made it up.

A habit not inclined to endear her to the literal-minded Charlene.

It didn't help that Louise Jane had a strong interest in what she calls the paranormal history of the Outer Banks in general and our library in particular. Charlene thought that nothing but rubbish.

"Noted," Charlene said.

"Car pulling up outside," Ronald said. "It's quarter to seven, so probably Bertie."

"Stations everyone," Charlene said. "Let's do her proud."

Louise Jane dropped into a deep curtsy, and we all—even Charlene—laughed.

Charles laid claim to his favorite chair, the comfortable wingback next to the magazine rack.

Three women arrived with Bertie. They were all of an age, all smiling broadly, but the similarities ended there. These three were Bertie's closest friends from her college years, and they'd met for a drink before coming here to join the rest of their class for the party. She introduced us.

Mary-Sue Delamont was short and slight, almost a perfect caricature of a librarian with her beak nose, thick eyeglasses under bushy eyebrows, slate gray hair tied into a stiff bun, and sensible shoes. She wore a brown pantsuit that looked as though it had been plucked directly from one of the photos Bertie had given us of them at college.

Lucinda Lorca towered over her friends, and was as thin as a runway model. She looked about twenty years younger than Bertie, the result, I thought, of some discreet surgery. She wore a yellow dress with a deeply plunging neckline and tight bodice, a thin belt, and flaring skirt; plenty of good jewelry; and sandals with dangerously high heels.

Ruth McCray was short and round, with pudgy red cheeks, a huge smile, and a mass of frizzy red hair heavily streaked with gray. She wore jeans and a red T-shirt under a blue denim jacket and had hiking boots on her feet.

After we'd been introduced, Ruth threw up her arms and declared, "I cannot believe I've never been to this library before, even when I was working in Manteo. I'm green with envy, Bertie. I saw a boardwalk heading for the marsh as we drove up. Maybe a walk down to the water later?"

"That can be arranged," I said. "It's lovely down there after dark."

"Ooh, a cat!" Mary-Sue exclaimed. "What a darling. What's his name?"

"Charles," I said. "After Mr. Dickens."

"Is he a Himalayan?"

"Yes."

Without another word she charged across the room and scooped Charles up. Charles never minded being scooped. As long as he wasn't eating.

"Can I get you ladies a drink?" Ronald asked. "I have wine, beer, iced tea, and peach juice."

They asked for wine, and Bertie said she'd have juice because she was driving. The guests followed Ronald to the makeshift bar on what was normally our circulation desk.

Cars and taxis began pulling up a few minutes later, and librarians of all shapes and sizes poured into our library. They squealed and hugged and exclaimed how they hadn't changed a bit, and phones were whipped out to show family photographs. Ronald was kept busy behind the bar, and Charlene showed the guests our historical display. The women laughed uproariously over the pictures of themselves and their school, and reminisced while looking at the photos of rows of card cabinets, and the books containing stamped withdrawal notices.

"They say when the wind blows from the south, he wanders the upper floors looking for playmates." Louise Jane was talking to one woman in a low voice. The woman's eyes were wide, and she leaned close to hear better. "Ronald," Louise Jane continued, "knows to keep a close eye on the children, and the gate to the upper levels is always locked when we're open, or who knows what might happen?"

"Louise Jane," I said, "do you have a minute?"

She peered down her nose at me. "I'm kinda busy here, Lucy. Sheila's interested in the . . . other life forms that live in the lighthouse."

Sheila nodded enthusiastically. "Ghost hunting's a passion of mine."

Oh dear. The last thing I wanted was Louise Jane leading a tour group through the upper levels in search of Frances, called the Lady, who, Louise Jane insists, was a young bride locked inside the building by her cruel, much older lighthouse-keeper husband.

To be specific, the Lady—according to Louise Jane—had been locked in *my* room. From which she escaped by throwing herself from the fourth-floor window. That I had not once in the year I've lived here seen the slightest trace of the Lady, or the little son of another lighthouse keeper who supposedly fell to his death when playing on the upper levels, where he'd been forbidden to go, didn't matter to Louise Jane.

"I believe," I said, "you were hired to help us tonight."

"If by hired, you mean paid for my time, I wasn't. And I am helping. I'm entertaining the guests."

"And very well too," Sheila said.

"But if you insist." Louise Jane emitted a martyred sigh.

"Ruth's telling everyone we're going for a walk to the marsh later," Sheila said. "Do you have stories about happenings in the marsh?"

"What an excellent idea," Louise Jane said, "I can tell you some stories on the walk. If you'll excuse me, duty calls."

She followed me into the break room, where the platters of food were waiting. "Is it time to serve?"

"Bertie wanted to wait for Ms. Sanchez, but she hasn't shown up yet, and it's almost eight, so she said go ahead. I hope Ms. Sanchez comes. Bertie's wanting to show her some of the things Charlene and I dug up from the storage rooms at the town hall."

We hefted the platters of canapes and carried them into the main room. The assembled women descended like a pack of wolves.

By eight thirty, the desserts had been decimated, and the canapes thoroughly picked over; only the usual celery stalks, sliced red peppers, and carrot sticks remained. I was clearing dirty glasses, getting no help at all from Louise Jane, who was regaling a group of women with details of her family's history on the Outer Banks.

"A taxi's pulling up outside," Ronald said to me, and I went to get the door as a woman walked up the path with firm, rapid steps. When she stepped into the light thrown by the lamp above the door, I could see that this must be the expected Helena Sanchez, previous director of the Bodie Island Lighthouse Library. She was of average height, but very thin, with small dark eyes and a face that was all sharp angles, deep shadows, and jutting bones. The skin on her face formed deep crevices, and her iron-gray hair was tied in a thick bun at the back of her head. She wore plain brown trousers, a red blouse with a white bow tied tightly at her neck, and no jewelry that I could see. A calf-length brown woolen cloak, far too hot for the warm night, was thrown over her shoulders.

"Good evening," I said. "I'm Lucy Richardson, assistant director here, and you're very welcome."

She studied me, top to toe. Then she nodded and held out her hand. I took it in mine, surprised at its strength. "I'm Helena Sanchez. I believe I'm expected."

"And so you are," Bertie said behind me. "Please come in."

I stepped out of the way, and the new arrival walked into the library.

"It's a pleasure to have you here," Bertie said.

"I'm sure it is," Ms. Sanchez replied.

"You must have missed the Lighthouse Library," I said.

"Not particularly." She glanced around the room. A few of the women smiled at the newcomer, but most of them were occupied with their friends.

Charles leaped onto the bookshelf behind us. Ms. Sanchez stared at him. "A cat," she sniffed, "roaming free in a library. Wouldn't have been allowed in my day. Standards are slipping, Albertina. You need to guard against that."

"Charles is a valued member of our library family," Bertie said. "The children in particular get a great deal of pleasure out of him, and he's an excellent therapy cat for some of the lonely elderly who come here in search of company."

"Can't abide cats myself. Thoroughly nasty creatures."

Charles hissed.

Ms. Sanchez hissed back.

Charles jumped off the shelf and disappeared in the sea of legs.

Ruth McCray broke out of the pack and approached us, glass of wine in hand. "Helena. It's been a long time."

Ms. Sanchez blinked at her.

"Ruth McCray? We worked in Manteo together before you left to work at the Lighthouse Library."

"Oh yes. I remember you. You've put on weight."

Ruth's eyes widened in surprise. "Well, it has been a few years. I think that's allowed. I hope you're enjoying your retirement. I can't wait until it's my turn."

"I keep myself busy." Ms. Sanchez pointedly didn't ask Ruth anything about what she'd been doing all these years.

"Okay. Well, nice to see you." Ruth wandered away, shaking her head.

Ms. Sanchez glanced around the room. "I recognize some of these women. Is that Lucinda Smith talking to the man in the yellow tie? What on earth has happened to her face?"

"She's Lucinda Lorca again," Bertie said. "After her divorce she went back to her maiden name."

"Looks like she's fishing for a new husband," Ms. Sanchez said as Lucinda laughed at something Ronald said.

I threw Bertie a look. She returned it with a shrug.

One of the other women broke away from the pack and greeted Ms. Sanchez with a smile and outstretched hand. "Nice to see you, Helena."

"Margaret Hurley." Ms. Sanchez did not return the smile.

"You must know some of these women," Margaret said. "Let me take you around."

"I'd rather have a drink." Ms. Sanchez headed for the bar. Margaret hesitated and then followed.

"She's rather . . . blunt," I said when Margaret and Helena Sanchez had melted into the crowd.

"So it would seem," Bertie said. "I didn't know her well. I didn't work here when she was in charge. I was hired from outside. She interviewed me, but that was the extent of our contact. When I arrived to start work, no one said anything, but I got the feeling the staff were not entirely unhappy to see her go. I'm going to show her the display. Excuse me, Lucy."

Bertie stepped away, but before she could reach Helena, another woman came up to her. "Great party, Bertie. I absolutely love your library. It was so nice of you to think of having our opening reception here."

"It's my pleasure," Bertie said.

"I happen to have some pictures of my grandchildren in here somewhere. Would you like to see them? My son Kevin's a pediatrician—did you know that?"

"I don't believe I did." Bertie politely bent over the woman's phone to see the pictures.

I chuckled and looked around for something I should be doing. Three women were at the circulation desk chatting to Ronald, who seemed to be having a great time. Helena Sanchez pushed her way through them and managed to give Lucinda Lorca an elbow in the ribs.

Lucinda stepped out of the way. Whatever she'd been about to say died on her lips. Her eyes widened and her face tightened. She stared at the newcomer.

Ms. Sanchez gave her a glance, dismissed her, and said to Roland, "I'll have a glass of white wine. If you have anything decent that is. I can't stand Chardonnay."

"We have a nice New Zealand Sauvignon Blanc," he said.

"That will do."

Lucinda gripped her glass and melted into the crowd.

Bertie finally finished admiring grandchild photos and caught up with Helena Sanchez. She said something to her predecessor and gestured toward the alcove. They headed for it, followed by a few others, including Sheila, Ruth, and Lucinda.

I spotted a dirty plate and crumpled napkin on a side table close to the alcove and hurried to pick it up. Ronald was pouring drinks and laughing at something a woman said. Charlene stood next to the historical display, ready to show it to Bertie's guests, and Louise Jane hovered at her elbow, prepared to leap in with interpretations of her own. I picked up the plate and had started to head down the hallway to the break room when Mary-Sue Delamont passed me, returning from the ladies room. I heard a sharp intake of breath and glanced at her.

She was frozen in place with a look on her face that I can only describe as one of horror as she stared at the women gathered around the display. No, she wasn't staring at the women. She was focused on Helena Sanchez, who'd pulled a pair of drug-store reading glasses out of her bag and propped them on her nose.

"Are you okay?" I asked Mary-Sue.

She started at the sound of my voice, and the expression faded. She gave me a weak smile. "Perfectly okay, thank you. I saw someone I didn't expect, that's all. That woman wearing the ugly brown cloak wasn't in our class. Why's she here?"

"That's Helena Sanchez, the previous library director. The one before Bertie. She's visiting Nags Head, and Bertie thought she'd enjoy the historical display we put together. Do you know her?"

"No. No, I don't. Never seen her before. Excuse me." She headed for the bar.